Verity Fibbs

cathy brett

Cathy Brett has been scribbling stuff for more than twenty years; as a fashion illustrator, as a jet-setting spotter of global trends and as a consultant to the behemoths of the British high street.

She now teaches in design and unashamedly plunders her students' lives for sensational storylines and characters.

Books by Cathy Brett

Ember Fury
Scarlett Dedd
Verity Fibbs

Verity Fibbs

cathy brett

First published in Great Britain in 2011 by
HEADLINE PUBLISHING GROUP

1

Cataloguing in Publication Data is available from the British Library

ISBN 978 0 7553 7947 7

Typeset by Jason Cox

Printed and bound in Great Britain by
Clays Ltd, St Ives plc

Headline's policy is to use papers that are natural, renewable and recyclable products and made from wood grown in sustainable forests. The logging and manufacturing processes are expected to conform to the environmental regulations of the country of origin.

HEADLINE PUBLISHING GROUP
An Hachette UK Company
338 Euston Road
London NW1 3BH

www.headline.co.uk
www.hachette.co.uk

For Mum

Thank you to my awesome friends and family for their support and encouragement. I'm also enormously grateful to members of the Phoenix Writers' Circle and to Emma Hamilton for their generosity and honest feedback

teenmag

VERITY FIBBS
on being a famous daughter

"Mum's my best friend. We talk about *everything*."

10 STEPS TO CLEAR SKIN

ADDICT? Have you caught the gaming bug?

200 pages of *sensational* spring fashion

truth or dare
hair-raising confessions

teen**green**
how **YOU** can save the planet

£2.50 teenmag

Interview

WEIRD 'N' WACKY WONDERFUL WARDROBES

What does the teenage daughter of a famous fashion designer love, hate and dream about? More importantly, what does she wear? *Teenmag* spent an afternoon with Verity Fibbs in her fave London haunts, then was invited back to her eccentric bedroom to goss about her mum, school, friends, dating — and for a serious clothes-trying-on sesh.

TM: What's it like having a celeb for a mum? Is it totally cool or a total nightmare?

VF: Urgh! Really embarrassing sometimes. But pretty cool, too. She's a cool mum and kinda my best friend . . . second best friend. I mean, I can tell Mum anything and we talk all the time about different stuff. AND we're the same size so I get to borrow loads of her clothes.

TM: Wow! That is a-maz-ing!!

The Mole and Fat Pig Face

Something, or someone, shifted in the dark, just moving weight from one foot to the other. If she'd not been searching for it she wouldn't have noticed the slight twitch of the inky black shadow beneath the fire escape, but a twitch was all it took. OK. He was there, waiting for her. The Mole. She closed her fist a little tighter around the reassuringly smooth mother-of-pearl handle in her pocket and took a step into the alley. Away from the brash, neon-lit street, the darkness now closed around her, pressing against her body like a heavy coat.

The Mole turned his head. He'd heard the hesitant tip-tap of her boots. Part of his face was now visible in a letterbox slit between the collar of his raincoat and a black fedora tilted down to the bridge of his long, twitching nose.

'Maisie Malone?' the Mole growled, lifting a shovel-sized hand. He pushed the fedora back with the tip of a claw-like fingernail to reveal nervous, pale eyes. She was shocked.

She'd assumed his name, the Mole, was a joke, a nickname, that simply described this clandestine activity, but this man actually looked like he might live underground.

'Yes, that's me,' she said.

'Password?' The Mole blinked at her.

Password? What password? She didn't know she'd need one of those. She had brought the small suitcase full of cash and she had the pearl-handled gun in her pocket and the tiny stiletto blade, tucked into the top of her boot, just in case. But a password?

The Mole cleared his throat. He was already getting impatient and she'd been there less than a minute. She'd have to be quick and work it out or he might get twitchy and back out of the deal. He looked the twitchy type.

'Password,' the Mole demanded again. 'Or I take the goods elssssewhere.' He hissed the last word through a gap in his teeth, then the dry skin of his cheeks creased up under his eyes like tissue paper. She couldn't tell if there was now a smile or an angry grimace behind his collar. *Creepy!* She shivered.

Password?

She stared in to the dark void of the alley behind him and tried to think. She mustn't let the Mole leave without handing over his package.

Password? Password?

Might he be asking for the password from Level 3? That was *Femme Fatale*, she remembered. But, no. That wasn't really a password, more the solution to a complicated riddle. And it had taken her *forever* to decipher.

Might it be *Black Orchid*? She'd used that password in

the Oyster Bar where she'd acquired the pearl-handled pistol from the barman. She'd been stupidly smug about guessing that one, but it had probably taken more luck than brainpower. The Oyster Bar had been busy and, while waiting to be served, her mind wandered. She had gazed at the flickering neon sign on the wall and noted that the shape bore an uncanny resemblance to the picture on a box in burlesque star Pamela Pout's bedroom on Level 5 – a fancy *Black Orchid* lingerie box. It wasn't uncanny, of course. It was a large, flashing, neon clue!

Should she try *Black Orchid* again? Or had she missed another clue? Might it have been something in the previous scene? What had been out of place? What didn't quite belong? Maybe it was that weird comment Veronica Vamp had made when she'd handed over the cash. She'd thought at the time that it was an odd thing for her to say: 'Go backwards into the alley.' Backwards? Get real! Walking backwards into a dark alley to meet an informant was a really stupid idea, so perhaps Veronica was referring to something less literal.

She looked around desperately for some inspiration. There would often be a hint in these situations – a discarded newspaper, a blood-stained banknote, a picture or a logo on the side of a pizza-delivery van. That's when she saw the sign, the name of the narrow street printed on a rusty metal panel, fixed high on the wall. *Murder Lane*. Murder.

'Redrum?' she blurted. 'Is the password Redrum?'

The Mole smiled and reached inside his coat. She flinched. Was he going for a gun? Had she got the password completely wrong?

+200 points
score: 7,700
Bonus Fact: Demons avoid Oyster Bars because of their Seafood Allergies
options
play
II

No, he was pulling out a small, brown package, thrusting it towards her, then making a 'hand it over' gesture with his other wide, flat hand. She relaxed a little, placed the suitcase on the ground and shoved it towards him with the toe of her boot.

crack!

-500 points
score: 7,200

options play II

Aahhh! What was that?

A brick behind the Mole's right ear shattered and sprayed grit and red dust all over him and the package.

We're being shot at!

Instinctively, she leapt sideways and crouched behind the fire escape, but the Mole didn't move quickly enough and the second bullet flew over her head and slammed into his chest with a sickening crunch – the sound of disintegrating flesh and bone. The Mole's body slumped against the wall and fell in a crumpled heap beside her, his startled lifeless eyes staring, straight up into hers. She turned, wrenched the pearl-handled pistol out of her pocket and waved it back down the alley.

Someone followed me.

As she peered into the gloom, a silhouette emerged through a cloud of neon-lit steam wafting from a restaurant kitchen vent. It walked towards her. She knew the dark shape instantly – the wide-brimmed hat, the sharp suit, the glowing red eyes. It was . . .

'Verity? Vee? VEE!'

'What?'

'So? What d'ya think?'

'Yeah.'

'You weren't listening, were you?'

'Yeah, I was.'

'Porky pies. You were playing that game again. You're addicted. You need help. Like, see a doctor or something . . . game addiction therapy . . . a support group.'

'Nah. I was only checking messages.'

'So what did I say then?'

'When?'

'Just now.'

'Um, something about jeans?' Verity guessed, tapping the screen to log out of the *Demon Streets* game.

Her best friend was tugging at the waistband of a pair of dark denim jeans and admiring their fit in the mirror, trying not to look at the muffin bulge of white tummy flesh. 'So? Mmm?'

'Yeah, they suit you,' Verity mumbled, ignoring the muffin top. She actually thought they were far too tight across her friend's backside, too.

'Ha! I *knew* you were fibbing, Fibbs. I asked if you could see my pants.'

'Oh, right. Nope. You're OK.'

'Why don't *you* try them on? They're your size.'

Verity shoved the phone into her bag. She'd deal with the Mole murderer later. The jeans were almost identical to the ones Verity was wearing and, although she had a notoriously vast wardrobe, twelve pairs of jeans was probably sufficient. Her friend, however, had just tried on at least that many in her search for the perfect fit. Verity had tired of the search hours ago. She was much more interested in the hat she'd spotted on a mannequin just outside the changing room – a black fedora with a white ribbon band.

'Meh!' She yawned and waved a dismissive hand at the jeans, then leaned out of the changing room and grabbed the fedora. 'Hey, Pye! I'm gonna get this. What d'ya think?' Verity rammed the hat down and tilted it forward like the Mole had done. She half-closed her eyes, pulled up the collar of her jacket and posed in front of the mirror.

'Not sure,' said Pye. 'I mean, what does the label say? You can't be certain that hats and stuff haven't been made by a starving child who lives on a rubbish heap and gets paid almost nothing.'

'Uh?'

'This recycled fashion malarkey is a fab idea and everything, but who made that hat *originally*?'

'Oh, shut up! Who cares?' said Verity. 'Does it make me look fat?'

She'd asked a question that, for most girls, is both completely normal and stupidly perverse – a trick question. *Does it make me look fat?* Verity and her friends asked it all the time. It just fell out of their mouths without anxiety, because there was only one possible answer: No, of course not.

Verity's friend Pye, however, answered without hesitation. 'Yeah, I suppose it does . . . but you *are* a bit fat, aren't you? Your face, I mean.'

'PIIIIIIIIIYE! Oh my gaaawwwd!'

'What?'

'You can't *say* that!'

'Why not, if it's true? You've got sorta podgy cheeks – like cute, squidgy dough balls.'

Verity rolled her eyes. 'Pye, babe, you are terminally tactless!'

Verity and Pye, though the best of best friends and equally obsessed with fashion, in all other respects were chalk and cheese. Where Verity was exuberant, Pye was reserved. Where Verity was hare-brained and erratic, Pye was thoughtful and deliberate. Pye was an eco-obsessed vegan while Verity ate almost nothing but meat-feast pizza. Vee was a glossy brunette and Pye a frizzy blonde. But perhaps the most striking difference (and apt considering her name) was that Verity was pretty much a compulsive liar while Pye couldn't help but tell the truth, even at the risk of causing offence.

'Why *shouldn't* I say it?'

'Because it's . . . because it's . . . well, brutal and just a little bit mental, that's why,' said Verity.

'Isn't it worse to tell someone they're pretty when they look like a pig?' Pye reasoned.

'*Thanks a lot!*'

'No, not you! But I don't like that hat.' Pye folded her arms and glared at her friend.

Verity smirked, puffed out her cheeks then pressed her palms against her face making her lip-glossed mouth into a round pout. 'Oinncchh!'

Pye collapsed on the floor with the giggles.

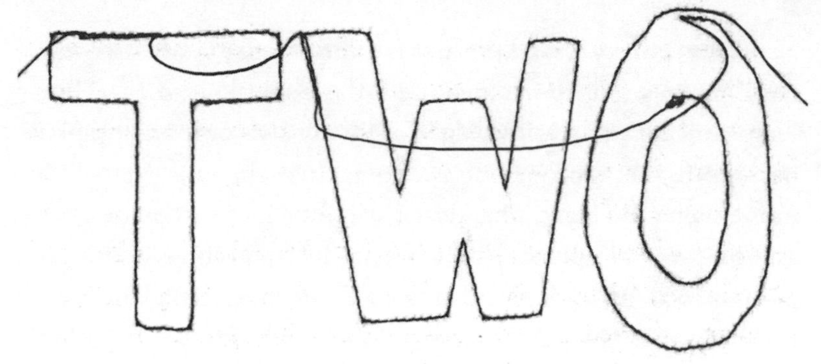

Jiggery-Pokery and the Huge Billboard

The changing rooms were sweaty, crowded and smelled of stale fragrance. The friends had found nothing so far that met their exacting fashion criteria – except the fedora, which Verity was going to get, despite Pye's comments – so they dumped their multi-limbed, multi-coloured pile of rejects into the arms of the nearest stressed-out assistant and headed back into the shop.

It was chaos out there. The enormous central-London branch of Jiggery-Pokery was always busy on a Saturday afternoon but today the new 'Flim-Flam' concept was being officially launched on the ground floor and the store felt like it was about to host a major riot. The threat of violence seemed to hang in the air like grease in a burger bar. Hundreds of teenage girls were yelling at each other over the pounding rock music and snatching at the vintage clothing while their agitated boyfriends twitched nervously in the testosterone-flooded 'Man Zone' watching Premier League football and playing car chase games on the touch screens.

Jiggery-Pokery wasn't the first fashion retailer to offer second-hand clothes, but it was definitely the coolest. And the Flim-Flam concept was acknowledged as totally awesome and original because it was more about swapping than buying. Very little money actually changed hands in the Flim-Flam part of the store, and that was its appeal. And it wasn't just recycling, it was up-cycling, too – up-cycling with a twist. Customers joined the Flim-Flam Club for ten pounds, brought their own unwanted clothes, and membership cards, to the Flim Counter where staff would decide if the item was clean and stylish enough to be exchanged for a Flam, credited to their card. The accepted clothes were then hung on a moving orange belt that circled the store like a Scalextric track or the food at YO! Sushi. You could stand in the middle of the shop and watch the progress of your grown-out-of pleated school skirt or loathed birthday present floral cardigan as it travelled up to the glass-fronted mezzanine floor above, where a team of young fashion designers would sort it, make a few funky enhancing alterations, press it and put it on a wooden Flim-Flam hanger before hooking it back on the belt. Eventually it would reach the racks to be fought over by yelling girls who could now 'buy' it with five or eight of their accumulated Flams. Some special pieces – major couture designer confections, worn-once red carpet evening wear or vintage originals from someone's recently-deceased gran's wardrobe – were assessed as Ultra-Flam items, costing *real* money as well as Flams (while earning the donor significantly less, of course), but these items were rare and could result in serious hair-extension pulling or acrylic-nail cheek-gouging when they reached the shop floor.

Pye and Verity (who was now sporting her one-Flam fedora) retreated to the other side of the store where a slightly less frantic crowd was oooing and aahhhing over the main Jiggery-Pokery Spring Collection. The rails were overflowing with gorgeous, ethically-sourced delights in delicious sorbet and ice-cream colours. In fact, the clothes were selling like ice cream in a heatwave – very chic and beautifully tailored ice cream – even though it was barely above freezing outside. But Verity wasn't seduced by the bias-cut, strawberry-ice dress with asymmetric hem or the fitted, cappuccino, glazed-cotton jacket with pistachio shorts. Nor was she interested in the mango denim pea coat with giant mother-of-pearl buttons or the vanilla jersey dress with raspberry trim. She was making for a side door, almost sprinting in her eagerness to get out. There was a buzz in the atmosphere – an increased rumble of noise and pop of flashing lights rising from the paparazzi who'd been waiting outside the front entrance – and it flipped her stomach. The store's glamorous owner and designer had arrived to officially launch her new venture. Verity caught a glimpse through the window of a woman emerging from a limo who was instantly mobbed on the pavement by the fashion media.

'Ooo, your mum's here!' Pye exclaimed, looking back over her shoulder while jogging to keep up with Verity's long, denim-clad strides.

'Yeah. Good time to leave then, I think,' said Verity, frowning and ploughing on through the shoppers.

'You still not talking to her?'

'Nope!'

'Can't you just say you were wrong, that you're sorry?'

'Me? *She's* the one who should apologise!'

'But would it kill you to kiss and make up?' Pye asked.

'Huh!' Verity scowled. 'Yeah, it would.'

'But it's her launch and the press are here! I wanna go say "hi".'

'You can do what you like,' said Verity, turning furiously to face her friend. 'I mean, she likes you more than me, anyway. I don't wanna be within a hundred miles of the evil bi—.'

'That's not true!' Pye yelled.

'It is. She obviously hates me and wants to completely control my life, make me into, like, a boring, loser, robot teenager or something. It's SO out of order . . . Total psychological abuse!'

Pye was exasperated but accustomed to Verity's over-dramatising and always dealt with her friend's moody outbursts in the same way – with the barefaced truth. 'I don't see how grounding you for bunking off school is out of order.'

They'd reached the street and now stood on the edge of the kerb in the weak sunlight, the last arctic blasts of winter slapping around their goosebump-covered limbs.

'Meh!' Verity flipped up the collar of her vintage leather jacket and pulled the fedora down over her eyes.

'And my mum would have called the police and had me

arrested or something,' Pye continued, 'if I'd bunked off school to go on a date with a really old fashion student.'

'Huh! Wouldn't have minded going to prison. Probably better than having to do cleaning chores for a month as punishment. It's inhumane torture. Look at my hands!' Verity waved her fingers in her friend's face.

'Only because she found out he wasn't fifteen, like you told her,' said Pye. 'And your hands look fine to me.'

'Yeah, well. So, he's twenty. So what?' She shrugged. 'She had no right to stop me seeing him.'

'She's your mum. That's what mums do.' Pye scrutinised her friend's face and waited for a flippant reply, but Verity shrugged again and began looking up and down the noisy street, scanning the numbers of the approaching buses, trying to ignore the fact she was losing the argument. She hated it when they argued. Verity and Pye's friendship had begun in the first term at primary school, Mrs Gladd's reception class, and had strengthened with each passing year. Neither of them had siblings and this deficiency in common seemed to have created a powerful connection between them – an unspoken, almost mystical bond, like they were twin sisters separated at birth who had miraculously found each other again. And, Verity supposed, like twin sisters, they were bound to disagree from time to time. As long as it wasn't too serious, their friendship could survive a little turbulence.

At last, Vee took a breath and delivered her closing statement. 'Well, she's happy *now,* isn't she?' She said it in an American accent she'd been perfecting since last year's school play. 'The creep hasn't replied to my texts, so she's not only responsible for me getting dumped by a future catwalk star, but also for the deep mental trauma . . . and the years and years of expensive therapy that she'll have to pay for . . . and I'll end up a delinquent or a sociopath or bulimic or something . . . and it will all be *her* fault, so she should be the one to apologise.' She nodded to indicate that the conversation was over and Pye sighed.

The brakes on their bus hissed as it juddered to a halt beside them and the doors rattled open. Verity and Pye climbed the stairs and manoeuvred around shoppers, legs and bags to get to the front seats, their preferred spot. If it was free, they always chose the front of the bus, upstairs, on the side nearest the pavement, so they had a perfect view of the bustling streets and passing shopfronts. Pye pressed her face against the window as the bus rumbled back past the Jiggery-Pokery store. Verity's mum was still posing for the cameras outside and the shouts and chatter of the overexcited crowd bubbled up like the effervescent wave in a glass of champagne. They had a wonderful view of the commotion from their high perch.

'Ooo! She looks *gorgeous!*' Pye cooed.

'Mmm,' Verity agreed reluctantly. Her mum *did* look pretty amazing. She was wearing the new collection (obvs): a dark chocolate suit, which she'd brilliantly teamed with a long iced-lime scarf. It skimmed elegantly over her willowy, supermodel figure.

'Those coffee suede boots are just edible!' said Pye, now in full-on worship mode.

Verity knew she couldn't stay mad at her mum for long. She secretly agreed that dating Darren, the fashion student, had been a bit of a mistake. The idea had been fun at first – an adrenalin rush. She'd sneaked her tight black minidress and platform heels out of the house stuffed into her school bag, then missed afternoon lessons to go to the Festival of French Cinema on the South Bank with him. Another time, she'd taken a bus to a pub in Camden to watch his fashion-student mates playing in a terrible post-punk band, when she'd told Mum she was studying at Pye's house. But when Darren had announced he'd won two free tickets to attend a swimwear show in Miami (first prize in a design competition), it had scared her. He was disappointed, and a little surprised, when she'd said she was 'far too busy' and declined his offer. 'The plane tickets are free,' he repeated. 'And our hotel.' Darren had no idea she wasn't a nineteen-year-old model with her own flat but was actually a fourteen-year-old schoolgirl with maths homework to do.

Verity smiled and threw her arm around her friend.

'You can borrow those boots when she's away, if you like.'

Pye gasped. 'Oooh no! Won't she mind?'

'She's not gonna know, is she? I'm gonna wear all her stuff the whole time she's in New York.'

Pye closed her eyes and smiled in rapturous contemplation of unhindered access to Saffron Fibbs's enormous walk-in wardrobe. The thought of endless racks of utterly delectable clothes and accessories was just *too heavenly!* 'Uuhh, we can't! She'd be sure to find out,' she moaned. 'And she'll probably take all the best stuff with her, anyway – like those yummy boots.'

The friends were thrown sideways as the bus rounded a tight corner and accelerated along Park Lane, losing sight of the Jiggery-Pokery pandemonium. Up ahead, through the trees, was a newly pasted billboard. They both shifted in their seats so they could get a better view and experience the full impact. The poster was so huge that it covered the entire side of an office building. Before they got there, however, the traffic slowed and then stopped at a red light for what felt like an eternity. Vee and Pye hunched forward in anticipation. They could see a fragment of the billboard through the trees: an ear, a hand. At last the lights turned green, the bus lurched onward again and the rest of the giant image loomed in to view.

It was an advert for the charity, Perfect Eden. The same picture was everywhere that week – on bus shelters, in Underground stations, on TV, pop-ups on websites – but this was definitely the biggest version they'd seen. It featured the ten-metre-high, ruggedly handsome face of ex-Hollywood actor turned fashion entrepreneur, Eden Greenfield – the man who had turned his TRULY clothing brand into a massive global chain of TRULYSuperstores and was now, through the Perfect Eden

Foundation, giving away large chunks of his vast fortune.

'Wow!'

'Cool!'

A chorus of adoring sighs echoed through the bus as they passed by.

'You seen this?' asked Pye, holding up the discarded free newspaper that had been left on their seat. There was another picture of Eden on the cover, this time coming out of a glitzy London restaurant.

'Mmm.' Verity frowned. She had been trying to ignore the celebrity gossip all week. She didn't want to look at another article about famous people dating each other. Especially not *those* famous people. She glanced at the headline.

SAFFRON'S TRULY PERFECT EDEN

The woman coming out of the restaurant with the billionaire was Verity's mum. Vee had been getting messages all day from school friends asking for confirmation.

eden gonna b yr nu dad? lol
wotl U wear 2 thr wddng???

Mum was even trending on Twitter.

'Uh!' Verity groaned. It had only been one date and already everyone was speculating like crazy. And it wasn't just questions like 'Will there be a second date?' or 'Don't they make a gorge-looking couple?' (which they did, of course). Oh no! They'd jumped right in to the intimate, embarrassing stuff. Eeuww! Not for the first time, Verity wished that she had a mum whose sex life wasn't scrutinised by the world's press.

The bus changed lanes and then pulled out to join the whirlpool of vehicles spinning around Hyde Park Corner. Verity sat back in her seat and the billboard disappeared as they headed down Knightsbridge. *One date*, she thought. *One date and everyone gets hysterical.* But she couldn't help wondering, too. Was everything about to change? Might the man on the billboard be a part of Verity's future? She chewed her lip.

The bus slowed to a crawl again in Sloane Street. There was another crowd milling about outside the TRULYSuperstore – perhaps not as big or frenzied as the one at Jiggery-Pokery, but no less remarkable. *Eden Greenfield must be doing another huge discount day*, Verity thought. She peered out of the window and her suspicions were confirmed by the fluorescent posters entirely covering the TRULYSuperstore windows.

'Look,' said Vee. 'Jeans for six quid. You could get yours there.'

'No way!' said Pye, screwing up her face in disgust.

'Why not? You could get ten pairs.'

Pye snorted. 'There's a reason they're so cheap, you know. Probably made by some blind, homeless orphan in some dangerous, rat-infested sweatshop somewhere, who gets no toilet breaks and is beaten if he complains.'

'A bit of an exaggeration, I think,' said Verity. 'Have you been watching documentaries again? This is the twenty-first century, not the Dark Ages. There aren't sweatshops with blind orphans anymore, like in Charles Dickens or something. Anyway, who cares who made them?' Verity asked. 'Where else in London can you get a pair of jeans for *six quid*? Nowhere, that's where. Bar-gain! It's flippin' bonkers and it's brilliant. Look how many customers they've got. No wonder Eden Greenfield is so rich.'

Eden Greenfield couldn't have been more different from Vee's bio-dad (a phrase he had invented himself) – the surf-obsessed sculptor whom she visited twice a year in his wind-blown beach-side cottage down on the North Devon coast. Eden was also significantly more impressive than all Mum's previous boyfriends – nice enough banker types who were OK-looking but ultimately tedious, Verity had decided. They simply couldn't compete. Eden Greenfield was in a whole different league and ticked every one of the boxes on Verity's Ultimate Stepdad Application Form (if she had one . . . which she didn't). He was incredibly witty and brainy (a first from Oxford and an expert in medieval warfare). He was impossibly handsome, had a warm chuckle in his voice and a flawless smile, ensuring that he stole scenes from his fellow actors from his first day on set. He was a phenomenon, seemingly admired and loved unconditionally by all, from little kids to grannies, from the High Street to Wall Street. Now he was dating Verity's mum.

She picked up the newspaper and looked at the photograph. Mum wasn't holding Eden's hand or anything, but she was looking at him and smiling. She seemed happy. Vee had to accept it. Mum deserved to be happy. She deserved success, deserved to be making lots of money. She'd worked hard, brought up a kid on her own, made sacrifices. And she deserved to have someone cool like Eden Greenfield as her boyfriend. Perhaps, Verity thought, Eden might even turn out to be the sugar on the cherry on the cupcake.

Fruity Toilets and Lying to Bliss

The figure emerged from the cloud of steam and stood in a pool of sickly yellow light seeping down from a first-floor window. Even with her face in deep shadow there was no mistaking the wide-brimmed hat, the sharp suit, the elegant designer shoes with the scarlet heels. It was Veronica Vamp.

What is she doing here?

'What did you kill him for?' Maisie asked, confused.

Veronica was the one who told me about the Mole. Veronica gave me the suitcase stuffed with money to exchange for the package. This doesn't make any sense. I hate how this game keeps throwing you surprises.

Veronica Vamp threw back her head and laughed. The sudden sight of her white teeth and wide, glossy mouth, painted the colour of blood, filled Maisie Malone with horror.

'Oh dear. You are slow, dear Maisie! Did it never occur to you that you were being set up?'

What? Maisie's heart fluttered.

'Poor Maisie!' Veronica pouted, lifted the still-smoking gun from where it had been resting on her haute-couture-clad hip and pointed it at Maisie's head. 'Thought I'd kill two irritating birds with one stone . . . or should I say bullet?' She sighed and lowered the gun. 'But, I suppose you deserve a bit of an explanation before I frame you for murder.'

Maisie Malone gulped. She didn't need an explanation. It was completely clear to her, now, how she'd been duped. She'd been used. Veronica needed to locate the Mole and Maisie had lured him out of his underground hiding place. She must have intended to kill him all along. Maisie Malone had been the bait. And now she was the *fall guy*, too. Veronica Vamp would shoot her, put the gun in her hand . . .

ha ha ha!

-1,000 points
score: 6,200

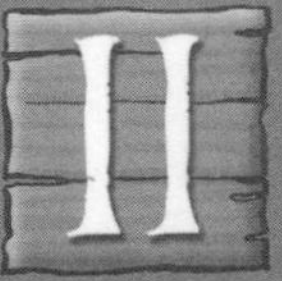

No – wait. There's something not right about this scenario. Veronica wants to make it look like I killed the Mole and the Mole killed me, but, when our corpses are discovered (hopefully before they get too putrid and bloated!), there will be autopsies, won't there? Both our bodies will contain the same bullets . . . from the same gun. So we couldn't have shot each other and the cops will guess it was Veronica. She'd be their number one suspect.

Maisie felt the weight of her pretty pearl-handled pistol in her pocket. There were sometimes weird little loopholes like this in Demon Streets and, when they came along, you had to take advantage of them.

'You can't shoot me,' said Maisie, smugly, ''cause you'll need *this* gun to kill me and I'm about to shoot *you* with it.' She prayed that she'd spotted a genuine flaw in Veronica's plan and that the small amount of ballistics knowledge she'd gained from TV detective shows was accurate.

'Go ahead,' said Veronica with a chuckle, the two, shiny red horns protruding from her forehead glinting in the neon lights.

'D'ya think I won't?'

'Come on! Pull the trigger!'

Maisie glanced down at her dainty pistol.

Would it dispatch such a powerful demon?

She shut her eyes and squeezed the trigger.

CLICK.

Nothing happened.

Veronica, still laughing, reached into her pocket and brought out a handful of small . . . . shiny . . . rattling . . . bullets!

'You should have been more observant when you collected my money, Maisie darling.'

Oh no! Another unforeseen twist. Every classic crime thriller had them in spades. Duh! How had she not predicted this? Why hadn't she noticed that the pearl-handled pistol was lighter when she'd left Veronica's luxury penthouse apartment? Eight bullets lighter. And how was she going to get out of this mess? She only had the tiny knife in her boot and that was no defence against getting shot in the he—

'You cleaned the toilet yet?'

'Yeah, just doing it!' Verity shouted. She wasn't. She was sitting on the side of the bath, bent over her phone. She jabbed her finger on 'pause'

then flexed her arms. She'd need some thinking time before making her next move, so she dropped the phone into the front pocket of her floral-print apron.

'When you've finished in there, you can whiz the vacuum around the hall,' Mum shouted from her basement studio.

'All right,' Verity huffed in reply.

'And get a move on. I can't give you a lift to school today.'

'It's OK. I don't mind.' She wanted the privacy of the fifteen-minute walk to search online for stuff about Mum and Eden. She'd decided she needed to check out the current celeb chat, but it was more as a defence against the inevitable taunts at school than because of any genuine interest. *I'd better fake that I've been cleaning the bathroom, then go,* she decided. She slopped a sponge around the bath then squirted the loo with tropical-fruit-scented pink bleach. As she leaned to close the lid of the toilet, her phone dropped straight out of her pocket . . .

PLOP!

. . . into the water.

'Oh, crapping crappety crap-fest!'

BRRRRIIIINNNNGGG!

'Argh!' She jumped away from the bowl, then realised the noise was coming from the front door, not the loo. She pulled a face and plunged her hand into the toilet. 'Eeuurgh!' She grabbed her half-drowned phone and wrapped it in a towel.

BRRRRIIIIIINNNGGG!

'Vee, sweetie! Will you get that?'

Verity closed the toilet lid and placed the phone on it (still wrapped in the towel) then stamped angrily on to the landing, wiping her wet hands on the apron. Why couldn't Mum answer the door? She was nearer.

BRING!

This time the ring was more tentative. The early morning visitor was probably about to give up and go away. But then Vee wondered if it might be the postman or a courier with a package. Perhaps it would be worth the effort to go and see. They might be delivering cool stuff.

She'd decided to answer the door as the Cleaner, a role she'd been playing to make the endless tedium of her punishment chores a bit more entertaining. The Cleaner was mopping-up after a particularly grisly murder – a murder that had left hard-to-remove bloodstains on the carpets and numerous bullet holes in the walls. And there was probably puke, too, she imagined. There was always a rookie cop puking at the sight of a bullet-ridden body in movies. The Cleaner had an Australian accent.

'G'day.'

'Oh, hi.' A red-haired girl wearing a crisply tailored, grey tweed suit stood on the top step, smiling. 'I'm Bliss. Bliss Meadows.'

'Roight-o,' said Verity. 'Aeend heow can oi . . . ?'

'I'm here for the interview?'

'Roight-o. Yi'd bitter cam een.' The accent was rubbish but Bliss Meadows seemed fooled by it. She probably thought Verity really was the cleaner – not the *crime-scene* sort, of course, but just the type who does ordinary housework (like the one Mum had paid *not* to clean their house for a month while Vee completed her 'sentence'). 'Oi'll gaw till missus Fibbs yeor heea.' Verity went to the top of the stairs that led down to the basement workroom and called out, 'Blees Midows's heea for the eentaveuw!'

'Oh, thanks!' said Mum's muffled voice from downstairs. 'Erm, show her into the kitchen, will you? I'll be right up.'

The kitchen's a weird place for a job interview, Verity thought. But maybe there were top secret Jiggery-Pokery design drawings in the studio that she didn't want a job candidate to see. Or maybe Mum, who was a *total* caffeine addict, just chose the kitchen because she needed a coffee fix. She sniggered as she imagined a bizarre scene – Mum's arm attached to the coffee machine via needle and plastic tube.

Bliss Meadows frowned so Verity managed a smile and pointed at the door through to the kitchen, then watched as the candidate tottered across the hall on zebra-stripe platform boots. She was just the sort of designer Mum liked – smartly dressed but with an eccentric twist.

'Vacuum?' said Mum as she came up the stairs.

'Jest about tow,' said Verity.

Mum pursed her lips and disappeared into the kitchen.

Verity opened the hall cupboard and pulled out the brightly-coloured vacuum cleaner, attached the hose and plugged the cord into the wall. Then she jabbed the *on* button with her foot . . .

VOOOOOOOOOOOOO!

. . . and machine-gunned three drooling zombies lurching down the stairs.

TA-TA-TA-TA-TA-TA-TAT!

'Eat lead, zombies!'

Their heads exploded across the wall.

'Die, you ugly undead losers!'

Dead! My phone! She'd forgotten her drowned-in-pink-bleach phone was in a critical condition, so she dropped the hose and sprang up the stairs two at a time. In the bathroom, she unwrapped the towel and pressed the buttons, like she was performing CPR. Nothing. She picked it up and shook it. There was a tiny sloshing noise and a smell of tropical fruit cocktail. She tried the buttons again but the screen remained blank. She turned it over and flicked out the battery, shook it again and put the dried-off battery back. The screen flickered, showed the time (8.43), then died.

Great start to the day: I'm late and I killed my phone!

She grabbed her school bag from her room and sprinted down to the hallway again, where Mum was shaking hands with Bliss Meadows.

'Thanks for coming over so early,' said Mum.

'That's OK. So I'll start when you get back from launching Flim-Flam in America?'

'Yeah. But I'll email all the details . . .

and send you keys and door codes and stuff.'

That was quick! She'd obviously got the job. Bliss and Mum were grinning at each other and seemed to have become instant best friends.

'I can't wait,' said Bliss.

'Well, like I said, I knew at your first interview that you were the best candidate and you did come highly recommended.'

That explained it.

Mum turned as Vee jumped noisily down the last step. 'Will you put that away before you go?' Mum pointed at the vacuum cleaner.

'Roight-o. Oh, and you're owt of dunny cleana.'

'What?'

'Yew naw. Thit smilly staf for the dunny.'

Mum pursed her lips again and rolled her eyes, then turned her attention to Bliss Meadows, who was still smiling and standing in the open doorway.

'Bye then,' said Mum.

'Hope you have a great trip,' said Bliss, beaming from ear to ear.

Uh, thought Vee. *All that grinning is making me nauseous.*

'Thanks. I'm sure we will.'

'Bye.'

'Baa-ee!' said Verity, making an *I want to vomit* gesture with two fingers down her throat.

The List, the Panther and the Boy

Terminal five at Heathrow airport was super busy, noisy and bustling with frantic travellers. The most frantic seemed to be the Jiggery-Pokery team of eight, fidgeting around the check-in point, waving their arms about, counting giant suitcases and sample bags and shouting into their Blackberries. At the centre of the chaos, the calm eye of the storm, stood Saffron and Verity Fibbs.

'Don't let your Aunty Tam pay for everything, OK?' said Mum, frowning and nervously brushing her hand through her hair.

'Right,' Verity grunted. She had just about forgiven Mum for her month of domestic torture.

'Here's cash for the taxi home tonight, then the train to Brighton on Saturday.' Mum handed Verity a thick white envelope.

Excellent! An envelope full of cash, thought Verity. *A top-secret pay-off.*

'Then there's emergency money and the credit card in the safe. But *only* in an emergency, OK?'

'Uh-huh.'

‘I trust you to use some common sense.’ Mum managed a smile and the pair hugged.

Unlikely, thought Verity. *Super-sleuth, Maisie Malone, let loose in London with an envelope of money: there is absolutely no chance of any common sense.*

‘I’ll be fine. You don’t have to worry,’ she said, stuffing the envelope into her bag. She was looking forward to counting it later.

Mum scraped her hand through her hair again. ‘Perhaps I should delay my flight, wait until the weekend. I hate leaving you on your own.’

‘Muuum!’ Verity protested. ‘We’ve discussed this. You’ve got to go today. You decided.’

‘Are you sure you don’t want Callista to—’

‘NO!’ Verity cut her off. There was no way she was going to let Mum’s evil studio manager spoil her plans.

‘She wouldn’t mind.’

‘I told you, I’m gonna be fine on my own. I’m not a kid any more. I’m not this baby bird with its mouth open waiting for its mum to feed it worms and stuff. I learned how to walk and talk and dress myself, like, at least a week ago,’ she said. ‘And, for your information, I’m actually potty-trained, too. I’ve been getting to school on my own—’

‘You make sure you do,’ Mum interrupted. ‘Get to school, I mean. The only reason I agreed to leave you alone is so you don’t miss any school. This year is SO important, Vee. You need to work hard and apply yourself.’

‘I am. I will. Now, get out of my life, you controlling freak, and go to New York!’ Verity grinned.

Mum grinned back. ‘You can come with us next time.’

'Mmm,' Verity agreed, while thinking how great it was NOT to be going with Mum. She'd be on her own in London for two and a half days of total freedom.

Mum's assistant was making weird hand signals at her. The last piece of baggage had been checked, they had their boarding passes and the team was ready to hit the bar in the flight lounge.

'I'd better go,' said Mum. 'Say "hi" to my sis . . . Get to school on time . . . and don't talk to journalists . . . and don't let strangers into the house . . . ' Mum was walking backwards towards the security gate. 'And switch the dishwasher on when it's full . . . and don't play those video games *all* night . . . and don't get into any trouble!'

Mum waved and Verity laughed.

'OK. I'll try.'

Four hundred pounds! Two and a half days of independence and four hundred quid to spend! Verity pushed the wad of twenty-pound notes back into the envelope. Mum had left her far too much. It was loads more than she'd actually need to get home from the airport and down to Brighton on Saturday. Vee drew out a folded sheet of paper that had made the parcel twice as fat. It wasn't more lovely cash for Maisie Malone to have fun with, as she'd hoped, but a typed note from Mum. How disappointing! Verity sighed as she read it. It wasn't just a note, but a long list of paranoid instructions covering both sides. Mum worried too much.

- DON'T talk to the press. If they follow you, say 'no comment' and pretend you're phoning the police or your lawyer.
- DO NOT use the emergency cash or credit card in the safe for anything other than an emergency! (like a nuclear war or something!)
- You are NOT old enough to drive my new car!
- Get to school on time – if you cut lessons again, they'll exclude you and, more importantly, I will be in serious trouble.
- The fridge is well stocked so PLEASE try to eat some real food, not takeaways! Your skin will thank you.
- Get a black taxi if you're out after dark – not a minicab or the night bus. Better still, don't be out after dark!
- Close the curtains at night (so nobody can see you're alone).
- No late night horror movies on school nights.
- Set the alarm when you go to bed or leave the house and don't forget it needs to be disarmed, too! (Remember the number is YOUR birthday and, if you set it off by accident, the code word you give the police is MANNEQUIN)

Verity rolled her eyes. *Duh! You're not supposed to write it down, Mum!* And she didn't need reminding of the number. She was always turning it off and on. It was like an automatic reflex action as soon as she got to the front door. Mum was treating her like a complete imbecile. She flipped the sheet over and read on.

•Keep your music down, particularly that moaning emo stuff that drives our neighbours crazy.

•Put the rubbish out on Friday morning, not Thursday night. I saw a four-foot rat last week! I'm NOT joking!

Verity laughed. Mum was a complete lunatic . . . and obviously exaggerating somewhat.

•Switch the dishwasher on when it's full.

•Don't let strangers into the house.

•Remember you can call Callista any time if you have a problem and Tamsin is only an hour away. Tam is expecting you in Brighton on Saturday. Phone from the train and she'll pick you up. Don't let my sister pay for everything. You've got plenty of cash, so offer to buy lunch a couple of times.

•We are due to fly back to Heathrow next Thursday, sooner if I can. Flight details on my desk.

•Should our plane be abducted by aliens or sucked into a black hole, all the insurance documents, my will and the number for my solicitor are in the safe. (Ha ha. That **was** a joke!)

Verity swallowed. That's *not at all* funny, Mum!

The list ended with the words:

BE SENSIBLE!!! I TRUST YOU!

Love you lots. Hugs and kisses.

MUM xxxxxxxxxx

P.S. Text me any time and I'll phone every night. I'll take you on my next trip and we'll have some girly fun, I promise.

PLEASE be good!

x

Be good? What does that mean? Be a boring old loser? No way was she going to waste the next two days being 'good'! Mum had said nothing about her friends not staying the night, nor had she forbidden a party. She turned the paper over and scanned the list. Nope. No party ban. Verity grinned. There was nothing to say she was forbidden to wear Mum's clothes either, or her shoe collection or jewellery or designer handbags or to use her make-up or her gorgeous luxury en-suite bathroom.

Verity began to plan. She'd invite her mates back after school each day and she'd order a 'party hamper' to be delivered by the fashionable deli around the corner. The deli's catering service had supplied several of Mum's fancy business functions and their phone number was stuck to the fridge. Maybe she'd hire their bartender as well, to come and mix cosmopolitans and Martinis. How far would her £400 stretch? she wondered. She and her guests would move the furniture back to the walls and blast music out of the new multi-platform media system in the lounge (tracks she was sure the neighbours would *love!*). She'd already downloaded the eighteen-rated *Demon Streets* online role-play game so she could play it on the giant HD TV screen (instead of her drowned phone). And it didn't matter what was or was not on Mum's list because Mum was never going to know, was she? She wouldn't know if Verity ate nothing but meat-feast pizza, danced naked on the night bus or invited her forbidden ex-boyfriend round to snog on the sofa and watch horror movies (although she had no intention of doing any of that!). She would simply have her party and put everything back where it should be by Saturday afternoon, then take the train to her Aunt Tamsin's, as instructed.

Although, why she had to go to Brighton at all, she had no idea. *Why can't I stay in London until Mum comes home? I'm not a child any more. I'm practically an adult. I don't need a minder or a babysitter to check I'm not drowning myself in the bath or sticking forks into plug sockets.* Mum clearly didn't completely trust her, so she'd have to make the most of the time she *did* have: two and a half days. Just enough time to have an *adventure!*

She began to walk back towards the taxi rank. *Which way did we come in?* She looked up at a yellow sign floating high above the sea of passengers, saw the word *Taxis* above *Trains* and *Underground*, and wondered for a moment if she should save some of the cash for her party and take the tube instead of a cab. Then she noticed what was written below: *International Check-in* and *International Arrivals.*

I won't go home just yet.

She began to walk with a confident stride, pretending to be one of the passengers, someone who caught flights to distant, glamorous destinations every day of the week. Then she was brought to a sudden halt by a slow-moving crocodile of grey-haired, brightly-dressed tourists, each of them dragging a wheelie suitcase the size of a small car in their wake and seemingly oblivious to Verity's urgency.

Come on! I need to get to my luxury, Louis Vuitton-interior-designed private jet so I can fly to my own secret tropical island with my totally gorge secret agent/rock star boyfriend.

While she waited for them to pass, she watched two bulky police officers, both armed with enormous guns and dressed in multi-pocketed, padded black suits that could have walked straight off the catwalk of her mum's 2009 Post-punk collection. They looked rather cool, she thought, but a little scary. It wasn't until she began to scrutinise their headgear that she realised one of them, the one with bigger biceps, was actually a woman. She scanned their foreheads for horns. *Were they demons disguised as police officers,* she wondered? *Are they looking for their next innocent human victim or searching the crowd for terrorists? I'd better not do anything weird in case they suspect I'm a heroin smuggler or a crazed assassin. Or act suspicious like that bloke over there.*

The bloke she'd noticed looked like he would have been more comfortable on a university campus or at a grungy rock festival. He looked out of place in his hooded, graphic-printed sweatshirt and wrinkled low-slung jeans. He wasn't even trying to look smart like most of the other passengers.

Perhaps he'd just returned from a drugged-up holiday with his drugged-up mates, Verity thought. He had a grubby canvas satchel slung across his body but no suitcase and he was shuffling about, looking furtive. Then he disappeared behind a tower of giant nylon bags, skis and snowboards. When she spotted him again, further across the enormous concourse, he'd removed the hood, had pulled up the jeans and was walking differently. It was really odd. His was transformed. By adjusting his jeans and changing his walk he'd managed to look like a completely new person. Why would he do that? *He's weird and probably a total psycho*, thought Verity. She decided to follow him.

The girl-sleuth silently stalked her prey like a prowling panther. The raven-haired beauty clung to the shadows and moved through their velvet blackness with the stealth and grace of a hungry cat.

Verity tailed him around the building – browsing along the bookshelves in WHSmith's, checking out the price of digital video cameras in an electrical shop, to Starbucks (where she followed his lead and ordered black coffee – latté being for wimps and trolls, as everyone knows) and then down to the lower levels.

Where is he going?

Into the deepest underworld the cat pursued her victim. Step by careful step she drew closer to her quarry . . . ready to pounce.

He stopped at a barrier, turned and looked up. She could now see his face more clearly and was surprised to discover that he wasn't a man at all but a teenage boy, perhaps not much older than she was. He had soft brown eyes, a full mouth, cute smile and a slight peach-fuzz moustache above his top lip. *A bit nerdy, but nice*, she thought.

The girl-sleuth gripped her gun, ready to dispatch the boy should his seemingly harmless, though attractive, appearance conceal his true, villainous, demon identity.

The boy was scanning the arrivals board. *Is he meeting a friend? A girlfriend? A fellow spy? A fellow drug dealer? Is he a chauffeur like the group of uniformed men standing over by the barrier? Probably not. Is he in fact a crazed terrorist about to make contact with his accomplice, the even-more-crazed terrorist?* Verity simply couldn't tell. He looked like a slightly geeky student to her, not someone who hung around international airports.

The beautiful and brainy girl-sleuth decided to draw on her lifetime of spying experience, her quick feline brain and razor-sharp powers of deduction . . . but they told her nothing. Zilch. Absolute zero. Peach-fuzz boy was a complete mystery to her.

Verity gave up her role playing (which was getting a bit exhausting) and began to read some of the handwritten signs clasped in the hands of the uniformed limo drivers. She giggled. Two of the signs were particularly amusing:

and

Surely these weren't genuine clients. Perhaps the chauffeurs got bored waiting for planes to land and came up with comedy signs for a bit of a laugh. *Cool!*

The boy had retreated behind a pillar and was tapping furiously at his phone. He was either deciphering a complex coded message from his terrorist accomplice, texting an epic novel or making a gazillion attempts to beat his all-time best score at *Paper Toss*, Verity thought. Suddenly, he put his phone in his pocket and backed away from the arrivals barrier. The boy pulled up the hood of his sweatshirt and returned to the slouchy walk, only this time he seemed in more of a hurry. Where was he going? Verity kept her distance again but found it hard to keep up and then almost bumped into him as he came back out of WHSmith's, where he'd bought some chewing gum and a computer magazine. He backtracked across the concourse and headed swiftly towards the far end and straight into a noisy bar.

Verity hesitated at a sign that read, *No Unaccompanied Children*. She obviously wasn't a child but tonight her lack of make-up and cherubic (dough-ball fat, according to Pye) face were a massive disadvantage. If she'd had a bit more time she could have got into character as the sophisticated girl-sleuth, and would have strode in like she owned the place. Right now, though, she looked totally underage and could pretty much guarantee she'd be thrown straight out. How had the boy just walked in there with so much confidence? *Bet he's ordering a quadruple Jack Daniels or something, without the bartender even asking his age.* But, before she could rummage in her bag for some lipstick, the boy was coming out of the bar towards her again. He was putting on a pair of geeky spectacles. She gulped. Had he stolen them, picked them up off a table, or something? *He's a shoplifter! A pickpocket!* Verity looked around for CCTV cameras or the two armed police officers rushing over, waving their guns, to arrest him. When she'd reassured herself that the airport's entire security strike force wasn't about to swoop, she turned her attention back to the boy. But he'd disappeared.

The girl-sleuth had lost track of her prey but, like a cat with nine lives, she would return to hunt another day. On panther's paws she padded back to her lair to lick her wounds.

Verity returned to the arrivals barrier. She'd decided to see if Mr Pong or Walter Fizz would make an appearance. She didn't hold out much hope.

I wonder where I could fly to for £400? Milan? Miami? Moscow? I could buy a ticket and be somewhere on the other side of the world in a few hours. How cool would that be? Hmm . . . s'pose I'd have to go get my passport though.

She was about to reach for her phone to ask Pye if she'd like to come to Miami with her, then remembered her phone was a fruit-flavoured corpse, lying lifeless on her bedside table at home. *And we'd need return tickets, which I guess might be expensive. Can I afford two return tickets? And we've got school tomorrow.* She sighed.

A flight from San Diego, via Washington, had landed and the first passengers were just beginning to emerge, with trolleys brimming with luggage, through the double doors on the other side of the barrier. Suddenly, right in the middle of the recently arrived travellers, there was the boy! At least she thought it was him. He'd completely changed his appearance again. He'd removed the funky sweatshirt to reveal a blue check shirt, to which he'd added a tie. Verity wondered if he'd bought it, pinched it (confirming her shoplifter theory) or had been wearing it all along. He'd pulled the jeans up and they now sat above his waist instead of hanging gangsta-style from his hips. The canvas bag was no longer slung across his body, but dangling from one shoulder, the strap shortened. He had dampened his hair and smoothed it down, giving him a geeky side-swept fringe. The glasses completed the look. He'd even altered his walk again. This time his hands were constantly fidgeting and his legs were sort of stiff, like he was clenching his bum cheeks together. *He's pretending he was on that flight*, thought Verity. *Excellent*! She moved closer, eager to see what he'd do next.

The boy approached one of the chauffeurs and pointed. 'Hey, that's me,' he said in a high-pitched Scottish accent, chewing gum between each word. Verity tingled with excitement. *That accent is brilliant but defo-lutley fake.* She'd heard him ask for his coffee just a few minutes ago and she was certain he wasn't Scottish.

The chauffeur was holding a board with removable white letters that spelled out the name,

Edgar Butterworth
Butterworth Digital

Verity was mesmerised. The chauffeur was clearly waiting for someone important, someone who shared his name with a company, Butterworth Digital. He was probably the director or the chairman or something. There was no way that peach-fuzz boy looked like he was the director of a company. How would he pull it off? And what would he do if the *real* Edgar Butterworth came through those doors? He was bound to at any moment. Vee's heart drummed against her ribs.

The chauffeur asked, 'Mr and Mrs Butterworth? I guess we're waiting for your wife then, sir?'

Verity gulped. *Uh-oh! Major disaster alert!*

But the boy's expression didn't flicker. 'Aye. She's just vizeteng the, y'knor, little girrrls rrroom,' he said, passing the computer magazine from one hand to the other. Verity could now feel her heart beating in her throat and was sure she was about to throw up, it was so exciting. The chauffeur looked at the boy, narrowed his eyes, then looked at the other passengers now streaming through the double doors.

That's when she decided to do it. She had to act quickly. She took the lipstick from her bag and, using the chrome rail of the barrier as a mirror, applied it. She leaned over and fluffed-up her hair, then she buttoned up her jacket and stepped forward.

Raven-haired and scarlet-lipped, Maisie Malone walked out of Murder Lane to join her accomplice and face their foe, the Demon Driver. This time she was ready for anything with her loaded pistol and what she hoped was the correct password.

When, for a brief moment, the chauffeur pulled out a copy of a computer magazine (the same one the boy had in his hand) and flicked to an inside page, she ducked down, pushed through the crowd, stood up again and took hold of the boy's arm.

'Hey, hun!' She kissed the boy on the cheek, leaving a scarlet smear, and prayed her Scottish accent, learned from the movie *Trainspotting*, was going to be convincing. 'Ay so heet those airrrplane bathrrrooms, don't yew? Ay've been simply bustin' since mid-Atlantic! So, you foond ower rrride.'

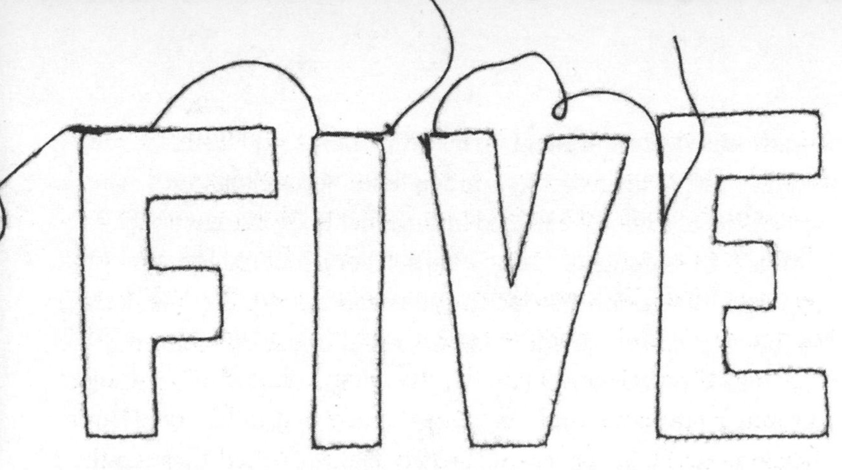

Being Married then Being Dumped

The sleek, streamlined limousine purred through the midnight streets towards their secret rendezvous. The gaudy, flickering lights of the decadent city illuminated the angelic face of Maisie Malone as she gazed through the rain-flecked window. Across the vast, empty space of the back seat sat Peach-fuzz-Boy, her accomplice, calm and seemingly untroubled, ignoring the air of menace and foreboding that hung between them like a bad smell.

Verity still could not believe the chauffeur had fallen for it. *This is SO COOL!* The boy, annoyingly, refused to catch her eye, though, and seemed instead to be reading the computer magazine. She wanted him to talk to her – in character, of course – so she could do some more of the excellent accent she had adopted. She also wanted him to thank her and acknowledge that what she'd done had been really impressive. Verity glanced at the face of the driver, reflected in the rear-view mirror, and his eyes flicked momentarily away from the road and straight into hers. She swallowed then smiled back. She had to stay focused. She was Mrs Butterworth, married to Edgar, and they were en route to their swanky London hotel. Something touched her hand. A jolt of adrenaline flashed through her body like electricity.

Maisie Malone flexed her fingers. Every muscle tensed and prepared to leap for the door handle and spring, cat-like, from the moving vehicle as soon as her secret cover was blown.

She looked down. The boy had put the magazine on the seat and pushed it towards her. *What is he doing? I don't want to read a magazine!* She shook her head. The boy opened his eyes wide then nodded at the magazine. Perhaps he'd written a message on it. Something like, *You're an awesome actress!* or *You saved my life back there. Thanks, babe.* She picked it up. It was open on one of the middle pages – an article entitled 'Edgar's Dark Worlds'. Not what she was expecting at all. Then Verity flinched. There was a picture that she recognised spread across the double page. It was a screen grab from *Demon Streets*. She read the strap line:

Edgar Butterworth, Scottish creator of the Demon Streets franchise . . .

'Woah!' Verity exclaimed.

The boy coughed, nervously.

She ignored him and flicked over the page to scan the rest of the article and found another picture with a caption below.

Edgar Butterworth and his wife, Flora, at the party to celebrate the launch of Demon Streets 4.

Verity read on and discovered that, not only did Edinburgh Uni drop-out, Edgar Butterworth, create her fave online role-play game of all time, but he was 'just twenty-two', a 'games millionaire' and ending a world tour with a 'visit to London for the games and animation convention, *Avatarama*'. She was furious.

'Uuh, you moron!' Verity moaned. 'The actual inventor of *Demon Streets* was at Heathrow airport!'

'Shh!'

'No, I won't shh! I was *there*!' She was furious. 'I could have *met* him, got his picture, an autograph, asked him about my favourite characters . . . how to avoid getting framed for murder by Veronica Vamp on Level 14!' Her voice had risen from a whisper to loud, bad-tempered muttering.

The boy looked worried now and held up his hands in a 'calm down' gesture.

'Huh; following you was a massive mistake,' she mumbled. 'FYI, you turned out to be a waste of good lipstick!'

The limo was the type with a partition between driver and passengers. In fact, it had two – a glass one and a solid one – which could be raised and lowered. That night, if either screen had been in place, the course of events might have been very different, but neither screen was raised.

Verity folded her arms, scowled at the boy, then continued. 'I was gonna have this fabulous evening at the airport and now look what's happened. I end up in a stupid limo with some weirdo who won't even thank me fo-uurgh!'

Verity was thrown forward and winded by her seatbelt. The chauffeur had swung the car over to the curb and slammed on the brakes.

'Right! Get out!'

'Oops!' She'd forgotten the driver could hear them and she'd completely dropped her accent.

Cover blown! Game over!

Before she had a chance to unbuckle her seatbelt, the chauffeur was at her door, wrenching it open and shouting, 'I knew there was something dodgy 'bout you two! Come on, out you get!'

Traffic on the busy road was having to swerve around the stationary limo and the night air was now filled with the sounds of squealing tyres and angry honking.

'My mate at Gatwick warned me there was some kid doing this. Never thought I'd . . .' He shook his head. 'Bollocks! The *real* computer geezer will be waitin' there like a right plonker. Soon as you got in the car I knew you wasn't married. I bloody knew it!' Then he tried to hide a smirk. 'What are you, 'bout fifteen, sixteen? I've got a nephew your age. Bloody criminal-in-the-makin' he is. Just like you two.'

Verity and the boy got out, then the driver stormed into the road, where he narrowly missed being crushed by a truck, before sliding back into his seat. As the driver waited for a gap in the traffic, they could hear him chuckling.

'He he! At least you didn't get any money out of me, like my nephew does.'

The boy leaned forward, smiled and asked, through the open window, 'Lend us a tenner?'

'Sod off!'

'Got a business card?'

'What?' said the chauffeur, astonished.

'A business card or something with your phone number? We might want to hire you again. I'll recommend you to *all* my friends.'

'You've got to be kiddin' me!' He laughed, reached into a cup-holder between the seats, then thrust a white card into the boy's hand.

'Thanks, James,' he said, reading the name on the card.

'Any time. Good luck stayin' out of prison, you two,' James yelled as the limo pulled out and disappeared into the night.

'Hey! Where you goin'?' Verity shouted.

The boy was walking away. She hadn't really meant what she'd said about him being a weirdo and a waste of lipstick. And actually, if she was truthful, she couldn't think of a better way to spend the evening than scamming a chauffeur and pretending to be someone else. She'd enjoyed it so much she was still shaking from the exhilaration of being found out. The boy had pulled his sweatshirt back on and returned to the hunched, student persona she'd first encountered at the airport. She sprinted to catch up with him as he slouched off down the street.

'Wait!'

He ignored her and kept walking.

'Don't I even get a thank you?' she said, panting.

He turned and scowled at her. 'What? For getting us thrown out of the limo?'

'I didn't! It wasn't my fault!' As she said it, she knew it probably was.

'Huh.'

She didn't like the way the conversation was going. Why was he being so gnarly? Couldn't he see how much they had in common, how they were destined to be firm friends? She had hoped that this boy would be different, more sophisticated, perhaps more mature and less annoying than the boys in her year at school, but now she didn't think he was. The boy thrust his hands into his pockets. She walked beside him, matching his stride.

'I guess that means divorce then?' said Verity.

He smiled. 'Yep. You get the papers drawn up and I'll sign 'em.'

Verity smiled back. At least he liked her joke. *G.S.O.H. Tick.*

The boy kept walking. She wished he'd slow down.

'Hey! Wait! Where you going?'

'I dunno. Bus stop? Tube station?'

'You gotta be somewhere, then?'

'Not really. Thought I'd go into town and see what's buzzin'. You?'

'Um,' Verity thought for a second or two. He didn't sound very enthusiastic but she didn't want to be on her own just yet. Anyway, Mum wouldn't be waiting for her on the doorstep with a look of dismay on her face. Not tonight. Who better to share her first evening of freedom? And he owed her an adventure, didn't he, after stopping her from meeting the *real* Edgar Butterworth? And he intrigued her. What sort of person got his kicks scamming chauffeurs at airports? 'Yeah, let's go and see what's buzzin',' she said and smiled, hoping she didn't look like a crazy psycho stalker. The boy groaned but Verity hoped he didn't mean it and that he secretly admired her part in the Edgar Butterworth scam. She comfortably matched his pace as they strode towards Earl's Court tube station.

'So, you've done it before then?' asked Verity.

'The chauffeur swindle? Yeah. Not at Heathrow, but Gatwick once and Stanstead.'

'Cool!'

'I look at the signs then all I have to do is search for the names on the internet and, if they've done interesting stuff, like they're musicians or writers, there will be loads of info. I look for pics and kinda personal stuff. It's great if there's video but that's usually really famous people, like footballers and movie stars, and it's probably not a good idea to pretend to be them. Too well known.'

Verity nodded. She was fascinated. *What an amazing idea! I wish I'd thought of it. He's a genius!*

'. . . And if they're kinda near enough to my age then I go for it. At Stanstead, I pretended to be this horror writer on a book tour. I only got a ride to a scabby Travelodge near the airport, though. Then, at Gatwick, I was this cellist – the one who was doin' a gig at the Royal Albert Hall – and I had to explain that my cello was on a different flight. I was dropped at the Dorchester . . .'

'Ooo, posh!'

'. . . and almost got as far as checking in.' He paused. 'Last week I was a New Zealand rugby player.'

Verity raised her eyebrows. The boy was pale and skinny – a physique more suited to chess than rugby.

'Yeah, I know,' he laughed. 'Hard to imagine? But, I promise, we do look alike. Same hair and nose and stuff. But, yeah, the real bloke is about twice my size. I padded out my jacket and the driver took me all the way to Twickenham. I was telling him all this crap about my knee injury on the way, like describing the surgery and all that, but it was all made up.' He shook his head. 'So cool.'

'Why d'you choose Edgar Butterworth?' asked Verity.

'I knew I could do him.'

'Do him?'

'Yeah, make myself look enough like him. You saw the picture.

Pretty close, right? He was on the telly last week and I thought I could probably get his accent and wave my hands around in that weird twitchy way he does.'

'Didn't know he had a wife, though,' said Verity with a smirk.

'Nah. Bit of a mistake, that. Wondered if you might step in.'

'Eh?'

'Yeah. I was watching you and thought you might.'

'*You* were watching *me?*'

'Uh-huh. All that sneaking about you were doing, turning up the collar of your jacket and talking to yourself.'

'I was NOT talking to myself!' Verity protested, her cheeks turning pink. 'Anyway, it's *role play*. It's called "Method acting," if you must know. I learned it at drama school. All the best actors do it. Well, I do, anyway. You draw on your own experiences and you really *live* the part you're playing. It makes your performance more authentic.'

'So what part were you *role playing* back there then? Mental girl who talks to herself?' said the boy with a sneer.

'Shut up!'

The tube train rumbled, whined and screeched to a halt at a crowded station.

'So you're an actress?'

Verity shivered with delight. He believed her! It must have been all that stuff about method acting techniques. Then an idea popped into her head. She'd show him what a real actress could do. She'd impress him with her own amazing ability to impersonate someone else – way better than his pathetic chauffeur scam.

'We're getting out here.' She grabbed his hand and dragged him from the carriage, just as the doors beeped and began to close.

Hades

Verity hailed a taxi outside the station and gave the driver an address in Soho. The journey would be just long enough for her to prepare. First she rummaged in her bag for some make-up and carefully applied eyeliner and lipstick as the taxi bounced and swerved through a maze of back streets. Then, when she was satisfied that she looked at least ten years older, she plunged her hand back into her bag for her mobile. But it wasn't there!

'Urgh!' she moaned, remembering that she'd drowned it that morning. She looked at the boy. 'Lend us your phone, will you?'

'What?'

'Phone.'

'What's wrong with yours?'

'I used it to murder the last person who wouldn't do what I asked. It's been logged in to police evidence. Come on! We don't have all night!'

She waved her hand at him, palm upwards. He pulled his mobile out of his pocket and passed it to her. Verity then extracted and unfolded a grubby flier for a photographic studio that had clearly been decomposing in her bag since the Jurassic period. Near the bottom of the flyer was the number she was looking for. *Bookings and enquiries, call Vincent on . . .* She tapped in a short text message:

vinnie
arrive Hades 5mins b redi
saff x

Then she keyed in the number and pressed *send. I hope Vince hasn't changed his schedule*, she thought. *I hope he's waiting in his usual spot, where he always waits, every night, with his camera . . . and his mobile switched on.* She handed the phone back and smiled.

'You got sunglasses?'

'Yeah. But it's eight thirty and dark out. Why do I . . . ?'

'Don't argue! You'll see. Put 'em on.'

The paparazzi were already jostling and barking at each other as the taxi pulled up outside The Hades Club in Soho. They were a pack of animals waiting for their prey. Having rested after their last celebrity meal, they were ready for the next victim to wander into their killing zone. Even before the taxi's door opened, the street was filled with the overexcited blinking of flashing lights and the growl of camera lenses auto-focusing.

The boy had found his sunglasses and pulled up the hood of his sweatshirt as Verity had instructed him to do.

'Ready?' she asked as she reached for the door handle.

The muscles of the boy's jaw clenched, a momentary twitch of nerves, but he quickly turned it into a broad grin. Verity felt a warm flush of pleasure in her cheeks. He was totally up for it. Excellent!

'Let's go!'

The boy stayed close behind as she dashed across the pavement towards the doors of the club. The hungry pack were not corralled behind a barrier or rope like they might have been at a movie premiere, they were right there, standing lens-to-face with them, so the pair had to push their way through.

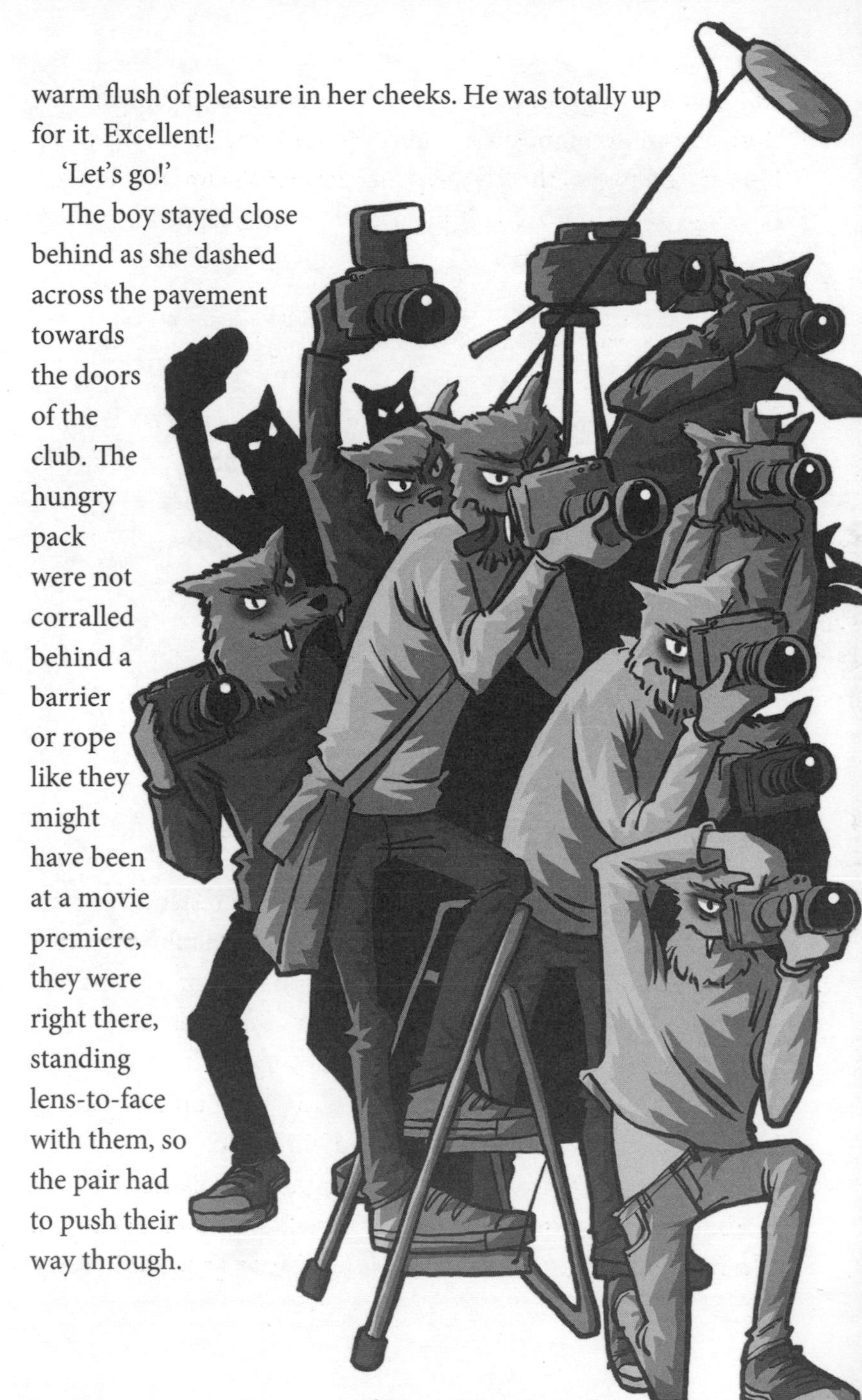

Verity had pinned up her hair, turned up the collar of her jacket and put on her own, oversized shades.

'Put your arm around me,' she hissed. 'And look concerned for my safety.'

He did as he was told. Verity raised a hand as if to cover her face, but then spotted Vince in the crowd – the photographer she'd once met at a shoot for Jiggery-Pokery. He was a studio assistant by day and a papper by night. She waved a friendly thumbs up-sign at him. Had he got her message? Vince smiled and nodded, but then frowned. He looked confused.

Uh-oh, thought Verity. *Better get inside before he realises I'm not Mum.*

'Saffron! Saffron, this way!' a photographer shouted. 'Who's your date?' barked another.

Verity put her head down and blundered forwards, hoping that the boy would do the same. They had to get inside before Vince informed his colleagues that it wasn't the famous fashion designer with a new mystery date after all. It was her teenage daughter with some geeky boyfriend. The doors to the club opened as if by magic and they tumbled into the dimly lit lobby. Verity didn't stop to chat with the doorman or the waiting hostess or to check in their coats, but stormed straight into the main bar, dragging the boy to a secluded table by the fireplace.

'Who *are* you?' the boy shouted over the loud music, pushing back his hood and grinning at her.

'Saffron Smith, pleased to meet you,' Verity replied, offering her hand for him to shake.

'So you're a famous actress? I didn't recognise you at the airport but now I kinda know your face.' His own face creased up in concentration. He'd obviously never heard her name but was trying to recall where he'd seen her before.

'Yep!' She tingled with pleasure.

'Would I have seen you in anything?'

'Well, I've done a lot of telly and some Hollywood movies, but I'm concentrating on the stage at the moment. You know, Shakespeare at the National and all that.'

'Really? What Hollywood movies?'

'Um. I was in that vampire movie last year. It was only a small part – one of the girl vampires.' She was speaking far too quickly.

'Wow! That's cool!'

'Yeah, it was. And it was great in LA – kinda fun to be working on a really big movie, you know. But there was loads of that *green screen* stuff, which is really difficult because you have to pretend you're in this, like, amazing landscape but it's not actually there because they put it all in later with CGI.'

'Mmm, that must be tricky.'

A warm fizz was growing in the pit of her stomach. He believed her. In fact, he was lapping up her story.

'I'm thinking of doing a musical next, you know. I'm doing voice training and dance classes and my agent is talking about maybe a part in *Chicago* or something. But I—' She stopped. *Chill out, Vee!* If she kept up this inane gabbling, she knew she'd say something really stupid. She always did. The faster she talked the more likely she was to make a mistake and then the whole performance would collapse. 'Anyway,' she continued, 'I don't even know *your* name.'

'Me?'

Verity nodded. 'I know you're not Edgar Butterworth, are you?'

'No. Obviously not.' He shook his head. 'Hi, I'm Peter Parker.' They shook hands again.

'Peter Parker? You mean like Spiderman?' She wasn't sure she quite believed him, but didn't want to suggest he'd made the name up in case he started to question her own story. 'I shall call you Pete.'

'What can I get you?' A waiter had appeared by their table.

'Oh, hi,' said Verity. 'I'll have an appletini.' She turned to her companion. 'Pete?'

'Scotch. No ice.'

'Um. I hope you don't mind,' said the waiter to Verity, 'but I'm going to have to ask your guest for some form of ID.' He smiled and shrugged.

'Hey, no probs,' said Verity. 'He does look younger than he actually is, doesn't he? Pete? Got your driving licence, babe?'

Peter Parker was already pulling something out of his pocket. *Great*, thought Verity, *he's carrying fake ID*. Every well-equipped teenager had fake ID. She had her own counterfeit student card – one that stated she was six years older than she really was – always ready in the side pocket of her bag.

'Thank you, sir,' said the waiter, glancing quickly at the card in Peter's hand, then walking back towards the bar.

'So, are you a student?' she asked.

'Nah. Left college a while back. I'm kinda freelance. Y'know – I travel around doing different jobs.'

'So what you doing now?'

'Snake-venom milker.'

'What?' Verity laughed. She thought she might have misheard him over the noise of music and bar chatter. 'What's that?'

'Snake-venom milkers milk snakes for their venom.'

'Well, obviously!' *He had to be making* that *up!* 'What do you need snake venom for?'

'Well, I work for this medical company as a kind of lab technician. We get the venom by taking them by the head like this . . .' He mimed grabbing the snake. '. . . and pressing their fangs against a sort of beaker thing. Then when we've got enough, we extract the key toxins which we use to make a sort of antidote serum. It's a really complicated process. But I mostly do the snake-milking part.'

'Is it dangerous?' She was starting to think he might actually be telling the truth. He seemed to know what he was talking about.

'It can be.'

'You ever been bitten?'

'Yeah. *Hundreds of times!* I'm sort of immune to it. If a snake bit me right now, I'd survive. Wouldn't matter how deadly the snake – you know, viper, cobra, rattle snake, I would still be fine because I've had venom in my veins so often. My blood is probably half venom, actually.'

'Appletini. Scotch no ice.' The waiter placed two paper coasters on their table followed by their drinks, a tray of nuts and olives and a bill for fifteen pounds.

'Thanks.' Verity had already extracted a brand-new twenty-pound note from her mum's envelope and placed it on top of the bill. She didn't mind too much that Pete had let her pay for everything so far, because tonight she was *loaded* and would enjoy *splashing the cash.* But he seemed distracted and was scanning the room. Then he flinched, his eyes popping wide with excitement. He'd just noticed the bar was full-to-bursting with celebrities. Verity was thrilled at his reaction and allowed herself a smug smile.

'What *is* this place?' he asked, incredulous, staring at a famous DJ who was chatting with friends at the next table.

'The Hades?' said Verity. 'It's a private members' club. You have to be someone quite important on the telly or in films or music to join. And you have to be recommended or nominated for membership or something and it costs *loads* of dosh. Cool, isn't it?'

'Yeah.' Peter had just realised that the pretty girl sitting on a stool at the bar was his favourite singer. A picture of her in a strappy red minidress was the wallpaper on his laptop. Verity was looking across the room, too. She'd noticed their waiter and the hostess were watching them from the bar. They were pointing and seemed to be arguing about something.

'Uh-oh! Looks like we're about to be rumbled,' she whispered.

'What?'

'Drink up!' she said more loudly. 'We need to leave.'

'But we only just got here.'

'I know.' Verity gulped the rest of her bright green cocktail, which made her splutter, and reached for her bag. 'Come on!'

Peter did the same with his scotch and grimaced, then they both got up and walked rapidly towards the exit. Their waiter began to wave and call after them. 'Hey! Wait a minute!' He lifted his other hand in which he held a saucer with their change on it. But it was too late. Verity had already grabbed Peter's arm and dragged him out into the lobby.

The waiter shrugged and returned to the bar.

Verity and Peter crashed through the doors, sprinted past the photographers and tore down the street. They kept running, crossing dangerously at a busy junction, then dodging strolling pedestrians until they couldn't run any more. They slowed their pace to a jog and at the last corner Verity clutched her side and leaned over, laughing. 'Ha ha! That was a close one!'

'You're not an actress at all, are you?' said Peter between out-of-breath gasps.

'Took you long enough to guess.' She smiled at him.

'And your name's not Saffron Smith, is it?'

'Nope. Yours isn't Peter Parker.'

'Nope.'

'That was fun,' said Verity as she hooked her arm through his. They turned down Shaftesbury Avenue and disappeared into the night, still chuckling.

The Night Bus and Neighbours

'I was raised by a circus troupe,' the boy (who wasn't Peter Parker) explained. 'Quentin the Clown found me in a ditch on Exmoor when I was a baby and Brenda the Fire Eater adopted me and named me after a nearby landmark.'

'You were left in a ditch? How awful! What happened to your mum and dad?'

'Dunno. We were never able to find them, even after a nationwide search and a poster campaign and offering a huge reward and everything.'

'You're an orphan.'

Verity wiped a hole in the condensation on the window with her elbow, and looked out into the darkness. The night bus was still several stops away from her street. She tried to imagine having Quentin and Brenda, a clown and a fire eater, as surrogate parents.

'Awesome! So what's your name then? Steep Hill?' She smiled at her own joke. 'Smelly Pond?' She chuckled.

'It's Merlin Stone, actually.'

'Merlin? You're name is Merlin?'

'Yep. After an ancient standing stone on the moor, where the druids go to sacrifice virgins on All Hallows' Eve.' He leered at her.

'Nice. Good thing to be named after, then – chunks of rock and virgins!' She couldn't tell if any of what he was saying was true. Was this another tall tale like the snake-venom thing? She didn't really care. It was pretty entertaining, as biographies go, and at least the name Merlin Stone was more original than that Peter Parker nonsense.

'Anyway, I stayed with the circus, learned about clowning and slapstick and how to walk in giant shoes and I did a high wire act 'til I was twelve, then I ran away.'

'You're supposed to run away *to* the circus, not *from* it!'

'Yeah, well I got too fat for the high wire and I discovered another way to make a living.'

'What was that?'

'Extreme eating competitions.'

'No way!' Verity was trying to picture him as a fat twelve-year-old but it was almost impossible. He was so skinny. 'What, like that eat-a-packet-of-crackers-without-a-glass-of-water thing you do at school fetes?'

'Yeah, kind of. More, sort of, eating the most pies or hot chillies or a bucket of mashed potato. I travel around, all over, wherever there's a competition. You can make quite a lot of money. Entered one yesterday, in fact.'

'Here in London?'

He nodded. 'Uh-huh.'

'What did you eat?'

'Jellied eels.'

'Eergh! Did you win?'

'Runner-up. Three kilos.'

The bus slowed then halted. They were nearing her street. She sighed. She'd have to get out at the next stop and say goodbye to Merlin, but she was desperate to hear him make up more of his fascinating life story.

'Didn't you go to school? You must have gone to school.'

'Well, I kinda learned stuff from the circus people.'

'Circus School.' She grinned smugly at her own wit again.

'Cy the Sword Swallower taught me applied maths, the Fabulous Flying Frogatelli Brothers taught me quantum physics, I learned drawing from Madam Mephisto, the circus costume designer—'

'Costume?' Verity had a brainwave. 'That's what I do. I'm a costume designer.'

'Not an actress?'

'No, that was just to get us into the Hades Club, remember?'

'So you're not at school or college?'

'I did a degree in fashion and now I design costumes for RPGs.'

'Eh?'

'Role-Play Games.'

'Oh, really?'

'Yeah. That's why I was pissed off about not meeting Edgar Butterworth. I could have asked him for a job, couldn't I? Ooo, this is my stop.'

Verity was annoyed at herself for having changed the subject. Why did she interrupt him? Why did she waste their last moments together talking about herself? She was such a moron. She sighed, stood up, pressed the stop-request button and started to move towards the exit door, but Merlin got up, too.

‘I’ll see you to your house. Make sure you get there safely. I’d feel terrible if you were mugged or murdered or something.’

‘Thanks.’

Yay! There was that warm glow in her stomach again. She’d been thinking about what her mum had said about not taking the night bus and how dangerous it was to walk home on her own. Now she smiled and enjoyed the tingle of pleasure that was running up her spine. *He’s going to make sure I get home safely. I’m glad I DID get the night bus.*

Verity took the smallest steps she could. There were only a hundred metres or so left until her front door and she wanted the walk to last as long as possible.

‘So, the costumes in these video games, do you come up with the characters as well, or is that the writer’s job?’ Merlin asked. She’d been unable to steer the conversation back to the circus or the eating competitions, but now she didn’t care. He seemed completely focused on her and, naturally, she was delighted by the attention.

‘Mostly, but I work *with* the writers. It’s a collaboration.’

‘Where do you get your ideas from . . . for the characters?’

Verity’s heart began to beat faster again. She was in *heaven!* She *loved* swapping invented stories with this boy. It was the most fun she’d had in ages. It was a sort of tournament of tall tales, both of them knowing that the other was probably telling lies, but not minding at all. In fact, she was beginning to think that there was no point inventing stuff that was plausible.

‘Ideas? From my neighbours,’ she replied. ‘They are my inspiration. They’re all freaks and junkies and serial killers.’

‘Yeah?’

‘Like here, at number fifteen,’ she pointed at the house they were passing, where a blue glow flickered behind the ground-floor curtains. Whoever lived there was watching television. ‘Dave and Margaret Banks are both over seventy and they’re vampires,’ she began.

'I thought vampires were young 'cause of drinking blood and everything.'

'Well, not Dave and Margaret. They prefer being old and ordinary so that nobody will ever suspect what they really are. They've been seventy-something for about four hundred years. If we waited out here for a bit, we'd probably see them transform into giant bats and then swoop out of the front door and flap down to the skate park under the flyover, where they suck the necks of the whizzed-up skaters and graffiti artists, then flit home again in time for the BBC Breakfast programme. Margaret loves that Bill Whatsit bloke.'

Merlin laughed. 'Excellent! What about that house?' He waved at a house across the street with a beautifully clipped hedge and immaculate front lawn.

'Ian Wilson lives there. He's an estate agent by day . . . and a drug boss by night. He has a dog called Satan who breathes fire and has lava for blood.
Ian feeds him live rabbits
and kittens three times a day.'

'What about number nineteen?'

'Karen Reed is a sea serpent. She practically has to *live* in her bathroom or her scales will dry out. She used to be a swimming coach until she drowned one of the kids for eating a tuna sandwich that wasn't line caught and dolphin friendly.'

'Number twenty-three?'

'The whole family hatched from giant eggs.'

Merlin was really laughing now. 'Twenty-five?'

'Maths teacher!'

'Uurgh! Scary! What about this one?

'This is my house.'

'Ha! The weirdest house in the street!'

Verity's heart sank. This was it. She was home. He'd walked her home and now he was going to leave. Their tournament was over. She slowly climbed the steps and Merlin followed. She stirred her hand through the contents of her bag, touching her keys several times, but then losing them again, on purpose.

'It's been . . . Um . . . it's b-been cool,' she stammered, looking at her shoes. *What would happen now*? she wondered. She shivered at the memory of snogging several boys from school on these steps. Matt. Henry. Josh. Henry had groped about under her top and Josh had tried and failed to slip his hand down the back of her jeans. Was she about to continue the tradition with Merlin? Maybe not. *Maybe he doesn't fancy me. Maybe my breath smells disgusting. Maybe the taste of appletini and the spiced cashew nuts stuck in my teeth will make him gag.* She didn't dare to look at his face. It was all far too embarrassing.

'Yeah, it's been f-fun.'

Phew! He sounded embarrassed, too. *Quick, do it now*, she thought. *Before it's too late. Kiss me . . . on the lips . . . the cheek . . .*

or just give me a hug . . . or shake my hand . . . or something!

He shuffled his feet.

This is unbearable!

She leaned forward slightly but he didn't move. *Oh, no!* He wasn't interested! He really didn't fancy her!

Dee deedle dee . . . deedle deedle deee . . .

She jumped.

What was that noise?

Dee deedle dee . . .

deedle deedle deee . . .

It was the phone ringing inside the house. *Mum! Could it be Mum calling from New York already? How long is the flight?* She took a step back, pulled out her keys at last and fumbled for the lock.

'Phone's ringing,' she mumbled. 'I'd . . . I'd better . . . It's probably . . . I'd better get it.'

'OK.'

The door clicked open and the *beep, beep, beep* of the alarm warning began. 'I umm . . . Thanks. See ya. Bye,' she said and, before she knew it, she'd stepped inside, closed the door on him and keyed in the alarm code.

'Uuhh!' she groaned. *I don't believe it! I closed the door in his face!* Her cheeks felt horribly hot. If she opened it again now it would be even more excruciating. She stood in the hallway staring at the front door.

Dee deedle dee . . . deedle deedle deee . . .

He's probably half way back to the bus stop by now, muttering about what a pathetic loser I am. He totally hates me. Merlin was SO cool to walk me home and I was a complete bitch in return. And he's got to go home on his own now. What if HE gets mugged or murdered?

Dee deedle dee . . . deedle deedle deee . . .

Then she gasped. She'd just realised something truly terrible. *Oh, noooooo! We didn't even swap phone numbers!*

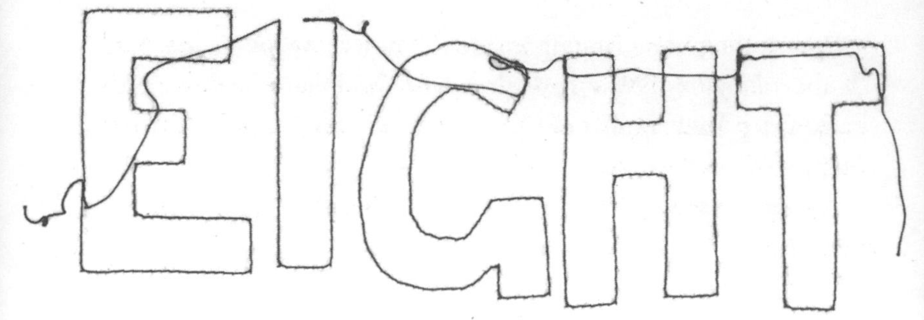

Raw Zebra and the Secret Weapon

'Yeah, I picked up this gorgeous guy at the airport and he gave me a lift in his limo and we went to the Hades Club for a few drinks and then he dropped me home at about three this morning and we snogged on the doorstep for just *hours* and he was just an *amazing* snogger,' said Verity, pulling on her grey hooded sweatshirt.

'Oh, wow! How cool!' Pye wailed from the speaker of the phone on Mum's desk.

She's so gullible, thought Verity. She was talking to Pye while dressing for school, eating a bowl of 'cat butt' cereal *and* trying to open the safe in Mum's office.

'Did he taste nice?' Pye continued.

'Yeah, I suppose . . .' She tapped her date of birth into the key pad. 'He tasted of whisky.'

'Ew, I don't like whisky.'

'It's better than Cheesestrings and Red Bull.' She was remembering the

awkward snog with Henry Harrison after the final dress rehearsal of the school production of *Bugsy Malone*. He'd breathed his packed-lunch stench all over her while attempting to unbutton her tight, pinstriped gangster costume.

'I prefer it when a boy tastes of mung beans or courgettes . . . or carrots.'

'You're weird!'

'I have a date, too, actually – a boy from my vegan cookery class, after school.'

Verity did a little joyful dance around the room. Yay! Alfie Parsons must have finally asked her out. Alfie was a very cute but shy boy, who had taken the lead role in *Bugsy Malone*, and had surprised everyone by completely losing his shyness on stage. He'd been following Pye around like a nervous puppy all term. *He must have finally found the courage to talk to her,* thought Vee. *Didn't know he was a veggie-vegan whatsit, though.*

'I'll tell you about him when I see. . .' Pye paused and there was a crackle on the line. 'Oo, I'm just going through the gates so I've gotta turn my phone off.'

'You at school already?' Verity panicked. She was later than she thought. She'd seriously overslept after spending most of the night awake, listening to the empty house creaking and imagining lunatic rapists or burglars breaking in downstairs. She'd even got up twice to check all the doors and windows.

'Yep. Miss Burton is scowling at me. She's *evil*,' said Pye.

'Complete psycho.'

'If I don't hide it now she'll grab it off me. You know what she's like. Talk later, OK? You can tell me all about the limo guy.'

The phone on the desk emitted a click followed by the disconnected tone. Verity reached over, jabbed the speaker button and returned to her search through the safe. She sighed, remembering the *actual* events of the previous night.

After slamming the door on Merlin, and by the time she had eventually crossed the hall and gone into Mum's office, the phone had switched to voicemail. She'd stood for several minutes in the dark, her heart thumping like a drum, red and hot with embarrassment, watching the blinking red light next to a glowing number three. Three missed calls. Three messages.

The first had been from Mum while she was still on the plane. Verity had groaned. *You're not even in America yet, Mum, and you're checking up on me!*

'Vee, I couldn't get you on your mobile. What's wrong? Why aren't you answering at home either? Did something happen? Did you have an accident? Are you all right? Are you in bed asleep already? I'm going to call Callista in case something awful has happened.'

Verity's stomach had leapt into her throat. *Something awful* had *happened!* She'd met an amazing boy and ruined the perfect snog moment and would never see him again . . . *ever! Major boyfriend fail!*

The second message had been Pye, also anxious about Vee's mobile.

The third had been Callista.

'Verity. Callista. Just to let you know your mum is worried and will call you before school tomorrow. I suggest you get your story straight by then.' The message had ended with a loud click.

Dee deedle dee . . . deedle deedle deee . . .

Verity jumped.

Dee deedle dee . . . deedle deedle deee . . .

She was ripped from her daydream back to the present. The phone was ringing.

'Hi, Mum.'

'Who were you on the phone to? I've been trying you for hours! I've had no sleep.'

Verity flinched and looked at her watch. She counted backwards from eight-forty. It would be the middle of the night in New York and Mum probably hadn't been to bed yet.

'Pye.'

'Veeeee! Can't you wait five minutes 'til you're at school to gossip with your friend? And why didn't you answer the phone last night? Were you in bed? You weren't out, were you? What's wrong with your mobile? When I got no reply, I called Callista and she couldn't get through either.' Mum's voice was becoming high pitched and slightly hysterical.

'My mobile? Oh, that,' said Verity, nonchalantly. 'I sort of killed it. Can I use the phone in the safe?'

'What? Yes . . . Um, I suppose so,' Mum replied. 'Wait. Something *is* wrong, isn't it? You've been looking in the safe. Did you need more money already? You're not keeping something from me, are you?'

'No. I just need a phone. Can I go to school now?' She tried to sound bored and let out a fake yawn. 'If I don't go now, I'll be late.'

'Oh, yeah, sorry. Do you promise me everything is OK?'

'I promise. Bye, Mum.'

Verity replaced the phone in its cradle and looked at the safe. Now that she had actually opened it and found Mum's old mobile, she'd also noticed the credit card and the 'emergency' cash. Lots of it. She stuffed it all into the front pocket of her sweatshirt and left the house.

Verity's Thursday timetable was full-to-bursting with tedium. European History tedium followed by Spanish Conversation tedium followed by Old English Poetry tedium. The only subject she'd actually enjoyed that year – probably the only reason she bothered to come to school at all – was Drama. But Drama was third period on Mondays and, apart from the bit of acting she'd done that morning (giving Mr Kemp an inspired 'gory traffic accident roadblock' excuse for her lateness), she'd now have to endure a Drama-free fortnight before they returned to school after the half-term break. This dreary Thursday was five hours of mind-numbing boredom, every lesson more pointless than the last. And there was the prospect of more boredom to endure on Friday, too. To make everything worse – if that were possible – she couldn't concentrate and had been winding up her teachers all day with her stupidity. If the questions they'd asked had been about the boy she'd met the night before, she would have been OK, because there was nothing in her head today *except* Merlin Stone and his snake-venom and circus stories. This was of no use whatever when her class was discussing Chaucer. By lunch break she wanted to rush to the playground and scream until her head exploded. Only her *Demon Streets* alter ego could now save her from imminent insanity.

Maisie Malone shoved the last chunk of raw zebra (chip) into her mouth and licked the blood (ketchup) from her sleek black paw. Her next ordeal was just moments away and she was now sufficiently fortified to face the Gremlin Hoards (Sixth Formers) crossing the Bridge of Death (hanging around the bicycle racks) and do battle with the Ogre (Mr Williams) in his dank, stinking swampy lair (ICT Studio).

Verity caught up with Pye halfway across the Bridge of Death. Pye had been talking to one of the Maths geeks and a pale girl in their year whom Vee had never even noticed before. She made a point of never paying any attention to the fashionably challenged.

'You survived then?' Verity asked as her friend sauntered over.

'Survived what?' said Pye.

'Your trip into the Fashion-Free Zone.' Verity nodded towards the geek and the pale girl.

'They're vegans.'

Verity snorted. 'That explains a lot!'

Pye frowned.

'What does he think he's wearing?' Verity chuckled. 'I mean, look!' She pointed at the Maths geek's shoes. 'Those are actually fluorescent laces! Argh!' Verity grasped her neck and made a choking noise. Then she began talking with a cockney twang. 'Prob'ly shops someplace called GeekWear an' lives in Geek Street in a suburb of Geekville. An' she's an 'opeless case. Terminaw!

Like, did she get vose cloves aaat ov a skip, or what?'

'Shhh. Don't shout. They'll hear you.' Pye was blushing a little. 'Anyway, I thought recycling was the hot look this season.'

'Yeah. Recycling *is*. Finding your clothes at the bottom of a green bin *isn't*.'

Pye was now eager to change the subject. 'When are you going out with the limo guy?'

'Out? Out where?' For a fraction of a millisecond, lost in her scornful rant against the uncool, Vee had actually forgotten Merlin, the 'limo guy'.

'You know – your new bloke.'

'Oh, *him*.' Verity's insides flipped over, churning the raw zebra in stomach acid.

'When can I meet him?'

Verity's heart sank. *Probably never*, she thought. *I'll never see him again because he loathes me.* 'Dunno,' she replied with a sigh.

'Why don't you invite him to your party tomorrow?'

'Mmm, yeah. I might. It's not really his sort of thing, though. He's more a posh-restaurant, swanky-bar, exclusive-club kinda guy.' She chewed her lip.

'Oh, right. Is he really old like the last bloke?' Pye continued. 'What will your mum say?'

'Shut your face, Pyewacket!' Verity snapped. 'It's nothing to do with Mum and if you tell her, I'll never speak to you again . . . ever!'

'Sorry,' Pye whispered. She looked close to tears. Nobody ever called Pye by her full name because she hated it. Pye's mum had been inspired by some really old movie she loved from the fifties. But lately Pye had discovered that 'Pyewacket' wasn't one of the main characters, like some glamorous fifties starlet, it was the name of a cat! Pyewacket the cat! Pye had always thought it ugly. Her mum had a lame obsession with old movies and, although Pye agreed the clothes were gorgeous, this was not a good enough reason to burden your daughter with a stupid name.

Verity wished she hadn't shouted. She'd obviously upset her friend. And, after all, it wasn't Pye's fault that Vee had made a complete mess of the potentially amazing goodnight snog. And it wasn't Pye's fault that Merlin Stone was so yummy that she could think of nothing else but his dreamy eyes and sexy, top-lip fuzz. And it wasn't Pye's fault that Verity's house creaked at night.

'No, *I'm* sorry.' She put her arm around Pye's shoulder. 'I didn't sleep much last night. I kept thinking there was someone breaking in.'

'You're forgiven.' Pye attempted a smile, then had an idea. 'Why don't you stay at mine tonight?'

'Nah. Thanks for the offer but I've got a date.'

‘With *him*?’

‘Yeah, we’re—’

Someone was chanting from across the playground, ‘Eden bonked your mu-um! Eden bonked your mu-um!’ It was a snotty kid sitting on a wall with his mates. The mates took up the chant, only they were customising, adding their own disgusting verbs. Snotty kid number one started doing obscene actions, too, which the mates thought were hilarious. Pye rolled her eyes and patted Verity’s arm.

‘Ignore them. They’re nauseating trolls.’

‘I know,’ said Vee, who was secretly grateful for the interruption. She had been digging herself a hole with the ‘limo guy’ story and hated how spinning an elaborate lie to her best friend was making her feel.

Pye stuck out her tongue at the trolls and Verity giggled. It was a very un-Pye-like thing to do, but completely brilliant. They turned and walked away, then the afternoon bell rang and they began to walk a bit faster towards the Technology Block. They strode arm-in-arm into the Ogre’s dank, stinky, swampy lair.

That evening, Verity was watching one of Mum's New York interviews on YouTube when she called. Vee was surprised at how pleased she was to hear Mum's voice.

'Hi, sweetie. How you doing without me?'

'Uh, it's *heaven!* I *love* being on my own. You should go away more often.'

She was lying, of course. Pye had left hours ago for a piano lesson, still believing Verity's story about going out on a date with 'limo guy', and now Vee was dreading bedtime and having to listen, all night, to the creaks and groans of the empty house. She wished now that she'd cancelled the fake date and had said yes to Pye's offer. She could have been sleeping on the couch in her best friend's room instead of shaking with fear in her own. Doing stuff for herself wasn't as much fun as she'd thought it would be, either. She had even decided that she missed Mum nagging her to do her homework, or to eat more fruit or to stop playing 'those brain-rotting video games'.

'Have you done your homework?' Mum asked. 'Did they give you lots to do over the break?'

Verity smiled. 'Pye and I were working on our ICT project and, now she's left, I'm just about to start my Chaucer essay.' She and Pye had actually been trying on Saffron's clothes. They had paraded up and down the landing as if it were a fashion-show runway, tottering on Mum's high heels and swishing silk scarves and chiffon skirts. The evening wear had been their favourite: Mum's glamorous red-carpet dresses. Verity was still wearing the grey Grecian-goddess dress that Mum had worn to the ELLE Style Awards.

'Did you eat some fruit today?'

'Yeah, loads. I had an apple last night and some grapes just now.' Verity grinned at the cleverness of her deception. The apple was the appletini she'd had at the Hades Club and the grapes was the half bottle of flat champagne she and Pye had found in the fridge and drunk with their Burger-King fries.

'Good. You won't stay up too late, will you?'

'No, I'm quite tired now actually . . .' This was entirely true, of course. ' . . . so I might go to bed soon.' Not true. She intended to play *Demon Streets* all night so she didn't have to think about being alone. 'What about you, Mum? I've just been watching your interview. You were fab!'

'Ooo, which one?'

'CNN.'

'Mmm, that was tricky,' said Mum.

The journalist had hardly talked about the Flim-Flam launch at all, preferring to quiz Mum about Eden and the seriousness of their apparent romance. Verity decided she ought not to mention that part of the interview.

'You looked beautiful.'

'Aww, thanks Vee,' Mum cooed. Then she groaned. 'I don't know how. I have bags under my eyes you could pack for a weekend break. It's been crazy here – a complete blur! I think I've done a million interviews already today.'

'I miss you,' said Verity, a lump in her throat.

'I miss you, too. *Mwa mwa mwa.*' Mum made stupid kissing noises into the phone. 'Ooo, is that the time?' Mum gasped. 'I'd better get changed.'

'You going somewhere?'

'Yeah – another couple of telly interviews this afternoon then a chat show and a party.'

'Sounds like fun.'

'It'll be *hell*, but it's all for Jiggery-Pokery and Flim-Flam . . . and for us, right? I'll call again tomorrow morning – tell you how it goes.'

'Goodnight, then.' Vee didn't want the call to end but she could feel a horrible pre-tears tightness in her throat and there would be nothing worse than blubbing down the phone to Mum. Mum was thousands of miles away and couldn't just reach over and give her a hug, could she? Being alone had become pretty horrible but she simply refused to admit that she was failing at it. It was just what Mum expected to hear, wasn't it? That Vee wasn't mature enough to be left, that she was still a kid. Verity had pleaded for months to be on her own. Now that she was, she would just have to SUCK IT UP!

'Night night, sweetie. Sleep tight. Be sure to lock the doors.'

'Bye, Mum.' Verity sniffed.

'Bye.'

CLICK.

The Sidekick

Veronica Vamp threw back her head and laughed again. Maisie Malone took a deep breath. She didn't cringe with fear or fall to her knees begging for her life. She just smirked. She'd had a bit of time to consider her next move and now she was going to make it. She was about to outmanoeuvre her opponent by deploying a secret weapon. She hoped it would work.

Select. Click.

Veronica Vamp tipped her hand and let the silver bullets fall like strange, glinting jewels on to the dark, wet cobbles at her feet. Then, suddenly, her body juddered and twitched in a peculiar way. Her expression had changed from an evil grin to one of complete surprise. Her chest thrust itself forward and she gasped.

'What the—?'

'Don't move or I'll slice you in two,' hissed a voice behind her in the darkness.

'I . . . I . . .' Veronica stuttered.

'Shut up and do exactly as I tell you!' said the voice.

'Yes. OK.' Veronica's face was frozen in terror.

'I said shut up! Drop the gun.'

She dropped the gun, which clattered on to the stones. Two black hands appeared from behind her and proceeded to pat her down – for concealed firearms, Maisie thought.

'Now, tell Maisie how sorry you are to have tried to frame her for murder.'

Veronica frowned. 'What?' Then her body twitched again. 'Uh!'

'Tell her!'

'I . . . I'm s-sorry I tried to frame you, M-Maisie.'

'Thanks,' said Maisie, not sure if that was the correct response. She wasn't interested in Veronica's stupid apology, anyway. She wanted to see what her secret weapon looked like. She had pressed the sidekick button, a weapon of last resort. You didn't play this weapon unless there was nothing else left in your arsenal, because there was absolutely no guarantee that your sidekick would save you. Nine times out of ten the sidekick would be friendly, but there was a small risk that they could turn out to be a selfish rival, another online player, a troll or a pixie, playing the game for their own benefit, or even a demon, with no intention of helping you.

'Now, walk away and don't look back.'

Veronica Vamp turned slowly to face the street and, as she did so, a figure, clad head-to-toe in black, shuffled around so that he stayed out of view behind her. Maisie could now see that the sidekick was holding a long, sharp sword pressed against the small of Veronica's back. The sword was huge, almost as long as the black shape was tall. Veronica began walking away and the shape turned to look at Maisie. At last, she had the first glimpse of his face. The sidekick wasn't an adult, but a teenager with soft, friendly eyes.

'Hi,' said the boy, transferring the heavy sword from one hand to the other and almost dropping it.

'Hello,' said Maisie Malone, hoping the friendly eyes weren't deceptive.

'I'm Ben Blades,' said the boy, and twirled his sword in the air.

Suddenly, Veronica Vamp, who'd only taken a few steps along the alley, crouched and threw herself to the ground. Then she rolled over, retrieved her discarded gun from beneath Ben Blades and began to lift her arm. She took aim at Maisie. Maisie had already reached down to the top of her boot and was clutching the handle of her knife. She flicked her wrist, sending the tiny metal spear whizzing into Veronica's shoulder, but it hardly penetrated her coat, causing no more than a scratch. Veronica barely felt it and brushed it harmlessly away. Caught off guard, Ben Blades fumbled and dropped his sword. He swore as it clanged noisily on the ground, but he quickly recovered his balance, bent his knees, did an acrobatic backflip, grabbed the sword handle with both hands, swept it around in an arc and sliced Veronica's head off! It tumbled down the alley, like a macabre football, and landed beside the slumped body of the Mole. Veronica's head stared up at Maisie with an expression of shock and extreme annoyance on her face. She'd been defeated.

Ben Blades looked equally surprised.

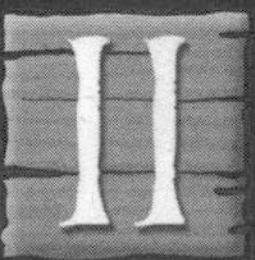

Warning:
Your Sidekick
may be friend
...or foe

+800 points
score: 7,600

Verity emerged, blinking, from the final morning session of double-tedium and texted Pye.

mall?
Vx

The immediate reply was,

C U there
Px

They weren't permitted to leave the school premises at lunch break (since a minor stabbing incident in the first week of term), but there was a new teacher on duty at the side entrance that day and they knew she couldn't tell the difference between the A-Level students, who were allowed more freedom, and the more mature-looking students from other years. Vee and Pye would sneak past and spend the forty-five minute break in the shopping mall instead of queuing with the disgusting snotty and sweaty trolls in the canteen.

There was a huge Perfect Eden poster just outside the entrance to the mall. Verity sighed. She almost couldn't tear her eyes away from that square jaw and those twinkling eyes. She wondered if her mum was missing him and decided that, if she had someone like Eden as *her* boyfriend, she'd miss him like crazy and want to get smoochie texts and emails from him every second of the day.

Pye was already sitting beside the central fountain, swigging from a bottle of water, when Verity arrived. Pye had stopped eating breakfast, and sometimes lunch, since someone had told her she had a pot belly. She would probably turn down the vegan, salad wrap from the burger bar that Verity was about to suggest, too. Vee had given up trying to convince her friend that, although she did have a very small pot belly, it was cute and gave her the sort of womanly curves that she and all their skinny friends craved. None of them could fill a bra like Pye could. Except Bella Brown, who was quite podgy, and consequently possessed a pair of enviable D-cups.

'You look half dead,' said Pye as Verity approached.

'I'm *completely* dead. Didn't get any sleep.'

'Was it *that* good a date then?'

'Oh, yeah, my date.' *My fake date.* 'We had a great time. Went to a movie then he bought me dinner at this fabulous Italian place and we went dancing at this club. I didn't get home 'til dawn.' She yawned. Why had she said 'movie'? Pye was bound to ask which one.

'Did you wear that grey dress? I bet you looked amazing!'

'Yeah, but my feet are *killing* me from those heels.' In reality, she'd worn bed socks and pyjamas all night. She groaned. 'Too much dancing.'

'And snogging?'

'And snogging. He's just the best kisser on the planet.'

'Pardon?'

'I said—'

They couldn't hear each other any more because the insistent sound of an engine was echoing around the mall and getting louder . . . and louder.

'WHAT IS THAT?' Pye shouted.

It sounded like a jet plane was about to land in Marks & Spencer. A very small, farty jet plane.

VVVVRRRROOOOOMMMMM!
PUTPUTPUTPUTPUTPUT!
VVVRRRROOOMMM!

'DUNNO.'

Just then, a white shape darted across the food court, skidding as it turned to head towards the fountain, then squealed to a halt beside them. It was a boy on a moped. The strange acoustics of the marble-floored mall appeared to have amplified the moped's tiny engine – amplified it to freakish proportions. Now that it was stationary, the noise softened to a throaty purr.

Rrrrrrrrrrrrrrrrrrrrrrrrrr . . .

The boy put out his feet to steady the machine and clicked up the visor of his helmet.

'Hi,' said Moped Boy. 'D'you wanna come for a ride? You'd better decide quickly.'

'He's talking to you,' said Pye.

'Whaaa?' Verity was shaking. As soon as he'd raised the visor she'd recognised him. It was Merlin Stone!

'Yes or no? I'm about to be arrested.'

'Arrested?' Verity asked. She was anxious but her heart pounded with excitement, too.

'Yeah, by them.' He pointed across the food court to a couple of red-faced, out-of-breath security guards who had obviously been chasing him through the mall. 'Get on, if you're coming. Here.' He offered her a helmet.

This is crazy, she thought. *It's like a scene in a movie or RPG where the hero has to make a choice that will change his life. It's the blue pill or red pill moment from* The Matrix. *Will the girl take the vampire's hand? Will the Hobbits take the meadow path home or continue their quest through the dangerous mountains? You always know what the hero will do. It's obvious.*

'OK,' said Verity with a grin and climbed on to the seat behind him, hitching up her school skirt and pulling on the helmet.

'Vee! What are you doing?' yelled Pye.

'This is him,' said Verity. 'The guy I was telling you about.'

'Limo Guy? What's limo guy doing on a moped?'

'Dunno, but it's brilliant isn't it?'

'No, it's not. Get off! You'll have an accident and be killed and you'll be late for registration.'

Merlin revved the moped, then took off in a noisy circuit of the fountain, Verity yelling at Pye from the pillion. 'Tell Mr Kemp I went home with period pain or something. You know how squeamish he gets about girl stuff,' she shouted.

The tyres of the moped juddered and squeaked on the slick floor as Merlin swerved to avoid a bewildered shopper and then to escape the hands of the younger, spottier security guard, who had very nearly managed to grab the strap of Verity's school bag.

'Hold tight!' Merlin shouted over his shoulder.

Verity circled her arms around Merlin's waist and nuzzled her cheek into the collar of his jacket. She wondered if he was able to feel the frenzied thumping of her heart through their layers of clothing. The moped completed the circuit of the fountain and Verity raised her hand and waved at Pye as they passed.

'See ya! I'll call later.'

A bewildered Pye waved back.

'OK.' Pye's final word was drowned out by the roar and splutter of the engine –

VVVVRRRROOOOOOMMMMM!
PUTPUTPUTPUTPUTPUTPUT! –

as the moped accelerated and disappeared along Sandwich Strip, through Pizza Plaza and, finally, out into the car park. All that remained were two exhausted security guards, Pye, her mouth wide open in disbelief, and a cloud of grey smoke.

On the way back to school, Pye sent a text to her friend's new phone.

moped boy may b
dngerous psycho
pls b crfl
Px

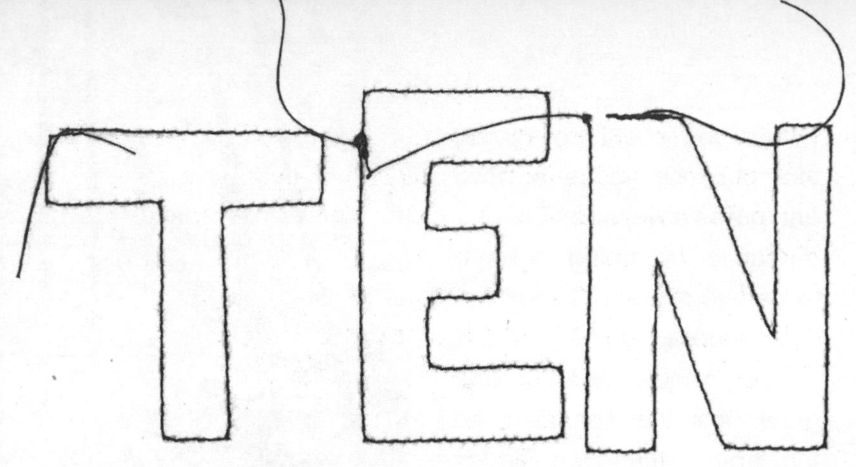

The Man with Winged Boots and the Party

Super-sleuth, Maisie Malone, and her sidekick, Ben Blades, ran out of the alley and into a dark, empty street. The wail of a distant police siren began to fill the air like the song of a strange, melancholic bird. Maisie knew then that they didn't have much time and wondered what her next move should be. With her sidekick's help, she had defeated Veronica Vamp and now possessed the secret – the Mole's package – which could bring down the Boss. But how would she do it? First, they had to get off the street – quickly. Maisie looked at Ben Blades and was about to suggest they run a little faster, when he sort of shrugged his shoulders and unfolded a pair of leathery wings from his back.

Woah! I didn't expect that, thought Maisie. 'You're a demon!'

'Nah. Winged pixie.'

'Uh!' She groaned. 'A pixie? I knew there'd be a catch.'

'Some of us are OK, y'know.'

'But you could be saying that because you're a *pixie* and *pixies* always lie.'

'You're just going to have to believe me, aren't you?'

'I suppose I am.'

The wings flexed and grew until the tips reached the ground, then Ben Blades slipped his arm around her waist.

OK. My sidekick is transport as well as a secret weapon. Multi-purpose. Useful to have around, even if he is a devious, not-to-be-trusted, *winged pixie*.

Bonus fact: Like humans, Demons have weaknesses

With a leap and a kick they were both in the air. Ben Blades flapped his strange wings and the pair rose high above Murder Lane and the bodies of their foes. Within moments they had left the grisly scene far behind and were soaring above the rooftops and out of the town. They swooped low over the bottomless *Dead Man's Lake*, then skimmed the top-most ash-white branches of the *Scorched Forest*. The vast, towering skyscrapers of *Demon City* loomed on the horizon – the Boss's domain. It was a city full of the worst type of

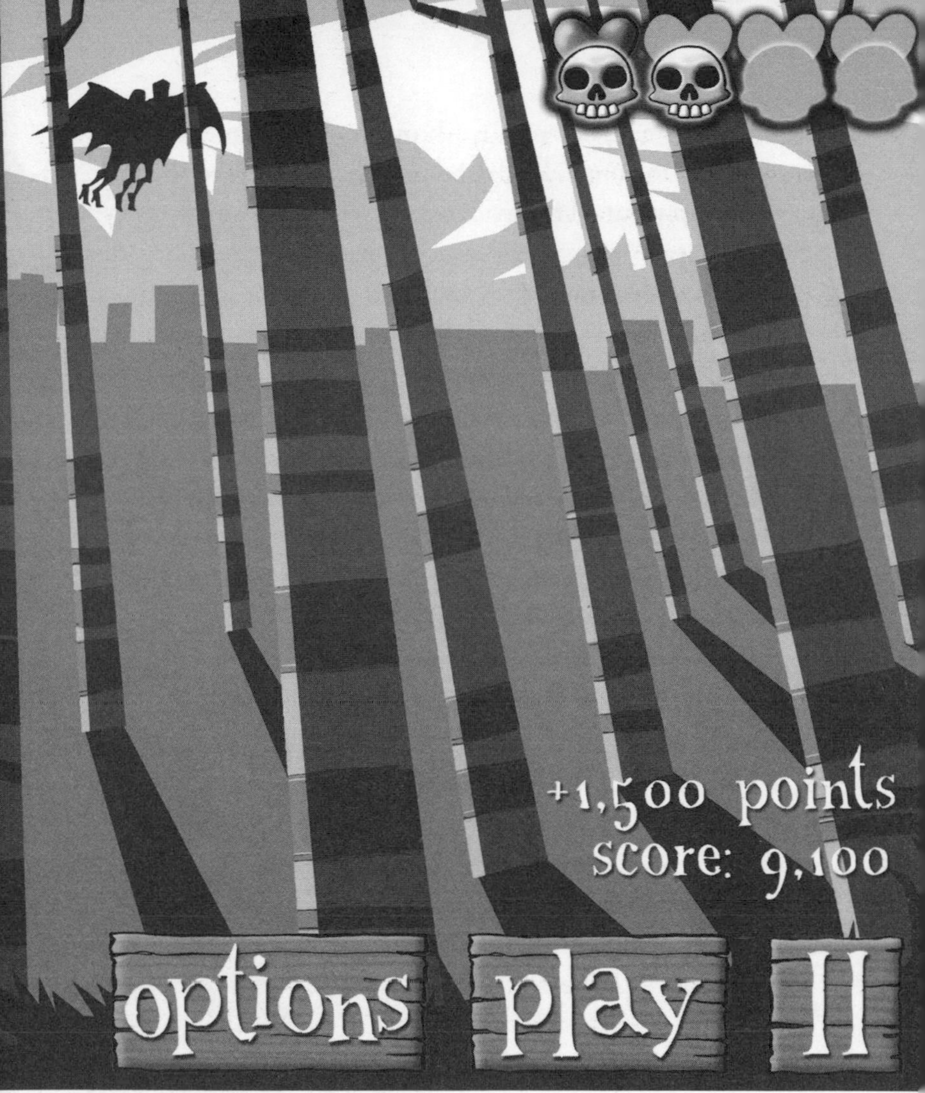

demons and horrific danger lurked on every street, in every innocent-looking park or playground, school or shopping mall. Nowhere would be safe.

What would they face as they tackled the next levels of the game? And would they both survive?

It didn't take Verity long to work out *how* Merlin Stone had found her and to conclude that he probably knew *who* she was, too. He'd simply put all the evidence together, like any detective would: the name 'Saffron', the famous face, the Hades Club, the lies. He'd done some online research and made the connections, just like he'd done at the airport. Then, when he'd discovered that she was neither an actress nor an RPG costume designer but the schoolgirl daughter of a famous fashion designer, he'd probably gone back to her house, found the nearest likely educational establishment, staked the place out, noticed her leaving the side entrance and followed her.

What Vee couldn't work out, however, was why he'd gone to so much trouble.

The moped screeched to a halt. A man wearing skin-tight blue Lycra had stepped into the road. He had winged boots, an enormous belly and a silver mask covering half his face. Verity gulped. Her heart thudded with excitement again. She'd barely recovered from the thrill of the moped chase through the mall and their snaking journey across London, the wind whipping up her skirt and slapping her face. Now she was confronted by this astonishing sight – not quite normal attire for a chilly Friday in West London. It told her, or she thought it told her, where they were heading. The clue was in the mask and the winged boots and she now hoped, with all her might, that she was right about them.

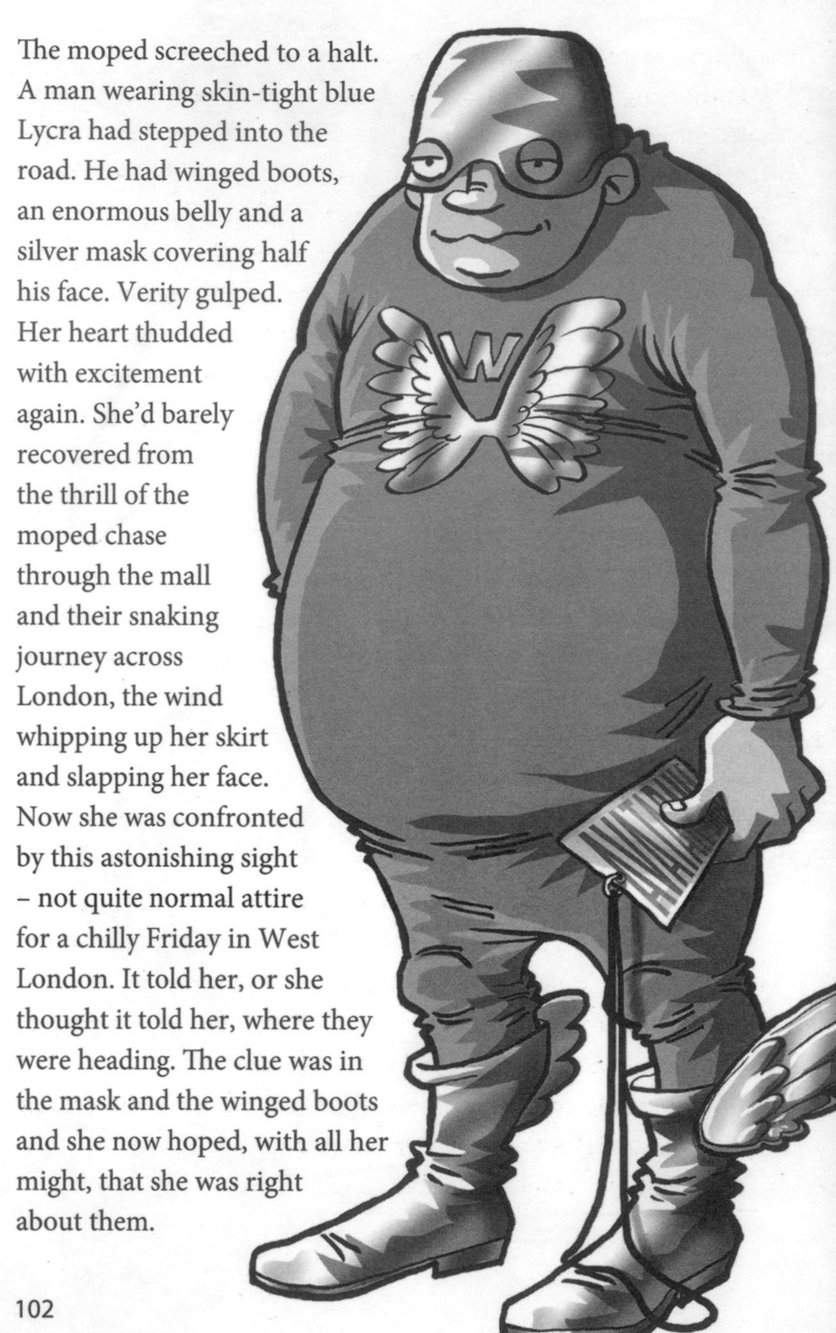

More weirdly dressed people were pouring out of a tube-station exit. There was Catwoman and a man with a dog's head and fur gloves, a six-armed alien and a woman in a purple bikini with thigh-length boots pushing a baby buggy. There was Edward Scissorhands and Spiderman getting off a bus. A little further on was another Spiderman, a Viking and a group of middle-aged men wearing suits, ties and knobbly orange faces.

Merlin steered the moped around the corner and an enormous exhibition centre loomed above them. A giant, illuminated poster announced what Verity had been chanting inside her head for the last few minutes.

AVATARAMA! AVATARAMA! AVATARAMA!

Merlin pulled into a motorbike parking space at the side of the building and Verity climbed off. All the questions she had been planning to ask him had evaporated from her brain. She was at *Avatarama! Awesome!*

Then she groaned. Everyone was clutching large, laminated entry passes.

'Uh, I think we need pre-booked tickets,' she said, pouting.

'Yep,' said Merlin.

'I suppose we could look for touts, buy a couple of tickets from them. It'll be illegal and expensive.' She was resigning herself to spending a large chunk of the money Mum had left for her. Maybe even the 'nuclear war' emergency money. *Avatarama* tickets were like diamond-encrusted gold dust.

'Or we could walk straight in with these,' said Merlin pulling two laminated *Avatarama* day passes out of his pocket.

'Oh . . . my . . . God! You genius!'

AVATARAMA
AVATARAMA

Scarlett Dedd

It was dark when Merlin and Verity made their reluctant way out of the exhibition centre, their goodie bags stuffed with the extraordinary giveaways and marketing freebies that had been thrust into their hands by all the games companies and film studios. Vee had bought lots of stuff, too. She'd downloaded a limited-edition version of *Demon Streets 4* (which came with an exclusive behind-the-scenes media pack), bought a Pamela Pout t-shirt, a box set of Wolf & Mandy videos and a signed sketch by her favourite fantasy costume designer. Verity smiled contentedly and lifted her bag full of swag on to her shoulder as they joined the bizarre stream of fans dispersing into the night.

Suddenly, Merlin stood still, causing a fish-head alien behind him to slap into his back in a floppy, cartoon-comical way.

Verity giggled then asked, 'What's the matter?'

'Let's get the bus.'

'But the moped . . .' she began.

'Forget the moped.' He pushed her back through the crowd.

'But . . .' Verity looked over her shoulder and caught a glimpse of the motorcycle bay where Merlin had parked their transport – the getaway vehicle. A police officer and a teenager were standing over the moped having an animated conversation. The teenager was waving his arms in the air while the police officer spoke into his walkie-talkie.

'You didn't steal it, did you?' Verity frowned.

'Borrowed it from a friend.'

'Borrowed? And you were late taking it back so your friend called the fuzz?'

'Yup! Very late. About a week late, in fact.'

They climbed aboard a bus and shuffled towards the stairs.

'You didn't steal the tickets as well, did you?'

'Won them in a poker game last night.'

She didn't believe him, but was momentarily distracted by a beep and vibration from her phone. It was a text from Pye. There were twelve other texts that she'd missed. She scrolled to the first.

whr R U?
Px

Then the next.

R U dead?
PLEASE txt me if U R!
Px

And the next.

R U @ hsptl?
morgue?

Then,

evry 1 is @ yr house
is yr prty off?
Px

The other messages were similar, only each one was more insistent and frantic than the last.

Verity looked at her probably criminal, almost certainly fugitive and undoubtedly untruthful sidekick. 'D'you want to come to a party?'

Verity's school mates were perched on the steps of her house or sprawled on the damp front lawn when they finally made it home. They'd started the party without their host and were well on their way to drunken stupidity, having opened assorted bottles of beer, cider and lurid-hued liqueurs, no doubt leftover from the festive season and pinched from their parents.

'You can't drink out here,' she complained, glancing around at the neighbouring houses. 'I'll get into trouble.' She ushered them all towards the steps and unlocked the front door. There was no beeping sound. She'd forgotten to set the alarm. *Woops!*

'So you're not dead, then,' said Pye.

'Apparently not,' said Verity, grinning.

Pye wrinkled her nose and, before Verity crossed the threshold, she grabbed her arm and dragged her down the steps again, to the end of a tall hedge. She seemed anxious to show Vee something. She pointed across the street, keeping her hand behind the hedge so her gesture wasn't too obvious. 'Do you know those two?' she asked.

'Who?' said Verity, looking in the wrong direction.

'There, under the tree,' said Pye, pointing again.

Verity peered over the road, into the dark shadow just outside the pool of light from a street lamp. There were two tall figures lurking by a fence. They both had long black hair and wore loose black clothes.

'The goths?'

'Yeah.'

'Nah. Never seen 'em before,' said Verity.

'Oh, I thought you might have invited them to your party, 'cause they've been watching the house the whole time we've been here.'

'Probably junkies got lost looking for their dealer, or something.'

'They're acting creepy,' said Pye.

'Ignore them and stop being such a worrier, Pye. You're worse than my mum. Come on, I want you to meet someone.' Verity dragged her friend back up the path and into the house. 'This is Merlin Stone. Merlin, this is my *bestest* friend, Pye.'

Merlin and Pye exchanged wary acknowledgements and proceeded into the lounge where someone had discovered the controls for the media system. Music began to pound out of the speakers and Verity beamed with satisfaction. She hadn't prepared any of the things she'd meant to. There were no decorations, no specially selected party playlist, no food hamper or cocktail-mixing barman, but her friends seemed to have brought all they needed with them. Everyone that was anyone had come to her house and her party was going to be legendary!

'You're making bells ring in my head,' said Henry Harrison, rubbing his ears then returning to his snog-athon with Bella Brown on the sofa.

'Ahh! Itsshh the phone,' Verity screamed and dashed across the room. It would probably be Mum calling to check that she was still alive and hadn't burned the house down. She grabbed the phone from the coffee table and ran to the kitchen, closing all the doors on the way in an attempt to block some of the expletive-filled rap track that was now throbbing through the house.

'Hull-o?'

'What's that?' said Mum. 'You're not having a party, are you?'

'Duh! 'Coursshh not!'

'Well, if you are, don't let people get too drunk or take drugs or anything. They'll fall out of a window or choke on their own vomit or something.'

'I told jeeuuww, I'm NOT 'aving a party. Itsshhh just the telly turned up loud.'

'And don't let your friends near my bed . . . or any of the beds.'

'Muuuum! Shuuut uuuup! There's nobiddee here but meee an' Pye. And we're wasshhin' telly.'

'Have you been drinking?'

'Mum, chill oouuut! Me an' Pye are 'aving a quaart night in, wasshhin' *Eastenders* and doin' aaaar homework. 'Kay?'

'Mmm,' said Mum. 'Well, you just be sensible, all right?'

'Awwiiigh.'

Torture, New Threads and the Masters of Illusion

Maisie Malone stared into the ink-black eyes of her torturer. How long would she be able to endure this torment? she wondered. She'd survived being hung upside down over a furnace, and the excruciating hammer-smashing of her fingers. Now he was squeezing her head in a vice.

'Uuhhh,' she groaned as the mechanism clicked again and her forehead throbbed.

'All you gotta do is tell me what you know,' the torturer hissed. 'And I'll stop.'

'I won't tell you,' she rasped. 'Not if you crush my skull and scoop out my brain. I'll never tell you . . . I'll never tell you . . .'

'Vee?'

'Uurgh.' Verity turned her head on her pillow and wished she hadn't.

'You OK?' asked Pye's voice from the sofa on the far side of Verity's bedroom.

'No. I'm dying,' said Verity, lifting the duvet off her face. It was too heavy.

'You were talking in your sleep.'

'Wha' d' I say?'

'Sounded something like "ever smell poo"!' Pye laughed.

'Ssshhh.' Vee rubbed her temples. 'Too loud.'

'Sorry,' Pye whispered, then she reached up and opened the curtains a nanometre.

Verity groaned. 'No! Sunlight . . . burning . . . holes . . . in . . . eyeballs!' She covered her face again. 'Uurgh! Why didn't you stop me drinking that chocolate stuff Bella brought? It was disgusting!'

Pye kicked away the blanket she'd been sleeping under and began to look for her shoes.

'You leaving?' asked Verity, watching Pye through one half-closed eye.

'Mmm. Meeting my new bloke.'

'Uh? Oh, Alfie,' Vee mumbled. She rolled over again and pressed her face into the coolest part of her pillow.

'Alfie who?' said Pye. 'I'm talking about the boy in my vegan cooking class. I told you.'

Verity could hardly move without excruciating pain and decided that, at that moment, she would prefer death to getting out of bed or questioning Pye further. 'Uh, have fun then,' she croaked into the pillow.

'Yeah.' Pye walked dejectedly towards the bedroom door. 'Great party.'

'Fffanks.' Verity knew she was being a miserable grouch, but she'd apologise to Pye later. After all, she'd just spent the night being horribly tortured in a dungeon beneath Demon City. Pye would be a grouch, too, if she'd had her brain squished.

By the time Verity felt able to crawl out of bed and venture downstairs in search of sugar-frosted cereal and a cup of strong coffee, it was past midday. She tried to ignore the debris from the previous night, stepped around the numerous glasses, bottles and items of clothing distributed across the hallway and pushed open the kitchen door. Inside, sitting on one of the stools, leaning on the black granite counter, was Merlin Stone.

'Hi,' said Merlin. 'I made coffee.' He lifted the glass jug out of the coffee machine and waved it at her.

'Hello,' said Verity, feeling a massive clench in her stomach. It wasn't nausea any more. In fact, she suddenly felt a *lot* better. 'Didn't know you stayed.' *But very glad you did*, she thought. *I wish someone had warned me, though, then I'd have washed off my panda eyes and put on some spot concealer before I came downstairs. I must look like one of the undead.*

'It's OK, isn't it? I guess you don't remember, but I kinda explained last night that I had to move out of my hotel at short notice and you said I could have the guest room.'

She wondered if the stuff about staying in a hotel was another lie. He probably lived in a suburban semi with his suburban mum and dad.

'Did I say that?' Verity frowned, shuffled over to the other stool and climbed on. 'No, I don't remember.' She rubbed at the congealed mascara under her eyes and stared at the stream of coffee that Merlin was pouring into a mug.

'Thought you might not,' said Merlin. 'You did go a bit loco last night.'

'Loco?' The kitchen tilted sideways, she wobbled on the stool and grabbed the edge of the worktop to steady herself. What had she done? She knew she'd mixed her drinks (orange, cherry *and* chocolate flavoured liqueurs) and had probably tried some embarrassing dance moves (she'd always assumed she was a cool dancer until someone had caught her on video once, looking like she was giving birth to an alien). But what else had happened? Had she done something *really* stupid? Something reckless? And had it involved Merlin Stone? She groaned. *Uurgh! I hope I didn't attack him and try to snog him*, she thought. She'd spent most of the previous day at school daydreaming about snogging him, so it was exactly the sort of thing she might have done. *Perhaps I even invited him to my bedroom. OMG!* She covered her pink face with her hands. Why couldn't she remember? Had it all been so horribly traumatic she had wiped the appalling memory of it from her mind? She peered at him through her fingers.

'Don't worry,' said Merlin, smiling. 'You didn't do anything too dumb. Pye put you to bed after you'd sung ABBA's "Nina, Pretty Ballerina" about twenty times, standing on the bench in the garden.'

That jogged her memory. She began to recall the scene from the night before. Around midnight, when most of her quests were starting to head home, someone had decided to reject Verity's music selection and scan through Mum's playlists, where they'd found ABBA's *Greatest Hits*. A horrific image formed in her mind. She had been standing on tiptoes and holding the edge of her sweatshirt like a ballet dress, using a beer bottle as a microphone and howling out the song at the top of her lungs. She groaned, folded her arms on the counter in front of her and buried her head.

'You were excellent!' he continued. 'In tune and everything.'

'Shut up! I don't want to hear any more.' She lifted her head and took a sip of coffee. Gradually, the heat in her cheeks subsided and she began to feel more human again. Her stomach still fluttered slightly every time Merlin reached for his coffee mug or flicked his fringe out of his eyes, but it was a nice flutter. Then she remembered something else.

'Did you tell me your real name last night?'

'Um, yeah. You asked, so I told you.'

'What did you tell me?'

'My real name.'

'I know, but I don't remember what name you said.'

'Oh, right.'

'So?'

'So what?'

'What is your real name?'

'Cameron. Cameron Catchpole.'

'Oh.' She couldn't remember what he'd said last night, but she was pretty sure it wasn't Cameron Catchpole. She decided to let it go. 'My friends call me Vee.'

Cameron spread Nutella on some toast for her, which she thought was very romantic. As she munched and swallowed, her eyes focused on the jumble of plastic letters and takeaway menus on the fridge door in front of her where she caught sight of two large, rectangular invitation cards held in place by a daisy-shaped magnet.

You are invited to
FASHION FREEDOM FIGHTERS
ANNUAL BOAT PA
Saturday 23

That's today, Verity thought.

There are two invitations. Genius! This is how I make amends for whatever hideous stuff I did last night. This is how I thank Cameron for getting those passes for Avatarama. *I'll get dressed up and take him to the uber-glamorous riverboat party, really impress him with my fabulous fashion friends and convince him I'm not a total weirdo loser or a drunken ballerina freak and that I might make a suitable girlfriend!*

In the taxi, on the way to the river, Verity had a brilliant idea. As she was dressed head-to-toe in her mum's most luxurious, exclusive clothing (which she'd taken several hours to assemble), she wondered if Cameron would like a new outfit for the boat trip. Even after her splurge at *Avatarama*, she still had some of the money Mum had left, since she'd failed to provide any of the catering she'd planned for her party the previous evening. And there was always the emergency cash and the credit card, too, if she needed it. Admittedly, there had been no rumours of impending nuclear disaster that Saturday, but Verity could think of no greater 'emergency' that would justify utilising the credit card than buying something for Cameron, her new bloke. Mum would understand.

She leaned forward, tapped on the Perspex partition and asked the taxi driver to pull over.

'Where d'you wanna stop, love?' he asked.

'Just there's fine,' she said. 'Outside Dolce and Gabbana.'

'What's up?' Cameron asked.

'Just need to do some shopping,' she said and thrust a tenner into the driver's hand. 'Come on.'

Forty minutes later, Cameron emerged wearing a black slim-cut suit, distressed-leather Victorian-style boots, a chunky grey scarf and a new pair of shades. *Urgh!* He looked SO cool. Verity sighed and shivered with pleasure. *Nom nom! Edible! Totally edible!* Pedestrians on the street were giving him admiring glances. *They probably think he's a movie star*, Verity thought. Cameron had been reluctant at first, uneasy at having clothes bought for him by a girl, but when he'd spotted the boots, he seemed to change his mind.

They hailed another taxi and set off towards the river again. There was no turning back now, thought Verity. She'd just put over a grand on the emergency credit card.

The invitation said '4pm cast off' and it was already forty-eight minutes past when Verity and Cameron's taxi finally turned into the narrow alleyway that led down to the jetty. But the boat was still there, as were the gorgeously-dressed passengers, who were having their photos taken by the assembled fashion fans and the ubiquitous paps.

'Thank goodness everything in fashion runs late,' said Vee as they climbed from the cab and joined the other guests on the chilly, windswept waterfront.

The flashing and whirring increased to a crescendo as the pair walked arm-in-arm along the red carpet, and a buzz of 'who's that?' rippled through the crowd. Verity stepped carefully on to the gang plank and wobbled down the steps on to the deck, wafting her invitation card at a publicist with a clipboard. The last of the celebs eventually tired of smiling and waving and did the same, and the large, top-deck saloon began to fill. Verity and Cameron grabbed glasses of champagne and went outside to the stern where people were watching the crew preparing to cast off. The publicity girl was flapping her arms and shouting into her phone. The boat couldn't leave yet. They were waiting for someone. The guest of honour hadn't arrived.

'Right,' said Verity. 'Here's the challenge.'

'Challenge?' Cameron's forehead creased.

'Yeah. Whatever I say from now on, you have to go along with. OK?'

Cameron hesitated. 'OK.'

'And then, later, you get to decide who we are and I'll go along with you.'

'Right. Got it.'

Verity always played this game at the fashionable events

Mum took her to – movie premieres, gallery private views, shop openings. They were usually cool for the first five minutes then mind-numbingly tedious for the rest of the night – the same old fashion designers and media celebs talking about the same old stuff, nibbling on the same old fish-egg appetizers or spoon-shaped canapés that looked like dog food. She had to find ways to amuse herself. This time she had an accomplice.

'Och, mine got!' she cried suddenly in an appallingly bad German accent. 'Ay hif dropped mine diamond ring into das wasser!' She threw her hands into the air then leaned over the rail.

'Och, darlink!' said Cameron, loudly, in an even worse accent. 'Niver mind. I vill buy you anuzzer, tvice as *gross*.'

'Vot an angel you are, *liebling*!' said Verity, blowing him a little kiss. She was really camping it up.

'Anythink for mine *kleine schnuples*!' Cameron seemed determined to outdo her campness.

'Don't you want to get it back?' asked a stylishly dressed, grey-haired man, standing beside them at the rail.

'I'm sure they could, you know,' said an anorexic-thin, red-haired woman. 'They could send down a diver and retrieve it.'

'Och, *nein*! I vil not have zem go to any trouble,' said Verity waving her hands. 'I hiv boxes and boxes of diamonds at home. Vot is one liddle ring?'

'Where's home?' the redhead asked, grinning and revealing a mouth full of impossibly white teeth.

Verity stepped excitedly towards her and held out her hand in greeting. 'Vee are Christoph und Lottie Schnitzelhoff of Las Vegas, Nevada. How do you do?'

Cameron clicked his heels together and nodded.

‘Nevada?’ the stylish man asked. ‘I thought you were going to say Berlin or something.’

‘Vee are yew ezz zitizens *von* ze last tree years,’ said Cameron.

‘You in fashion in the US?’ asked another woman. They were beginning to draw a crowd.

‘More zee costumes then zee fashion,’ said Verity. ‘Vee are *Zee Amazing Schnitzelhoffs, Masters of Illusion*.’

‘You do a magic show in Las Vegas? That’s fabulous!’

‘Meh-jick? Vee don’t do meh-jick!’ Lottie Schnitzelhoff was horrified at such an insult. ‘Ektually it *eez* febulous. Vee do zee

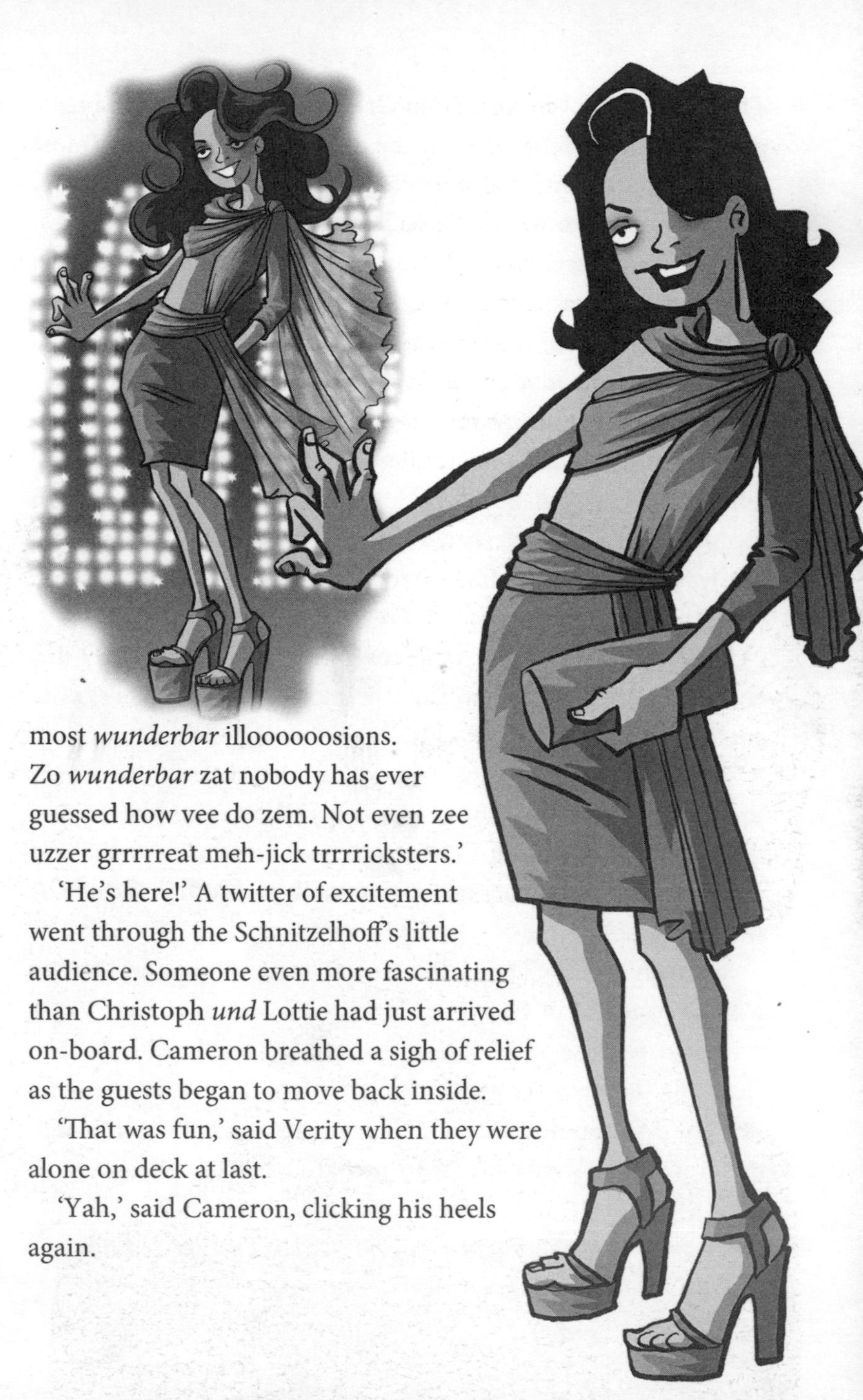

most *wunderbar* illoooooosions. Zo *wunderbar* zat nobody has ever guessed how vee do zem. Not even zee uzzer grrrrreat meh-jick trrrricksters.'

'He's here!' A twitter of excitement went through the Schnitzelhoff's little audience. Someone even more fascinating than Christoph *und* Lottie had just arrived on-board. Cameron breathed a sigh of relief as the guests began to move back inside.

'That was fun,' said Verity when they were alone on deck at last.

'Yah,' said Cameron, clicking his heels again.

The guest of honour was Eden Greenfield. Verity should have guessed it would be him. After all, he turned up at almost every fashion event and particularly leapt at any opportunity to increase his 'youth cred'. Today he was supporting Fashion Freedom Fighters, two talented girls straight out of college, who were the coolest pioneers of ethical fashion and were admired for their campaigning as well as their gorgeous designs. Eden had donated tens of thousands to the girls' various schemes and was always praising their stance on safer, greener manufacturing and fairer trade. In return, FFF applauded his well-publicised efforts to reduce his carbon footprint (solar panels and wind turbines on the roofs of all his warehouses) and had made Eden their sort-of patron. Greenfield: the Godfather of Green.

In the saloon, Eden was completely surrounded by his entourage and a growing huddle of adoring party guests. Verity could only just see the top of his head through the noisy throng. It was *so* exciting. A real, live global megastar! If she could squeeze through, she thought, perhaps today would be a good day to introduce herself to him. It would be sensible if she and the Potential Stepdad actually got to know each other, right? She should check him out.

Suddenly, as if by magic, the crowd seemed to part and Verity was swept forward. Her heart hammered on her ribcage like a tiny mad percussionist. Eden was shaking hands with people, clutching their elbows and looking them in the eye, in the same way she'd seen politicians do. He was working his way through the crowd and Verity began to prepare what she was going to say.

Hi, I'm Saffron's daughter . . . no . . . Hi, I'm Verity Fibbs . . .

No . . . I'm Vee, your future stepdaughter . . . NO, not that! They'd had ONE date!

Eden was standing in front of her, holding out his hand. He was even more handsome in the flesh. He smiled and she gasped at the flash of his brown eyes and his impossibly cute dimples, then took a deep breath.

'Hi, I'm—'

'This is Lottie,' the red-haired woman interrupted. 'Lottie Schnitzelhoff, the famous illusionist from America. You may have heard of her.'

'Very pleased to meet you,' said Eden Greenfield, grinning and doing the elbow-clutch handshake.

Verity was mesmerised and dumbstruck. All the blood had drained out of her brain and seemed to have relocated to somewhere near her feet. Her head was empty and her limbs felt like lead. She couldn't remember how to speak or move and simply gaped at him. Then, when Eden released her, she stumbled back through the guests and dragged Cameron outside.

'I just met Eden Greenfield!' She shivered with pleasure.

'Cool!'

'Let's be someone else now.'

The Bridges and the Box

The girls of Fashion Freedom Fighters had been pretty clever choosing a riverboat for their party because their hundred-or-so guests were now trapped on-board until the boat returned to the jetty. They wouldn't be released until they'd spent several hours cruising the Thames. Not that they'd want to leave such a cool party, of course, where there was a delicious vegetarian buffet, a well-stocked bar and a famous DJ providing the atmos. But FFF also had a message for their captive audience. A giant screen in the saloon flicked into life and began to play a video – *Educating the World about Ethical Fashion.*

First there was a very beautifully filmed report about textile factories polluting water supplies, then another about the exploitation of farmers by big cotton manufacturers. There was some stuff about how children as young as seven were working illegally and even a mention of how second-hand and recycled clothing had become really popular among affluent teenagers.

Verity groaned. The videos, which had obviously been made

by talented film makers, were wonderful to watch – like art house movies or perfume ads – and Vee completely agreed with what Fashion Freedom Fighters were trying to do. It was just that she'd heard all this stuff before – grown up with it, in fact. These were all the issues her mum worried about, too. Mum had been a pioneer, rejecting the production methods of 'fast fashion' before any other designer and ensuring that all the factories that made her collections were fair, safe and child friendly.

Verity and Cameron grabbed a couple of veggie samosas from the buffet and sneaked out on to the deck again. The boat was just passing under Albert Bridge.

'That's my favourite,' said Verity, her mouth full of samosa.

'Favourite what?'

'Bridge. It's pretty, isn't it?'

'Mmm. S'pose,' said Cameron with a shrug.

'I like Hammersmith, too,' she added.

'I prefer Tower Bridge myself.'

'That's 'cause you're a boy. Boys always like Tower Bridge best. That one's Chelsea.' She pointed up ahead.

'D'you know *all* their names?'

'Yeah, I do. I learned all the bridges along the Thames, but I can't remember why. School project or something. After Chelsea is the Victoria Station one, which is a rail bridge and I think it's called the Grovesnor. Then it's Vauxhall, Lambeth . . .' she began to recite. 'Westminster, Golden Jubilee and Hungerford.' She took a breath then continued. 'Waterloo, Blackfriars, then the Blackfriars train bridge.'

'Yeah, yeah. Getting nerdy and weird now,' said Cameron, laughing.

She ignored him. 'Millennium footbridge, Southwark, Cannon

Street – that's a railway bridge, too.' She paused and chewed her lip, then suddenly straightened her back. 'Aah!'

'What's up?' Cameron asked. She'd made him jump.

'I'm supposed to be on a train to Brighton.' She got the iPhone out of her mum's expensive evening bag and stared at it. 'What excuse shall I give my aunt?'

'Who?'

'My aunt – my mum's sister, Tamsin.'

'You had an accident?' Cameron suggested, unsure why she was asking.

'Mmm.' Verity tapped the screen, found the number, put the phone to her ear and waited. After three rings, Tamsin answered.

'Hello.'

'Hi, Tam. It's Vee.'

Cameron could hear the aunt's faint voice on the other end. 'Verity! Hello, sweetie! You on the train? When do you get here?'

'No, something's happened.'

'Oh. You OK?'

'Yeah, I'm all right but my best friend had this accident. She's in hospital and I'm calling from her bedside.'

'Oh noooo!' Tamsin wailed. 'I do hope it's not serious.'

'Nah. She's OK. She was knocked off her bike by this lorry and I think I should stay in London. My friend's dad says it's all right if I stay with them at their house. He's here so you can speak to him, if you want.'

'Oh, OK.'

Verity thrust the phone at Cameron who cringed then took it.

'Hello, this is . . .' he said in a deep, rumbling voice, then stopped. He looked at Verity with wide eyes. He had no idea who he was supposed to be. He flapped his free hand at her.

'Pye's dad,' Verity whispered.

'. . . Pye's Dad. We'd be very happy to have Verity stay with us while our daughter . . .' He hesitated again.

'Pye,' Verity hissed.

'. . . while our daughter, Pye, is . . .'

'Recovering from her accident.'

'. . . recovering from her accident.'

'Yes, of course, I can see that that would absolutely be the best thing for both of them,' said Tamsin. 'I hope Pye gets better soon. Poor girl. You must all be awfully worried about her.'

'Indeed, we are, but she's in marv—' his voice squeaked and a deep flush appeared at his collar and crept up into the soft patch of bristles below his ear. He coughed and continued in a deeper voice again. '—ellous, really marvellous hands here.'

'Will you talk to Verity's mum, or shall I?' asked Tamsin.

'Um, I think Verity has spoken to her mother already.' Cameron raised his eyebrows at Vee. Vee nodded vigorously. 'Ah, yes. Verity informs me that Mrs Fibbs has been notified.'

Verity grinned and jabbed her thumb in the air in a gesture of approval and delight. He'd said just the sort of stuffy, dumb, pompous thing Pye's dad would have said if Pye really had been in hospital after a bike accident. Cameron was really good at this – almost as good as she was. *Now, if he was equally good at snogging*, she thought, *he was going to be an awesome boyfriend.*

Maisie Malone and Ben Blades clung to the rickety and oarless rowing boat as it drifted silently down the evil-smelling river that wound through the middle of the Demon City. Ben Blades steered their unsteady craft with the blade of his sword as they passed under bridge after bridge, unnoticed by the menacing populace above. They should be safe. Maisie knew demons hated and avoided water (according to an on-screen hint on an earlier level) but there might be other villains on the river – smuggling weapons, transporting contraband or dumping bodies.

Maisie peered into the churning slime. Had she just seen the tip of a pale tentacle? Or maybe it had been the fin of a large, colourless fish . . . or a human foot.

'Verity?' A female voice wafted across the surface of the river.

Verity looked up. She and Cameron, standing at the stern rail, were directly under the central span of Lambeth Bridge, so had momentarily been plunged into darkness. The lights of the Houses of Parliament shimmered on the water just ahead, but for now they were invisible. Vee wondered who at the party might know her real name.

Then she saw Callista.

'Oh, no!' she moaned. 'We've got to hide. Come on.'

She pushed Cameron and, staying in the shadow, they staggered over to the far side of the boat. Verity pointed towards the bow.

'Hurry,' she hissed.

'Where?' Cameron was confused. Verity seemed to be pointing at the river.

'Climb over.'

They both climbed over the metal railing and balanced on a narrow ledge. There was no proper walkway to the other end of the boat, just a slippery wooden shelf the width of a shoe. They had to shuffle sideways along the ledge, clinging to the roof, past the giant picture windows, their legs in full view of the guests in the dark saloon. Thank goodness the lights were out, Verity thought, and that the party guests were all looking the other way, staring at the floodlit tower of Big Ben like awestruck tourists.

'Who are we hiding from?' Cameron asked.

'Callista, the snake-haired Medusa. If she finds us, she'll ruin everything . . . and turn us to stone with one look.'

Callista was Mum's super-efficient studio manager. She ran the day-to-day operations of Jiggery-Pokery*'s* London headquarters like a military boot camp and was one of the few people who hadn't gone to New York for the launch. She was far too important for that. The studio simply couldn't function without her. *But, what on earth is she doing at a party*? thought Verity. Callista was not at all the party type. In fact, Verity was amazed she actually owned any party clothes. Surely, Callista wore her immaculate trouser suits for everything, including working out at the gym and sleeping. That's if she ever *did* sleep. Verity suspected that she hung from the rafters of the studio at night, chewing on dead birds and small rodents.

Callista's face appeared at the far end of the boat, standing at the rail they'd just climbed over. Vee and Cameron froze and held their breath. The lights from the bank now illuminated the stern and they could see Callista quite clearly, but their side of the boat was in shadow and they were invisible. Callista did not have snakes for hair, of course. Her hair was short and neat and she raised a hand to tuck it behind her ears. She peered into the darkness but, seeing that the stern was empty and there was no obvious escape route, she turned to go. Perhaps she'd been mistaken.

Poo-pi-pi-di-da-da-di-poo-pi-pi-di-da!

The comical ringtone of Verity's phone echoed across the water. It was so loud, the chattering people on the terraces of the Houses of Parliament would have heard it.

Poo-pi-pi-di—

Verity flinched then wobbled and clutched the evening bag to her chest in an attempt to muffle the sound.

—ma-ma-m-moo-m-m-m-ma!

Callista stood still.

The phone stopped.

The boat engine chugged and the water lapped.

Callista shrugged and went back inside, but Verity suspected she wouldn't give up and might search the boat before she was completely convinced. They weren't out of danger yet. Cameron and Verity started moving again, shuffled to the end, climbed over on to the deck of the bow and crouched down. The phone rang again.

Ma-ma-m-moo-m-m-m-ma!

'In here,' said Verity pointing at a large wooden storage box.

Ma-ma-m-moo-m-m-m-ma!

Cameron lifted a tarpaulin and they both climbed inside. The box was full of bulky life jackets and not at all a comfortable place to hide.

Ma-ma-m-moo-m-m-m-ma!

Curled up in a ball, her cheek pressed against a damp, rough nylon jacket cover, Verity extracted the iPhone and tapped the screen.

Two missed calls. Pye.

Vee wondered where her friend was. *Probably smooching in a vegan café or making tofu smoothies with Alfie Pearson*, she thought. She glanced over at Cameron. His face was illuminated in the soft blue glow of her phone and she could just make out that he was grinning at her. He seemed to think that hiding from Callista was hilarious. She managed a half smile back, which became more of a sneer. This impress-the-boyfriend date was not going exactly to plan. She sighed. Squashed together in a box of life jackets might have some romantic potential, though. It could even turn out to be quite cosy.

'I'm a little bit uncomfortable in this corner. Is there more room over there with you?' Vee attempted another smile.

The boat began to lurch and turn around. At last, they were heading back. Verity had tried, initially, to crawl across the box to be closer to Cameron, but there had been too many life jackets in the way. She could have climbed out, removed some of the bulky orange jackets, then got back in again, but that would risk revealing their hiding place to Callista. The sooner they returned to the jetty, the better.

Vee had been counting and naming bridges to pass the time. Just before they'd turned, the echo of the boat engine had changed and the shard of light at the edge of the tarpaulin had disappeared (so she knew they were under a bridge) and she'd announced, 'Tower Bridge: your fave.'

Cameron had grunted. He was bored and uncomfortable, too.

It was another agonising hour before they finally docked back in Richmond.

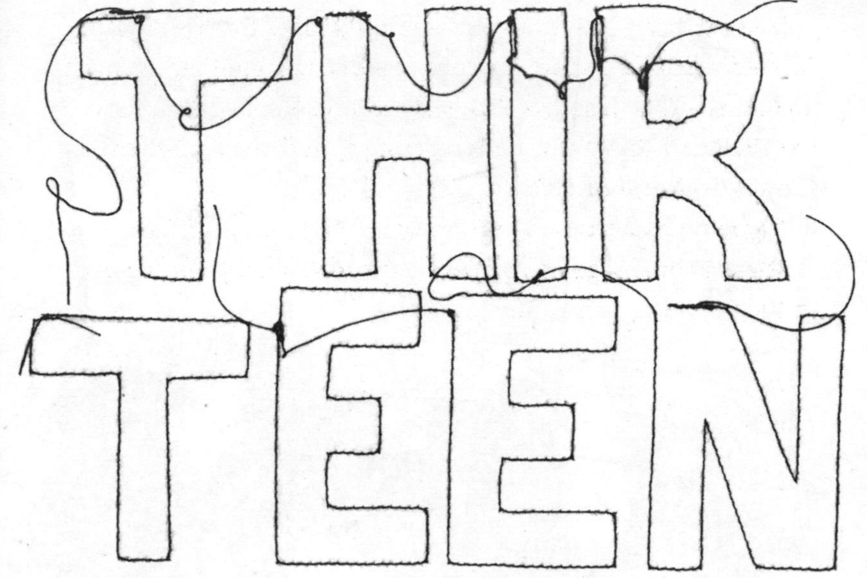

Koshi, Kissing and the Cleaner

It wasn't just paparazzi, limos and taxis that were waiting for the boat to return. The guests were surprised to find themselves disembarking to the sound of chanting protesters. A group of awkward-looking teenage geeks and eco-crusties were waving banners and blowing whistles on the waterfront and one of them was a girl with candyfloss, blond hair.

'Isn't that your friend?' asked Cameron, pointing at the dock. He had lifted the tarpaulin just enough to determine whether it was safe to venture out.

Verity grabbed his hand and yanked it down.

'Don't do that! Callista will see us!'

'That girl.' He pointed again. It's Cupcake . . . I mean, Pizza,' said Cameron, trying and failing to amuse her.

LIAR
THE TRUTH
about ethical fashio
STAR WARS
PYE
KOSHI
GRACE
JELLY
HAMISH
OLLIE
CHEN

'Pye. You know it's Pye.'

'Oh, you mean the one who's just had an accident?'

'Uh.' She'd lost her sense of humour.

'She made a quick recovery, then.' Cameron chuckled.

'What's she doing here?' Verity muttered. 'She's supposed to be on a date with her new boyfriend.'

'He must be that beardy with his arm around her, then.'

'Oh my God! *Weeooweeooweeoo*!' She imitated a siren. 'Call the Fashion Police! Have those people arrested and put in style rehab.' Verity was trying to hide her surprise and annoyance with sarcasm. Pye's new boyfriend wasn't Alfie Parsons at all. He was about as far away from Alfie Parsons as it was possible to be. He was tall, shabby and trying to grow a beard. Verity sort of recognised him from school but couldn't recall his name. *It might be Liam or Lewis or something lame like that*, she thought. But he was definitely one of the fashionably-challenged. Was he that swotty A-Level student who'd caused a commotion earlier in the term by getting into Cambridge?

Once the boat had begun to empty and Verity was satisfied that Callista the Medusa had driven off in a taxi, she and Cameron crept back into the saloon and strolled casually out on to the gangway, brushing the dust and dirt from their ruined designer outfits. The protesters jeered and whistled and chanted at them but, unlike the other guests, who were ducking into their limos and making a rapid getaway, Vee and Cameron walked straight over to the Fashion-Free Zone.

'Veeeee!' screamed Pye when she recognised her friend.

'You didn't tell me you were coming here,' said Verity, giving her friend a hug.

‘Eew! You’re all dusty,’ said Pye, wrinkling her nose.

Vee grunted. The disastrous boat trip had plunged her into a gnarly mood. She’d ruined Mum’s dress, had pretty much missed the entire boat party and now she’d discovered her best friend was dating a supergeek.

‘I came with Koshi,’ said Pye, grinning. ‘This is Koshi.’ She looked up adoringly into the beardy’s face and he grinned back. ‘And this is Grace, Jelly, Hamish, Ollie and Chen,’ she said, introducing the rest of the group. Verity recognised the pale girl Pye had been talking to at school (Grace) and her equally unremarkable friend (Jelly). And there was the maths geek from the other day, too (Chen). These were the school’s misfits – the swots, the nerds, members of the Vegan Cookery Club. Pye thrust a flyer into Verity’s hand and blew a whistle at Eden Greenfield, who was climbing into his limo.

Verity looked down.

LIAR

the flyer announced. Then below was,

THE TRUTH
about ethical fashion

A website address followed. The image behind the text was a very familiar one. It was the picture of Eden Greenfield with the apple-cheeked children.

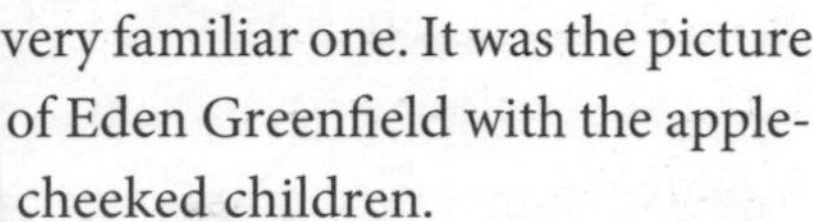

Verity's stomach lurched. 'What are you doing? You're gonna get into so much trouble using that pic. You'll be sued!'

'We're going to expose the lies,' Pye replied. 'And we know exactly what we're doing 'cause Koshi's doing Law for A-Level.'

'But that's a picture of Eden! He's not a liar!'

'Don't worry,' said Koshi. 'Your mum is squeaky.'

'What?'

'She's clean – your mum.'

'Well, I could have told

you that!' Sweat began to prickle Vee's forehead. Bad publicity like this could be disastrous. The smallest hint of something dodgy could be catastrophic for Eden's charity, never mind the damage to the TRULY clothing sales. This stupid flyer could turn into a complete public-relations nightmare. She'd listened to Mum often enough talking about maintaining her company's 'brand image' and all that other stuff publicity and marketing departments obsess about.

'Koshi's done loads of research,' said Pye. 'They've found out—'

'I don't want to hear about Koshi's stupid research!' A hot boiling rage was rising in Vee's body. It reached her ears, made her head spin and all her thoughts jumble together. 'You are wrong about Eden. He's not a liar. Mum wouldn't have anything to do with him if he was and you know it!' She flapped the leaflet in her friend's face.

'That's what makes it so sinister,' said Koshi. 'He's done such a good PR job that people actually think he's a saint.'

Verity couldn't take any more. Pye's new misfit friends were morons. They obviously didn't know what they were talking about. What did they know about the fashion business, anyway? Clearly nothing, going by what they were wearing. And what was cool, funky, stylish Pye doing with them? She was a moron, too.

'I'm not gonna waste my breath explaining how totally wrong and idiotic you are,' Verity spat angrily, then she turned and stomped along the dock towards a waiting taxi. 'I'm going home!' she yelled over her shoulder. She reached the cab, gave her address to the driver, wrenched open the door and looked back at Cameron. 'Come on!'

'See you Monday?' Pye shouted, her face now crumpled in anguish. 'I'll text you later.'

Verity pretended she hadn't heard and climbed into the taxi.

Cameron stole a glance at Pye, who looked like she'd just been punched. He hesitated but Pye shrugged and attempted a smile. 'Go on. She'll go without you.'

'Yeah.' He laughed. 'Bye, then.' He jogged over to the taxi and got in. As the cab pulled away, Verity noticed two crow-like black figures standing in the shadows. They were watching the protesters.

Verity looked into Cameron Catchpole's soft brown eyes, a delicious tingle of anticipation rippling over her skin. They were standing in her bedroom, the eerie sound of their abandoned *Demon Streets* game wafting up from the living room downstairs. At last, the moment seemed to have arrived – the longed-for *snog moment*. She'd already kissed him several times in her head, rehearsed it, tried different scenarios, but this wasn't quite what she'd imagined. It was *way* better. Maybe it was their having been thwarted and interrupted so many times that was now making the adrenalin rush around her body. Perhaps it was because she *knew* that Cameron wanted to kiss her, too.

He had followed her upstairs when she'd mentioned the sketchbook of *Demon Streets* characters in her room and, while he'd been flicking through her drawings, Verity had stood behind him, looking over his shoulder, her cheek close to his. Now he put the book down and turned to face her. He looked up into her eyes. She observed that they weren't completely brown, but had interesting flecks of green and orange. Their faces were so close,

she could feel the heat of his lips and almost taste his mouth. Her heart was racing and she'd forgotten how to breathe. All she had to do was lean, tilt her head, knowing he would do the same, and then, if she didn't faint from a lack of oxygen, their lips would meet. She wondered what his barely-there moustache would feel like. Would it be soft or scratchy? Would he part his lips or hungrily chew at her mouth like people did in movies? If it didn't happen soon, more dumb questions would seep into her brain and she might begin to panic. Were her own lips too wet? Too dry? When had she last brushed her teeth? She closed her eyes and felt the delicious fizz in her stomach again.

'What was that?' Cameron asked.

'What was *what*?' Her words forced her lips into a pout. *Don't stop now*, she thought.

'There!' A puff of his breath tickled her mouth.

She'd heard it, too, this time. *There's someone in the house!*

Cameron stepped back and they both listened for the sound again. The house was silent. The *Demon Streets* game had obviously timed-out or switched to screen saver.

TAP-TAP-TAP!

There was the sound again. Verity was surprised she could hear it above the whoosh of over heated blood pumping loudly in her ears and the air rushing in and out of her lungs.

TAP-TAP!

'It's a burglar.' She gasped.

'In *heels*?' asked Cameron.

'Go and see.' Verity's heart was thumping for a different reason now.

'*You* go and see,' he whispered. 'It's *your* house.'

She frowned. 'OK. But you come with me.' She grasped his arm.

From the top of the stairs, they could see part of the hallway. They listened and, after a minute or two of silence, they heard the tapping sound again and caught a glimpse of a flash of red hair and a pair of boots crossing the hall and disappearing into Mum's office. They were zebra-print boots!

Verity breathed out. 'Hhhh, it's not a burglar! It's Bliss Meadows!'

Cameron frowned. 'What's this Bliss person doing creeping around your house at eleven o'clock at night?'

'Good question.' Verity frowned, too. 'I suppose I'd better go and find out.' She began to walk down the stairs.

'Be careful,' said Cameron.

Verity chewed her lip. *Shouldn't Cameron have volunteered for this*? she wondered. If your boyfriend cares about you enough, he's supposed to step in to protect you, get in fights for you, risk everything. But, maybe he didn't care for her . . . and was Cameron officially her *boyfriend* yet? She looked up at him cowering at the top of the stairs, then crossed the hallway and pushed open the office door.

Bliss was sitting at the desk, prodding at the computer keyboard.

'Aahh!' Bliss screamed and clutched her chest. 'Uh – you made me jump.' Then she smiled.

Verity was about to ask her why she was there at eleven o'clock, just like Cameron had said, but Bliss rushed into an explanation before she could get a word out.

'Hello! We met the other day, do you remember? I'm the new

junior designer. It's OK, don't worry, I've got permission to be here. I didn't realise you'd be working so late but I suppose, with your boss away, you can clean the house anytime, right? And it looks like you've got a lot to clear up.' Her eyes flicked towards the door to the hallway. She was referring to the party mess that Verity still hadn't tackled. 'I was just doing some stuff for her, actually, for Saffron. She said I could call her Saffron, which is nice, isn't it? Because she doesn't really know me that well yet, since I only got the job last week . . .'

She still thinks I'm the cleaner, thought Verity.

'Anyway, I was just picking up some messages and running some errands for her. She called me from New York. I already had the door codes and everything; actually, I was surprised that the alarm wasn't on, but you're here, so that explains it.' Bliss wrinkled her nose and took a breath.

Verity was confused. Bliss was acting weird and the door to the safe was open.

'I don't suppose you know if there's another safe in the house?' Bliss asked. She'd seen Verity glance at it.

Vee was about to ask if Bliss had tried the lockable cupboard downstairs in the design studio, but stopped herself. For some reason, she didn't think she should be aiding her in her search.

'You see, Saffron asked me to find something and it's not there so I wondered . . . uuummm . . .' Bliss was tapping on the keyboard again. 'And you wouldn't happen to know the password for this thing, would you?' She pointed at the screen and looked up at Verity.

Verity shook her head. Something wasn't right.

'No, of course you wouldn't – you're the cleaner,' said Bliss, laughing. 'Never mind, I'll just give Saffron a call later and ask her.' She jabbed the computer's off button and stood up.

Verity followed her back across the hall to the front door.

'Bye, then,' said Bliss, stepping out into the darkness, still smiling.

'Bye,' said Verity and closed the door behind her. She pondered for a second, then went to the keypad on the wall, put in the alarm code and returned upstairs.

Verity moved the vibrating toothbrush around her mouth and scowled at herself in the bathroom mirror.

'Stupid Bliss Meadows,' she muttered. 'Mucked up my snog moment. Urgh! Stupid Bliss Meadows!'

She'd known, as soon as she'd climbed the stairs after seeing Bliss out, that the mood had changed. There was no electricity in the air, no adrenalin pumping and no exciting fizz in her stomach. What hung in the air instead was a hideous awkwardness. They could hardly look at each other. The snog moment had gone. They'd sat in silence, watching a rubbish 1940s gangster movie on Vee's telly. Then, instead of pulling her into his arms and kissing her, Cameron had *fake* yawned, said the film was 'totally lame', that he was tired and was going to bed. He'd then slouched off into the guest room.

Verity spat, wiped her mouth, threw her towel on the floor, stamped back to her room and crawled under her duvet. She stared up at the ceiling. How had her day become such a disaster? She'd woken to torture and now it appeared she was back in the gloomy dungeon again. In fact, right now, she'd probably prefer to have her fingernails extracted than the agony of having a full-on crush for Cameron Catchpole. She rolled over, wrapped her arms around her pillow and sighed.

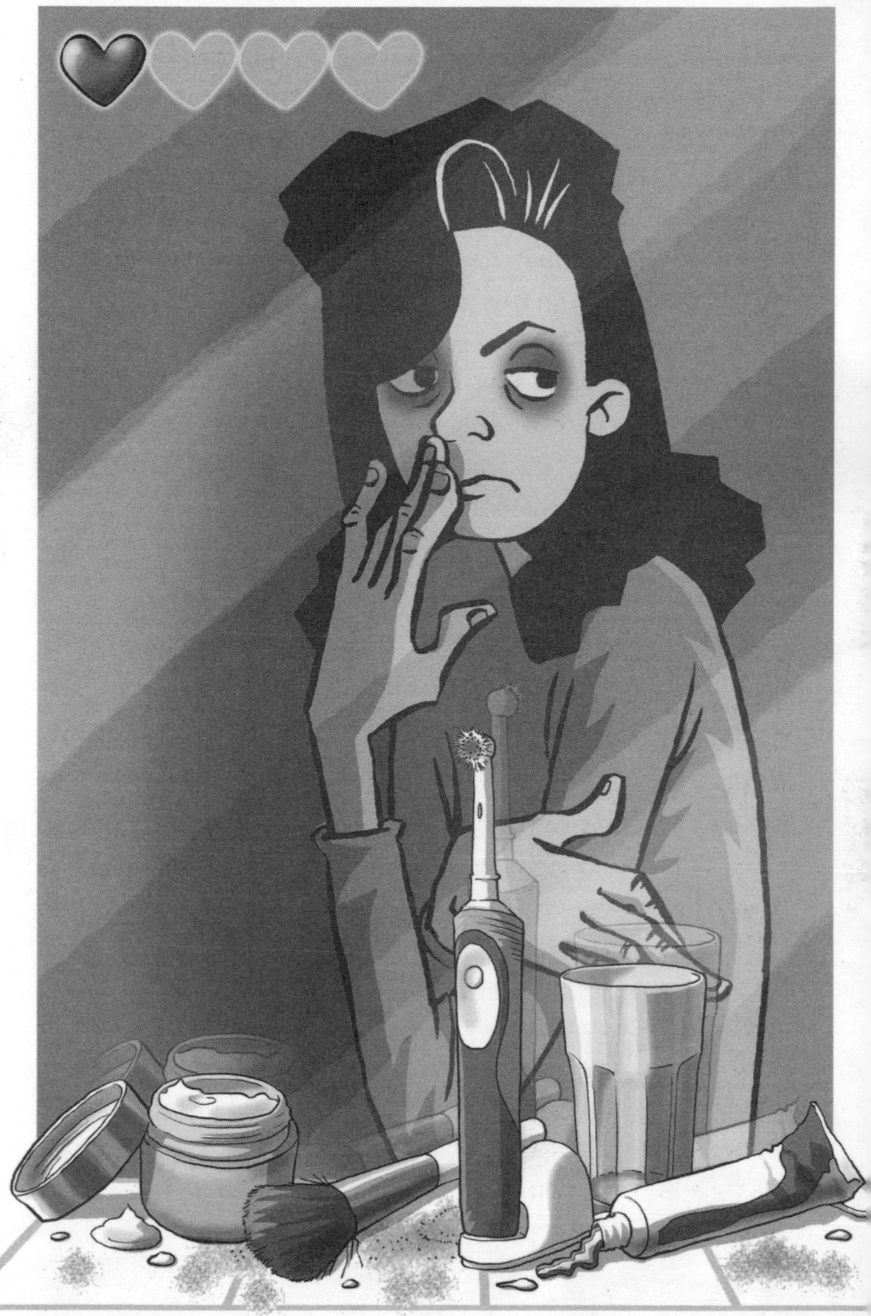

It was always night in Demon City. By the weak light of a sickly demon moon, Maisie Malone and Ben Blades dragged the rowing boat up a ramp. They would hide it here, they decided, as they might need the boat later, if they had to escape . . . should their plan fail. They climbed a flight of wet stone steps and crouched in the shadow of a bridge for a moment. The sound of a far-off siren echoed across the city, but the waterfront was silent. It seemed deserted. They crept forward, hugging the wall of a warehouse.

'Wait,' said Maisie. She thought she heard voices. Yes. Footsteps and two voices in the gloom up ahead. They stood still then ducked behind a discarded crate.

'My feet hurt,' said the first voice.

'Your feet always hurt,' said the second.

'I'm having bacon and sausages for breakfast when our shift is over.'

'All you ever think about is your feet and your stomach.'

'Well, feet and food are the only things that matter.' The first voice paused. 'And football,' he added.

Maisie and Ben Blades watched as two cops, one tall and the other short, sauntered around the corner and walked past them just a step or two from their hiding place. Their discussion of breakfast continued as they disappeared along the waterfront.

Cops were not always the 'good guys' in Demon Streets and you had to be careful. Some were on the Demons' payroll and others might pretend to help, then steal your weapons when you weren't looking. Ben Blades took a tentative look around the corner then whispered, 'All clear. Let's go.'

Maisie followed him along the alley until they approached another junction. Ben stopped and took a pace backwards into the concealing darkness. He'd spotted something across the street and had halted just in time. A short distance away were three large parked cars, bumper to bumper outside a huge warehouse. They could make out the shapes of several bulky figures, too, leaning on the vehicles or standing guard in pairs at either end of the street. They were armed and they were demons. Maisie could see the shapes of machine guns, long rifles and even baseball bats. Some sort of demon meeting was going on inside the warehouse – a meeting that warranted heavily armed security.

'We should get out of here,' said Ben Blades. He reached down, took Maisie's hand and they crept towards another dark alley opposite, staying out of the pools of lights from the few dim street lamps and keeping to the shadows of the buildings. Suddenly, the central double doors opened and Maisie found herself yanked to the ground. A massive figure staggered into the street and began to move towards the furthest car. He was followed by another, slimmer but equally enormous demon who turned and walked in the other direction. The demon meeting had ended and the demon bosses were leaving. The armed thugs scanned the street before reaching to open the car doors.

CLANG!

Bonus fact:
Avoid groups
of Demons
at all costs!

options play II

The sound of Ben Blades' sword hitting the pavement rang out along the street like a bell. Eight pairs of glowing demon eyes snapped around and glared at them.

The thugs raised their weapons and aimed them straight at the patch of shadow where Maisie and Ben were squatting.

'Oops!' said Ben.

SLAM!

A third massive demon came crashing out of the door, rammed straight into one of the henchmen and fell back against the door, making the building shudder. The demon eyes instantly disappeared, like someone had flicked off a switch. With the thugs distracted for a moment, Maisie and Ben Blades seized their chance. They leapt to their feet, dashed across the road and into another alley.

BANG! BANG!

'Aargh!' Ben grabbed his wings.

BANG!

A third bullet ricocheted above Maisie's head. She was getting a bit sick of being shot at. A sound like thunder was following them down the alley. She looked over her shoulder and was horrified to see dozens of glowing eyes, like distant headlight beams getting bigger and bigger. The demons were after them and they were closing in. Ben's wings hung in tatters. The bullets had ripped two holes in them the size of fists. He would never be able to take off with that much damage. Maisie had a flash of inspiration. Now was the moment to use what she'd got from Pamela Pout on Level 1, she thought. The feather-trimmed slippers. 'I know they don't look practical . . .' Pamela had said, '. . . but they'll get you out of trouble'.

+1,000 points score: 10,100

One click later, Maisie was wearing the slippers, had grasped Ben's arm and was running like the wind. Her feather-clad feet seemed to fly above the ground.

'You need . . . to learn some . . . sword skills,' said Maisie, through gasps for breath.

'Yeah. I think we both need training before the next level,' said Ben Blades, being dragged through the air like he was Maisie's scarf.

'How do we . . . do that?'

'We find other players willing to teach us.'

Maisie didn't stop running until they were streets away, the glowing demon eyes left far behind them. As she slowed her pace, Maisie stumbled on the heels, but Ben Blades caught her with both arms. She regained her balance and looked up into his soft, brown eyes. She was out of breath and terrified but her heart was pounding with excitement, too.

'Uhh!' Verity flinched and woke with a thumping in her chest like a tiny engine. She'd heard a noise. She released the pillow that she'd been hugging and rolled over. The house seemed silent, then a car passed in the street outside and Verity watched an arc of yellow light as the headlight beams cut across her ceiling. *Was that one of the demon cars? Have they caught up with us?* Then she heard it again, a sort of growl. Demons? It was the sound of voices but not from the street outside. *It's not* demons, she told herself. *Don't be such a dope, Vee. That's just in the game. This is real life. These are real voices and they are coming from inside my own house!*

Burglars, Calico and TRULY Towers

'There's someone downstairs again,' Verity whispered in the dark, shaking Cameron's shoulder.

'Uh . . . Wha' you wake me for? I was having a lovely dream.'

'Someone broke in. I can hear them. They're in the basement – in the design studio.'

'Chill out! It's probably that Bliss woman come back.'

'I don't think so. It's three o'clock in the morning and there's more of them this time and at least one is a man.'

She actually sounded quite scared, but Cameron already knew she was a pretty plausible actress, so he didn't believe her. 'Uhhh,' he groaned and ducked under the covers.

'Cameron, I'm serious! They're moving stuff and stomping about. I think they're *real burglars!*' The terror flooding her body was making her feel quite sick.

Cameron sat up. 'So what do you want me to do about it?'

'I don't know.' She really hadn't thought about it. Just getting Cameron awake and convincing him there was a problem had been her goal. Now she was unsure what to do next. Might he be a hero and volunteer to go downstairs, she wondered? However romantic a gesture that might be, she wasn't sure she wanted him to go. What if he *did* go down and the burglars were armed, like the thugs in the game? What if they murdered him and then came upstairs and did evil things to her? Mum would be so annoyed if she returned from New York and found a burgled house *and* two dead, mutilated teens.

Cameron got out of bed. Vee took the iPhone out of the pocket of her sweatshirt, which she'd grabbed and put on when she'd heard the noises, and began to punch in numbers.

'Who are you calling?' Cameron asked, his face now white and frightened.

'Police.' She stared at the three nines glowing on the screen.

999

'No! Don't call the police.'

She jumped and was about to ask 'why not?' but paused and thought for a moment. *Maybe he's right. What if it's Bliss again? I'll get into so much trouble for wasting police time or something. But, if it* is *burglars then won't the police catch them or frighten them away?*

Her finger hovered over 'call'.

But there will be an investigation. The police will ask questions about why I'm here on my own . . . and about Cameron . . . and Bliss . . . and I haven't cleared up after the party so they'll ask about that, too.

Verity groaned.

Mum will have to fly home . . . then the story will get out because she's a celeb . . . a corrupt cop will leak it or something . . . and it will get splashed all over the papers and Mum will be furious! Wait a minute, why didn't Cameron want me to call the police? Is he a crook? Did he steal those glasses at the airport . . . and that moped . . . and the Avatarama *tickets? Is he a thief . . . Or a terrorist on the run? Has he been lying about everything and I've let a major criminal stay in our guest room?*

She gulped. She didn't even think Cameron Catchpole was his real name!

CRASH!

Verity and Cameron both jerked like they'd been electrocuted. The burglars had knocked something over . . . in the hallway! They'd obviously finished ransacking the basement studio and were now doing the same on the ground floor.

'They're working their way up, aren't they?' said Cameron.

Vee nodded then said, 'I don't understand.'

'What?'

'How they got past the alarm.'

'Never mind that now. We should hide,' said Cameron.

Verity looked around the guest room. *Hide? Where would be safe? Where could we go that the burglars won't search?* 'Wet room,' she hissed and dragged him out on to the landing.

They hugged the wall and inched their way around to the far side and the door to Mum's bedroom, then froze. The voices were now at the bottom of the stairs.

'Let's try the bedrooms,' said the scariest voice – a deep, masculine growl.

'Yeah, most people hide stuff in their underwear drawers,' said a slightly higher-pitched voice.

'I don't . . .' said the third.

Verity recognised this voice. It was Bliss Meadows. *That* was how they'd got past the alarm. Bliss had keys and the code. But why had she come back? And why had she brought two accomplices with her?

'. . . I put mi—'

'Well, we've already established that you're an idiot and couldn't find your own head if it was handed to you on a plate, so we won't be listening to your opinion, will we?' said the second voice. 'You're probably one of those twits who thinks the freezer is the safest place to hide your valuables and you'd be wrong 'cause it's the first place a thief will look. The freezer and your underwear drawer.'

They were climbing the stairs and Verity and Cameron were still paralysed at the top.

'You sure Fibbs is away?' said the low growl.

'Yeah, like I said, the cleaner was here earlier but must have gone by now,' said Bliss. 'Although she didn't tidy up much.'

If Vee and Cameron didn't move soon, they were going to be discovered.

'And the daughter is in Brighton.'

At last, Verity felt Cameron's hand touch hers and she shuddered back into action. They ducked into Mum's room just as the tops of the burglars' heads came into view. Vee ran straight across to the en suite bathroom.

'In here,' she panted. 'Let's hope they don't bother to look in the shower.'

She and Cameron darted inside and crouched in a dark corner of the luxurious wet room on the limestone tiles, behind the frosted-glass screen, breathing as quietly as they could . . . and waited.

They could hear Bliss and the burglars moving from room to room, opening cupboards and pulling out drawers. Then a pair of heavy footsteps crossed the thick carpet of Mum's bedroom and the door of her walk-in wardrobe was wrenched open. The clatter of wooden hangers knocking together caused a sickening image in Verity's head of two enormous rough demon hands slapping through her mum's beautiful clothes.

It was too late to call the police now. Any sound would expose them, for sure.

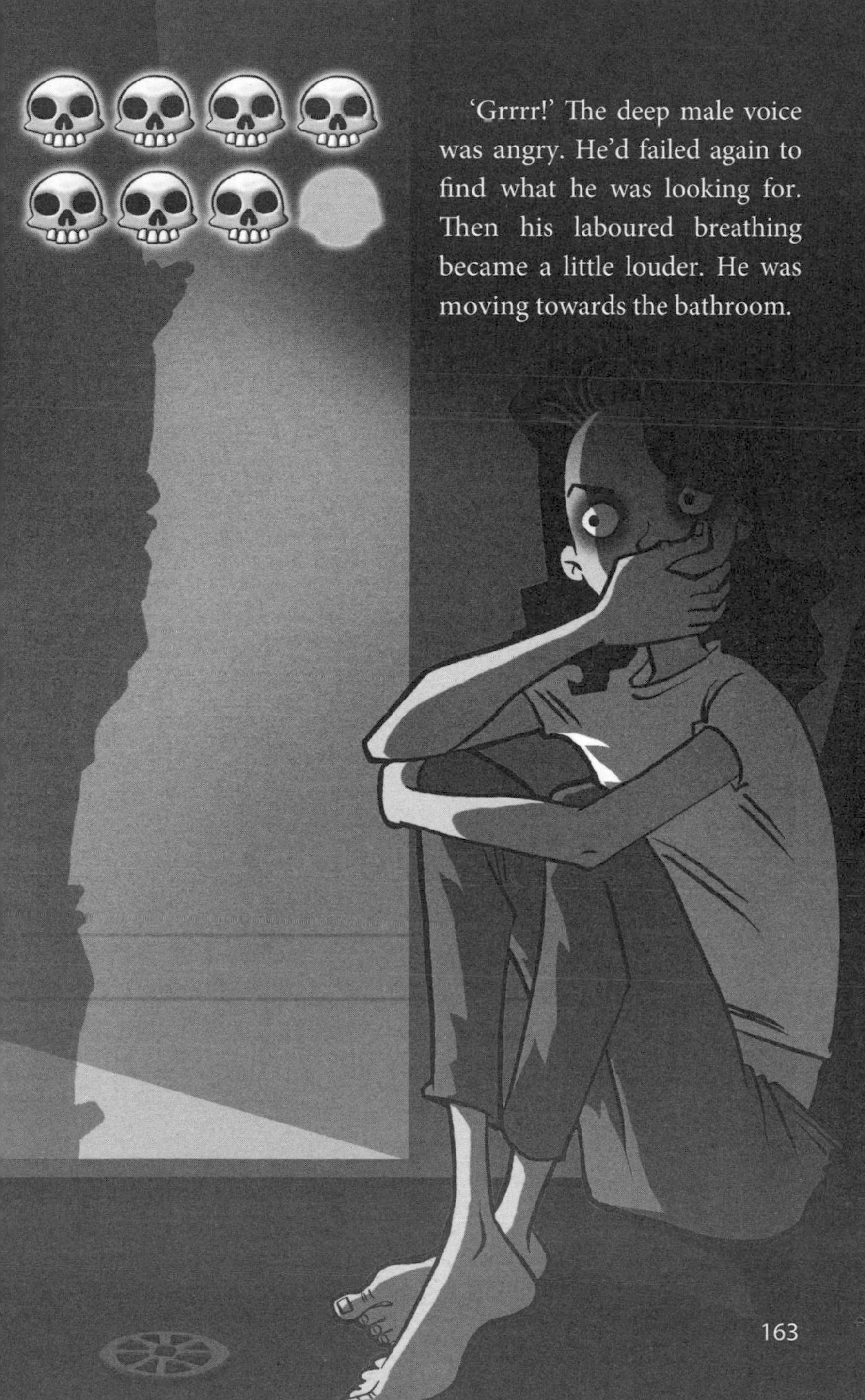

'Grrrr!' The deep male voice was angry. He'd failed again to find what he was looking for. Then his laboured breathing became a little louder. He was moving towards the bathroom.

In the gloom, Verity and Cameron watched, terrified, as a sliver of light appeared on the shower screen, grew into a rectangle and was then distorted into an ominous shape – a tall, male shape. He took a few steps inside and stood by the sink for a moment. His intimidating presence seemed to fill the room. There was a smell – a sort of damp-clothes smell mixed with sweat. Vee and Cameron held their breath but the man didn't leave. What was he doing? Verity's head began to spin and she raised her hand to her mouth to stop herself from moaning with fear. Then she flinched. A strangely familiar sound was echoing around the tiled room – the sound of a stream of liquid hitting water.

The burglar was having a wee!

'I don't think they actually stole anything,' said Verity.

'You sure?' said Cameron.

'Well, I think so.' She closed the safe and pushed shut the top draw of the desk. 'They just made a bit of mess.'

'Doesn't make any sense,' said Cameron, frowning.

'Not unless they were looking for something in particular and it wasn't here,' Vee suggested.

'Like what?'

'I dunno. But perhaps my mum took it to New York with her.'

Cameron nodded, picked up another book from the floor and put it back on a shelf. They had decided not to call the police. Or rather, Cameron had decided and Vee had gone along with it. They hadn't been beaten up or murdered or worse and the burglars hadn't broken the door down, Bliss had let them in, so Verity could see no reason to involve the police. It would make her life far too complicated. Admittedly, there was a bit of mess, but a lot less than had been caused by her party. In fact, Verity thought the burglars might have been slightly more respectful of their property than some of her friends! The burglars hadn't thrown up on the sofa, had they?

Cameron followed Verity down the steps into the design studio. Mum's basement studio was always messy, so Vee wasn't quite sure if the burglars had been responsible for the rolls of fabric thrown on the floor and the sketchbook pages scattered all over the cutting table.

Verity loved the studio, especially the smell of calico – the stiff cream fabric used to make the mock-ups of garments, the toiles. When she was a kid, she would always do her homework sitting on a high stool at the vast cutting table so she could inhale her favourite smell. She'd watch the ghostly pieces of calico transform as Mum ran them through the noisy sewing machine, smoothed them with the big steam iron and draped them over the headless mannequins. Then Mum would snip with her enormous shears, and fold and pleat and pin, until a complicated new garment would appear. Mum would sketch some more, add to the hundreds of colourful drawings that covered the walls and begin to mark out and cut pieces for another calico toile. Verity hardly ever came down here any more, preferring the sanctuary of her own room, her books and her gadgets, now that she was older. Fourteen-year-olds needed more than offcuts of calico and boxes of buttons to amuse them, she had explained to Mum. She stood in the middle of the studio and sniffed.

'You OK?' asked Cameron.

Verity nodded, but she wasn't. She was scared and tired and angry with herself. And, worst of all, she missed her mum so much that it was making her chest hurt. There was a horrible tickle at the back of her throat and she wanted to cry.

'I know you don't want to call your mum,' said Cameron.

Verity jumped because, actually, it was exactly what she *did* want to do.

'But, do you think we should warn someone about this Bliss Meadows person?' Cameron continued.

Verity nodded. 'Yeah, s-s'pose so.' Her voice cracked.

'I mean, if these people are involved in some sort of espionage, like, stealing exclusive designs or something, then you should tell someone at your mum's company, shouldn't you?'

Verity shrugged. She didn't want to risk speaking in case it came out as a sob.

'What about that snake-haired studio manager woman?'

Verity took another deep, comforting breath of the calico smell then smiled at him. Cameron was a genius! Super-manager Callista would sort everything.

'Well, obviously I'm having trouble believing you,' said Callista, peering at Verity over her enormous chunky-framed glasses. 'What did you expect?' They'd found her, as Vee knew they would, working on a Sunday, at her desk in the Jiggery-Pokery office. Callista had no family, no life and therefore no need for a weekend. She seemed always to be in a foul mood, too.

'But, it's *true!* Bliss Meadows *is* a spy! I *saw* her!' Verity whined.

'Well, I saw *you* on the boat last night.' Callista rested her elbows on her desk and clasped her hands together. 'And I know that you were passing yourself off as some cabaret-act magician.'

Callista sneered. 'I heard about that sick story you told your aunt, too, about an injured friend on her deathbed or whatever.' She pursed her lips.

Verity was astonished. How had Callista found that out?

'So this rubbish about Bliss Meadows is just juvenile. Why you should want to spread nasty little rumours about a new member of staff, I really don't know. It's spiteful. And childish. As is that despicable lie you told just so you could spend the weekend with a boy. One day, Vee, you're going to go too far. Luckily, some of us can see right through your ridiculous tales. In my opinion, your mother allows you far too much freedom. If I was raising you, young lady, things would be very different, that's for sure.'

'Well, you're not!' Verity spat.

'You wouldn't get away with that sort of rudeness, for a start!'

Verity's face burned with fury. She'd been about to explain that the boy waiting just outside Callista's office could verify everything she had just said about Bliss breaking in and trying to steal secret designs from Mum's studio, but now she was too angry.

'Well, it'll be *your* fault if Bliss Meadows leaks the next collection or wrecks the launch or something, won't it?' she yelled. 'I'll tell Mum that you ignored my warnings about a mole in the company and she'll blame you!'

Verity stormed out and slammed the office door like a bad-tempered kid. She was angry with herself as much as frustrated at Callista's scepticism. She must have explained badly, not told it right, and Callista had just assumed it was another of her elaborate inventions.

'Well?' asked Cameron. He'd been walking in circles around the deserted Jiggery-Pokery reception area, too agitated to sit on one of the leather sofas.

'Come on, let's get out of here,' said Verity.

'Did she sort it?'

'Nope!'

Cameron had to jog to keep up with her as she strode through the glass doors and took off down the street. She crossed the road, went through a set of gates into the miniature park in the middle of Soho Square and sat down on a bench. She breathed deeply and tried to calm herself. Who else might she go to for help? Who would believe her? The wind whipped litter around her feet as she pulled out her phone. It was obvious. Why hadn't she gone straight to her first? She called Pye.

'Veeeeeeee, you in Brighton?' sang Pye's voice. 'You calmed down yet?'

Verity smiled. 'No, still in London and yeah, sorry. I didn't mean it. Any of it. Do you forgive me?'

Pye laughed. 'Absolutely, matey! We friends again?'

''Course.'

'Come and join us, then,' Pye went on. 'We're pretending to superglue ourselves to a building!'

'What?' Verity frowned. Had she misheard?

'Wait! I'll send a pic.' The line went silent for a few seconds, then the phone beeped and an image began to appear. It was slightly blurred, but it seemed to be of smiling people with their hands pressed against the glass front of a sleek office building. There were Squashy and Chin, Ollie and Custard . . . or whatever their names were! Behind them, on the other side of the glass, was the angry, snarling face of a security guard.

'What are you *doing*?' Verity shouted into the phone. She'd just worked out where they were. 'That's Eden's building! Unstick yourselves!' Then she looked up at Cameron. 'We've got to go and stop them. They're going to get into SO MUCH trouble. The supergeeks are gluing themselves to *TRULY Towers!*'

TRULY Towers, the nickname for Eden Greenfield's enormous, modern, skyscraper office building, headquarters of his TRULY fashion brand and his various charities, was a short bus ride away. However, it was Sunday, and Verity and Cameron found that, although there were plenty of buses going in the other direction, none seemed to be heading towards TRULY Towers. They jogged and arrived in the plaza at the base of the building exhausted and dripping with sweat, despite the chilly wind. Pye, Koshi and the supergeeks turned and waved at them with their free hands.

'Hiya!'

'What are you doing, you idiot halfwits?' Verity shouted as she staggered towards them.

Pye's face dropped from a smile to a pout. 'There's no need to be insulting.'

'Yes, there is. You have to unstick yourselves and stop being giant morons, right now!'

'You know we're not going to do that, don't you?' said Koshi. 'Look, the paparazzi are here.' He pointed at a group of photographers and a TV camera crew who had just arrived and were already taking pictures. 'This is all great publicity.'

'It's *terrible* publicity, you mean,' said Verity.

'What's the point of doing it today?' said Cameron. 'I expect Eden Greenfield's down at his country estate or relaxing on his yacht or something.'

'No, he's here,' said Pye. 'We saw him arrive.'

Verity groaned and looked at the growing pack of photographers and journos. It was about to turn into a disaster. Pye was going to get into so much trouble. Her new fashion-free friends were obviously deluded and hopelessly misinformed. Then Vee realised that some of the camera lenses were pointed straight at them and covered her face with her hands.

Oh no! I'll be spotted with the supergeeks . . . and if Mum sees me at a protest against Eden she'll kill me!

She pulled up the hood of her sweatshirt, then nudged Cameron, indicating that he should do the same.

'Actually, the paps were here before us,' said Koshi. 'There's something going on.'

'What? Like a party or something?' asked Verity.

'Yeah. We think he might have recruited some celebs to promote his charity,' said Koshi.

'You know that chef you think is fit, Vee?'

Verity nodded.

'Well, he went inside just before you got here.'

'Tom Wilde is here?' Verity adored Tom Wilde. He was cool and rebellious, was on the telly all the time and, at only twenty, was one of the youngest ever chefs to run a top London restaurant. He was famous for his astonishing knife skills and also for being utterly, gorgeously edible. *Completely delish! Nom nom!*

'Look, there's someone else,' said Pye, unsticking her hand and pointing towards a limo that was approaching the kerb.

Verity folded her arms and shot her friend an exaggerated look of disapproval.

'What are you pissed off about now?' said Pye. 'Oh, yeah . . . my hand.' She waved her *not*-superglued hand. 'The glue we got is a bit rubbish and doesn't stick very well on the glass, but we're not letting anyone know that.'

Verity rolled her eyes but was then distracted by the noise behind her. The photographers had surrounded the occupant of the limo as he emerged. All that was visible was the person's shiny black hair.

'It's Flash Campbell!' cried an excited voice. 'Flash! Flash!' The gathering crowd took up the chant.

Freddie 'Flash' Campbell was a phenomenally gifted racing driver. He was well on course to win the Formula One World Championship that year, streaking ahead of the opposition, having won five races and achieving a place on the podium in every other race so far. Flash was another seriously scrumptious celeb that Verity drooled over. *What was going on*, she wondered? Was Koshi right? Had Tom Wilde and Flash Campbell been recruited to do something for the *Perfect Eden* charity? It would be a huge publicity coup if they were. And *so* cool!

Cameron wasn't at all interested in the arrival of the racing prodigy. He was deep in a discussion with Pye. 'You could try the door handles,' he suggested. 'They might stick better. Why don't you attach yourselves to the sculpture?' He was pointing at the enormous, abstract metal structure at the centre of the plaza. 'It would make great news pictures. Have you got handcuffs?'

'CAMERON!' yelled Verity. She was furious. 'You're not . . .' She stopped. She was wasting her breath. The paps were swarming over another expensive car that had pulled up. Vee watched them for a second, wondering who was inside, then something strange and alarming caught her eye further down the street – a person emerging from a taxi. Her heart thumped in her chest. *It can't be.* She could hardly believe what she was seeing. While everyone else had their eyes fixed on the sleek, silver Daimler, Verity watched the door of the black cab . . . Legs unfolding . . . A pair of boots . . . stepping on to the pavement. *A pair of zebra-print boots.* Bliss Meadows slammed the taxi door, walked rapidly across the corner of the plaza and, unnoticed by the paparazzi, pushed through a side door into the glass atrium. The photographers were far more interested in the occupant of the Daimler. Verity looked over at Cameron to see if he'd spotted Bliss, too, but he was transfixed, like the others. A gasp of delight rippled through the crowd, which was now at least a hundred strong. The new arrival was Bethany London. Bethany was the skinny, cockney supermodel, famous for dating dubious, drug-crazed rock stars, but who was now creating a stir in Hollywood. She had surprised everyone by turning out to be a brilliant actress, mostly playing cockney supervillain roles. Award nominations were rumoured.

Cameron sighed but Verity grabbed hold of his sleeve and pulled him away.

'You won't believe who I've just seen,' she hissed.

'I know. Bethany London,' said Cameron, a stupid grin spread across his face.

'Not her!' she said, angrily. 'Oh my God, Cameron! Get your brain out of your pants for a minute, will you? I've just seen Bliss. I think she might be stealing stuff from Eden, too. We've got to warn him!'

Exposing Bliss

As soon as they were satisfied that Bliss and Bethany had left the atrium area and stepped into a lift, Vee and Cameron headed for the main entrance. They were almost through the door when Pye, who'd unstuck her not-stuck hand again, saw where they were going and ran after them.

'Here,' she said, pushing a stack of flyers into her friend's hand. 'If you're going inside to visit your future stepdad, will you give him one of these?'

'*One date!* They've had *one date!*' Verity moaned.

'So take them because you're my friend, then,' said Pye.

Verity tutted, took the leaflets and pushed Cameron the rest of the way through, into the atrium. They didn't get far. Two steps in, Verity was face-to-chest with a security guard.

'Out!' he barked.

'But we need to speak to Eden Greenfield. Urgently!'

'Oh yeah?' sneered the security guard. 'Well I need you to sod off . . . urgently!'

'You don't understand. We have some really important information to give him.'

'One of your leaflets?' He grabbed the flyers out of Vee's hand. 'I'll show you what to do with these.' He waggled them in front of Verity's face then tore them in half. The pieces fluttered to the shiny marble floor. 'Now, bugger off, you two!' He pointed at the door and thrust out his chest. A second guard was running towards them.

'But—'

'OUT!'

Back outside in the plaza, Verity was furious with herself again. They should have planned that better, instead of just barging in like a couple of deranged hoodies. Of course the guards weren't going to let them in, never mind actually getting up to the penthouse suite, which was now full of celebs! She would have to think of something much more convincing, much more imaginative.

An hour later Pye got a text and unstuck her not-stuck hand again to read it.

Saffron Fbs abt 2 arrv
pls prtnd 2 B fan Vx

Another taxi pulled up outside the building. The paparazzi surged forward and focused their lights and lenses. Superstar fashion designer Saffron Fibbs and her young companion emerged and walked towards the entrance. This was turning out to be quite a party!

Although she was infuriated at her best friend's complete dismissal of their protest, Pye did as she had been instructed and announced loudly, 'Ooo, it's Saffron!' starting a sort of chain reaction among her fellow protesters and the gathered fans. The hiss of 'Saffron! Saffron!' echoed across the plaza.

Saffron Fibbs looked stunning, as usual, in a black trouser-suit teamed with high-heeled boots, a long pink scarf and enormous shades. Her companion looked pretty cool, too – also in a black suit and similar shades. As the pair pushed through the revolving door, the excited crowd pressed against the glass and a voice called out, 'Who's your new hunk, Saff? Did you dump Eden?'

Verity (for it was she) grinned from ear to ear as the security guard actually tipped his hat at her. She had obviously made the right choice of outfit and done her make-up and hair well enough to look A-list glamorous and totally convincing.

'I'll give 'em a buzz, shall I, Miss Fibbs? Say you're on your way up?' said the guard, picking up the phone on the reception desk.

She nodded at him then walked confidently towards the elevators as if she'd been there a hundred times. She couldn't let him scrutinise their faces too closely, though. They had to get safely up to the top floor before the guard began to think how much they resembled the 'hoodies'.

The lift doors closed with a sigh and Verity glanced at Cameron. His face, behind the giant shades, was fixed in a fake grin like it was held there by Pye's superglue. 'That's level one completed, then,' he said.

'Yep!' Verity pressed button 44 for the penthouse suite.

21 . . . 33 . . . 39 . . . 40 . . . 41 . . . 42 . . . 43 . . .

Her stomach lurched as the lift came to a stop. The doors parted with another, longer, sigh and the pair stepped out into the light.

'Hi, Saff! Didn't know you were back.'

Verity wasn't sure where the voice had come from at first because her eyes were adjusting to the piercing winter sunshine bouncing off the white marble floor. Then she saw Eden coming out of a sumptuous room through a huge pair of double doors. Inside, his celebrity guests were draped across elegant sofas, drinking champagne.

Verity looked at Cameron again. He nodded and his mouth twitched into a tiny nervous smile, so she took a breath to calm herself and walked forward. She'd prepared herself for Eden's domain and his likely reaction, so she didn't worry when he stopped walking towards her and said, 'You're not Saffron. Who *are* you?'

She was ready with her answer.

'Mr Greenfield, I'm sorry for the deception but we had to find some way to get in and warn you. Someone really dangerous is in your building right now!'

But she wasn't ready for what he said next.

'Ha! You're Lottie Schnitzelhoff the illusionist. And who's this?' Eden looked at Cameron. 'Your glamorous assistant?' He smirked and beckoned them through another set of doors opposite.

This other room was lined with white marble, too, just like the lobby, and it was decorated with enormous chunks of gleaming white and chrome that were more like sculptures than furniture. On the far side, in front of a wall-of-glass window, was a large white desk. It was his office. Eden walked around the desk and sat down.

'Um, well, my name isn't Lottie, actually,' said Vee.

'Oh, really?' Eden stopped smiling.

'No, that was just a role-play thing we do at parties . . . sometimes. Well, I do.' She was starting to flounder. It was going wrong again.

Eden looked up at Verity. 'So, this *dangerous person* warning must be pretty serious if you've gone to so much effort to get up here.'

'Well, it is. This designer – junior designer, actually – called Bliss Meadows, got a job with Saffron last week and, well, she tried to steal something at our house last night—'

Eden reached across his desk and pressed a button. 'Would you come in here, please?'

Who had he called? she wondered. *Flash Campbell? Unlikely. Bethany London? Probably not. Tom Wilde? No*, she thought, *I expect he's called the security guards*. She knew she wouldn't have much time now, so began to talk faster.

'Anyway, I just saw her come in downstairs and take the lift. I think she might have managed to get a job here as well and she's planning to steal from you, too. She could even be doing it now—'

The door opened behind them, so Verity paused and glanced over her shoulder, expecting to see the two guards from downstairs. She froze. A pair of zebra-print boots tap-tap-tapped across to stand beside Eden's desk.

Verity was baffled.

'Are you planning to steal from me, Bliss?' Eden asked, a sinister smile creeping across his face. 'Were you at this young lady's house last night?'

'No.' Bliss looked worried. She stared at Verity and frowned, then her expression changed from confusion to surprise. 'It's the cleaner!' Bliss looked around at Eden. 'You remember I said there was a cleaner there the first time, which was why I had to go back.'

Verity felt sick. Why had Bliss told him about the burglary? He knew she'd been there. *No, wait! I don't understand. This can't be right . . . it's all too confusing! How did Eden . . . ? There was some mistake. Could Bliss Meadows be . . . ? No. Eden couldn't have hired Bliss and* sent *her to burgle her mum! Could he? He's Eden Greenfield and Eden Greenfield wouldn't do something like that!*

She shivered. The room had suddenly become ice cold. She could sense an evil presence and there was a smell that was a mixture of damp clothes and sweat. Verity looked over her shoulder again. Two crow-like figures stood in the doorway. Eden nodded at them and the black-clad goths stepped inside. They brought a horrible feeling of gloom with them.

'Rain, Mud, I need you to deal with two more *irritations* – the cleaner and her sidekick.' Eden flapped his hand dismissively. 'I don't need details, but just find out what they know, then you can add them to your plans for those *irritations* downstairs.'

'All right,' said Rain from behind the long black hair that covered her face.

'OK,' said Mud. His voice was a low growl which turned Vee's blood to ice.

She knew them! She recognised their voices, that smell and the threatening aura that they carried with them, because she'd felt it before. Mud and Rain were the goths she'd glimpsed in the street, at the airport, on the dock. And, last night, they had been Bliss's accomplices! It had been Mud who had whizzed in her mum's loo.

Eden's office began to spin.

'No, wait!' she protested as the goths grabbed them by the arms and began to bundle them out of the room. 'Oww! That hurts! You don't understand. I'm Verity! Verity Fibbs! I'm Saffron Fibbs' daughter!' she shouted desperately across the white marble lobby.

Rain put her hand over Vee's mouth and shoved her backwards into the waiting lift. Mud threw Cameron inside but he tried to push his way back out, so Mud punched him hard, straight in the face, and he landed in a heap on the floor. Verity was horrified. Cameron's mobile tumbled out of his pocket and clattered into the corner of the lift.

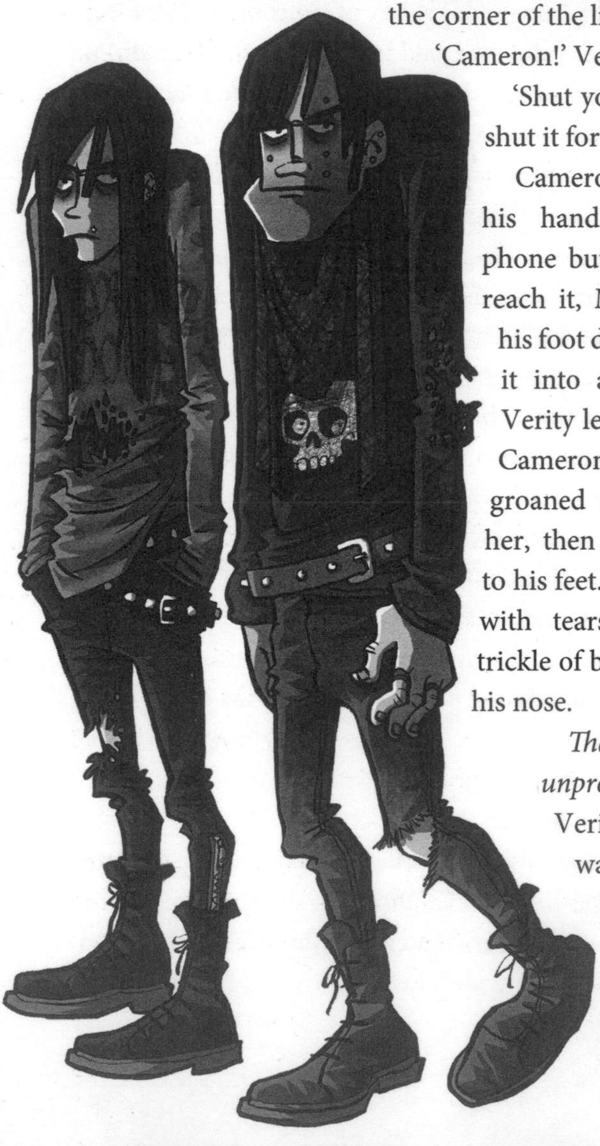

'Cameron!' Verity screamed.

'Shut your mouth or we'll shut it for you,' said Rain.

Cameron stretched out his hand to retrieve his phone but, before he could reach it, Mud had stamped his foot down and smashed it into a hundred pieces. Verity leaned over to see if Cameron was all right. He groaned and looked up at her, then began to struggle to his feet. His eyes glistened with tears and he had a trickle of blood coming from his nose.

That was completely unprovoked violence, Verity thought. She was stunned. Mud had just punched Cameron for no reason and now he was bleeding. Actually bleeding! This was like a scene from a movie!

'Don't try that again,' said Mud hitting the button marked LG. 'Or you'll get another fist.'

The lift doors sighed closed.

Verity tried frantically to straighten out the thoughts that were whizzing through her head. She had to think . . . think . . . think! *How did everything go so horribly wrong? How could I have made such a stupid mistake?*

23 . . . 22 . . . 21 . . . She watched the numbers blink on . . . then off . . .

20 . . . 19 . . .

Her eyes leaped ahead to their destination, LG. LG was Lower Ground. The basement level. Why were they heading there? The exit was through the lobby and the atrium on the ground floor. L for Lobby. Unless, of course, they wanted to throw them out of a private exit. Well, that made sense, she supposed, because the paparazzi were outside the atrium entrance and ejecting Saffron Fibbs, or a woman who looked like Saffron Fibbs would probably cause a massive commotion. So . . . OK . . . they were being escorted to a basement exit.

Verity took several deep, calming breaths. She didn't feel so panic stricken any more. Once they were out in the street again, she'd call Callista – although she had no idea how she would convince her of *this* new revelation!

16 . . . 15 . . . 14 . . .

Lower Ground? she wondered. *Basement Level? Dungeon Level! What if they weren't going to an exit at all? What if Rain and Mud had something else in mind?* Then she remembered what Eden Greenfield had said.

Deal with two more irritations.

What did he mean, 'deal with'?

Find out what they know.

How would Rain and Mud do that if they were simply going to let them leave? Perhaps they *were* being taken to a dungeon where they would be interrogated . . . maybe even tortured!

The feeling of panic returned to her chest. A cold shiver ran down her back. She looked at Cameron's face. The bridge of his nose was already turning from red to purple and he'd managed to smear the blood across his cheek. It made his injury look much worse – much scarier. Cameron's damp eyes blinked at her then he mouthed the word, 'phone?'

She began to move her hands towards her pockets but stopped. She wasn't wearing the sweatshirt any more. She didn't have it! She'd been in such a hurry when they'd dashed back to the house to get dressed up that she'd thrown her sweatshirt off without thinking. On the way out, she'd grabbed her front door key and twenty quid for the taxi, but the iPhone and all the 'emergency stuff' she had put in her sweatshirt pocket – the cash and credit card – was still in a screwed-up ball at the bottom of the stairs!

She shook her head.

Cameron twitched his head sideways and looked at the grid of buttons a few metres away. He was trying to tell her something. She creased her forehead, then raised her eyebrows to say, 'what?' He nodded towards the numbers again and she looked at them, too. *The buttons? Should I press one of them? Yes, that's it! I need to stop the lift. I should press the 'L' button. If we can get the doors to open at the lobby, then I'll push Rain out of the way, sprint across the atrium, shout at Pye and the others to tell them we're in trouble, alert the paps, then these evil goths wouldn't be able to hurt us.* Verity started to shuffle sideways.

12 . . . 11 . . . 10 . . .

Rain and Mud were both facing the doors so she hoped they wouldn't notice her tiny movements.

9 . . . 8 . . . 7

Rain looked over her shoulder and Verity, caught with her hand in mid-air, pretended to wipe at Cameron's blood with her sleeve.

6 . . . 5 . . .

Then Mud's mobile buzzed in his pocket.

4 . . . 3 . . .

Verity was almost close enough to reach the button. She could stretch . . .

'Right,' said Mud into his phone. 'We'll come back up, then.'

. . . 2

Verity jumped as Mud thrust out his hand and slammed it on the red STOP button. The lift lurched and juddered to a halt.

Verity looked at the numbers. The 'L' was lit. They were at the Lobby but the doors didn't open. Mud raised a finger and jabbed number 44.

They began to climb towards the penthouse again.

Getting Up Close in the Back of a Car

'Are you really Saff's daughter?'

'Yes and she's going to be *so* mad that you're being such a creep!' Verity's fear had become anger. 'And I'll tell her all about you.' She looked at Bliss. 'And how you were going through her stuff . . . and them . . .' She turned to Rain and Mud and snarled, '. . . beating up my friend like that. It's *so* out of order. Stop laughing! It's not funny!'

Mud was sniggering but Eden Greenfield's face had turned to stone. He was now deadly serious. 'Can you prove it?' he asked through clenched teeth. 'Got a student card or something?'

Verity shook her head. 'Nope.'

Eden sighed and rubbed his hand over his eyes. 'Urgh,' he moaned. 'You look exactly like her. I thought you were making it up, but you're not, are you? You really are Saff's kid.'

'Yeah, and we've found you out and I'm going to expose you and make sure my mum knows that neither of you can be trusted.' She was fizzing with fury.

'Mmm.' Eden swivelled in his chair and brought his hands together. He tapped his lips with his fingers and gazed out at the late-afternoon sun, which was now pale and sickly and dipping behind the city rooftops. 'Well, that's why it's awkward, Verity, sweetheart. Because I can't allow you to do that, can I?'

'What do you mean?' said Cameron.

'I mean, we are now going to have to come up with something a little more inventive, aren't we?' He looked at Mud. 'Something plausible? Something believable? A tragic little accident for Verity Fibbs and her devoted boyfriend.'

Verity felt sick.

'I assume you *are* her boyfriend?' Eden asked.

'Actually, I'm Axel Ramsbottom and I'm Verity's driving instructor.'

Verity grinned. He was brilliant! Even after having his nose smashed, he was brave enough to construct a new fake persona, a really funny one this time. She had fancied Cameron Catchpole like crazy, but now she fancied Axel Ramsbottom even more!

'Yeah, right,' said Eden, dismissively waving his hand at Axel. He knew it was another lie. 'Probably best I don't know who you are, anyway. I can act more surprised when I'm helping poor Saffron to deal with the shock . . . and the grief.' He swivelled back to face the window and gazed out again. 'I can picture the headlines: *Eden Comforts Distraught Saffron. Eden Mourns Saffron's Teen Tragedy*,' he mumbled.

'You're a psychopath!' said Verity.

'And you'll never get away with it,' said Axel Ramsbottom.

'But, I will,' said Eden, still looking out at the city skyline. 'I always do.'

EAKING NEWS: Teen Tragedy

Their fourth and final journey in the lift was silent. Silent as the grave. Neither Verity nor Axel Ramsbottom could get anywhere near the buttons this time because Rain stood right in front of them all the way down. They watched the lights blinking on and off like a countdown to disaster.

10 . . . 9 . . . 8 . . . 7 . . . 6 . . . 5 . . . 4 . . . 3 . . . 2 . . . L . . . LG.

The doors opened with a sad groan. They'd arrived in the dungeon. Mud shoved Axel while Rain took Verity's arm and dragged her out into the darkness. Slowly their eyes adjusted to the gloom. With some relief, Vee realised it wasn't a dungeon after all. It was a car park.

Verity looked around her, searching for a chink of daylight that would indicate an escape route. If there was a exit nearby, she would grab Axel's hand and they'd make a run for it. But the car park seemed dark and endless; the only glow was from a couple of flickering lights attached to the concrete pillars like pulsing alien pods.

Rain pulled out a black key fob and pressed it. *Beep!* A pair of orange eyes blinked at them from a short distance away.

'Right,' said Mud. 'Just in case you're thinking of making a run for it.' He waved something in the air. Verity thought it looked like he had a handful of rice noodles.

'OK, face to face and put your arms around each other,' said Rain.

'What?' said Verity and Axel at the same time.

'Come on. Hug, like you're gonna give each other a kiss.'

Verity blushed then felt a hand in the small of her back.

'Don't be shy,' said Rain. 'He's your boyfriend, inni?'

Suddenly she was pressed against Axel, chest to chest, his sweat-beaded temple touching hers, her panicked breath on his cheek.

Then Rain grasped her hands, pulled them around Axel's hips and Vee felt a plastic band being tightened around her wrists.

Mud began to push the two of them through the car park but, fastened together as they now were, it was hard to move without treading on each other's feet or crunching their knee caps together. Eventually, as they approached the back of a large black car, they found they were starting to get the hang of it, moving in unison, a strange, shuffling sideways dance.

Ooof!

Their knees slapped into the bumper. A final push from Mud sent them toppling over into the open cavernous boot of the car. Verity grunted. She'd hit her head and her arm was now trapped painfully under Axel's hip. The door slammed shut above them, locking them in thick, claustrophobic darkness.

Verity listened to the sound of her own pounding heartbeat for a few seconds then whispered, 'Axel?'

'Yeah?' said Axel.

At last, she could feel his chest expanding and contracting against hers. *He must have been holding his breath*, she thought.

'Are you OK?'

'Yeah. Are *you* OK?' His mouth was right beside her ear and his hot breath tickled her neck.

'I think so,' said Verity, shifting her arm and wriggling her hand. The rice-noodle plastic tie was too tight and her wrist was already sore. She wasn't OK. Not even slightly OK. She was worried that she'd got them into some serious trouble, but she was also furious. Once again, she was up close and personal with Peter/Merlin/Cameron/Axel and something was spoiling the atmos! Something dangerous and horrible and scary. Another perfect snog moment ruined!

'It's like an episode of *The Sopranos* isn't it?' said Axel with a chuckle, his body jiggling against hers.

'I can't believe you're laughing about this.'

'Sorry. It's panic.'

'So you're scared, too?'

''Course I am.'

She didn't really want to hear that. She wanted him to be fearless and reassuring and to have a plan to get them out of their dire predicament. She wanted him to be Ben Blades, to use his sword to break their bonds and to leap out of the boot carrying her in his arms and . . .

BANG!

The car doors slammed and the engine started.

This wasn't Demon Streets and Axel wasn't Ben Blades. He

was just a boy. A really cool, nice-looking boy, but he didn't have powers or skills or an 'extra life' bonus.

'What do you think they are going to do to us?' She wasn't thinking straight and the question sort of fell out of her mouth before she could stop it. She instantly regretted it. She didn't want to know the answer. Luckily, Axel understood and remained silent.

Unfortunately, Rain and Mud were anything but silent. As soon as the engine rumbled into life and the car started moving, they began to talk. It was a loathsome and terrifying conversation. Even through layers of nylon carpet, metal panels and the deeply padded seats, Verity and Axel were able to hear every blood-chilling word of their diabolical scheme.

It soon became clear that Rain and Mud had been planning the demise of all the supergeeks – the *irritations* – for some time. Koshi had been the first name on their 'termination' list, then they'd added the others – Hamish, Ollie, Grace, Jelly, Chen and, more recently, Pye too. They had devised a plausible death scenario for each one of them, which they discussed with ghoulish delight. Hamish and Ollie would have the brakes of their bikes tampered with, no doubt causing the sort of messy squashed-by-a-lorry accident Verity had imagined for Pye the previous evening. Grace and Jelly would get a dose of something tranquillising in their cappuccinos and end up in an alley with lethal heroin-filled hypodermic needles in their arms. Chen would be discovered in the Computer Science classroom, in a vast pool of blood, with multiple wounds, another sad victim of knife crime. Creepiest of all, Pye and Koshi would be found lifeless one morning, slumped on a park bench, their stomachs full of pills and surrounded by empty bottles of vodka. All horribly plausible 'accidental' deaths and all completely terrifying.

Koshi and the supergeeks must have been telling the truth after all, Verity realised. They really had uncovered something that could damage Eden Greenfield's reputation – something his enormous public relations machine couldn't cover up – and they had to be silenced. Why hadn't she believed them? Why hadn't she listened to her best friend? Her always-truthful best friend. Now it was too late.

Then Mud and Rain started to discuss their new plan – how to dispose of Saffron Fibbs' teenage daughter and her boyfriend.

'Something romantic,' said Rain.

'Awww, sweet.' said Mud. 'Something theatrical?'

'What about a suicide pact?'

'Ooo, yes! Double hanging!'

'He he! Or cut their wrists in the bath.'

'A multi-storey car park death plunge!'

'Classic! Or we could tie weights to their feet and have them jump off this bridge together.'

Verity shivered. The vibration from the car's tyres rumbled and juddered through her back. They were driving over a bridge. *What bridge?* she wondered. She hoped it wasn't one of the pretty ones. She'd hate to be thrown off one of *those* with weights tied to her feet.

'I know,' said Rain excitedly. 'I've got an idea. We'll write a suicide note and send it to her mum.'

'Excellent! That'll make it perfect.'

'About how they are SO in love and couldn't bear to live without each other and they'd rather die than go to different unis, or something.'

'Awwww, cute!'

'My mum would never believe that!' Verity shouted from the boot.

'Oh, crap!' whispered Rain.

'Did you know they could hear us?' hissed Mud.

''Course I didn't, you idiot!'

'*Nobody* would believe it,' Verity continued. 'They'd be suspicious and the police would investigate the bridge and you'd probably have left your DNA everywhere so you'll get caught and go to prison for ever!'

'Shut up!' Rain shouted.

'She'd believe a suicide note if it was left on my own laptop, though.'

'What?'

'If I wrote that me and Axel were going to throw ourselves off a bridge in my secret diary . . . on my own computer . . . at my house . . . that only me and my mum know the password to . . . *then* Mum would probably believe it.'

For a moment, Rain and Mud said nothing. They were thinking. Then Verity thought she could hear whispering.

'Uurgh! Why did you tell them about your secret diary?' asked Axel's voice in her ear.

'What secret diary?'

'The one on your computer . . . at your house.'

'Doesn't exist.'

'So what are you planning to do when they find that out?'

'Don't know,' said Verity. 'I suppose we'll decide when we get there.'

lose all points
score: 0000
options
play
II

GAME OVER

Maisie Malone and Ben Blades walked into the cafe and sat opposite each other in a booth beside the door. If they needed to leave in a hurry, they were only a few steps from the exit. The flyer had given this address but they hadn't expected a cafe. A race track or a garage, maybe, even a car park, but not a cafe. Why would Steve Speed give the address of a cafe on his 'Learn to be a Getaway Driver' flyer?

Learn to be a Getaway Driver

This sort of thing happened quite often in Demon Streets. You'd be trapped in a water-filled basement with a burst pipe and a plumber's van would appear. You'd need to follow someone on a bus and have no money, then you'd find a coin at your feet. Your weapon of choice would be stolen by a demon, locked in a hotel room and a chambermaid would offer to sell you her skeleton key. No sooner had Maisie mentioned they wanted to learn some skills than Steve Speed's flyer had fluttered down the alley.

Even though they didn't actually have a vehicle, Maisie and Ben had agreed that they would take advantage of every new opportunity. You never knew what new challenge would be waiting around the corner. Ben Blades scanned the cafe while Maisie re-read the flyer. Yes, they were at the right address. Apart from the waitress and that demon chef, there were only two other customers. One was a round-faced woman feeding bits of sausage to a small black dog. The other was a young, tanned man with shimmering, greased-back hair moulded into a giant black quiff and tattoos all the way up both arms – definitely the most likely candidate, Maisie decided.

+350 points
score: 10,450

Bonus Facts:
Not all skills are useful... but some will be

options play 

'D'you think that's him?' asked Ben, pointing at the youth.

Maisie nodded. 'Shall we go over, then?'

Ben nodded back and they both eased themselves out of their booth just as the waitress was approaching. She frowned at them.

'Um, we'll both have black coffee,' said Ben. 'But, over there.'

The youth looked up as Ben and Maisie sat down opposite him.

'You Steve Speed?' Maisie asked.

'Yep.' Steve moved the toothpick he was chewing to the other side of his mouth and grinned. 'You after lessons? Wanna learn some of my drivin' tricks?'

Maisie and Ben nodded.

'What you got to trade for it?'

After some negotiation, Maisie traded her feather shoes and Ben gave up his lucky double-headed coin (it hadn't been particularly lucky). Then Steve Speed took them out the back of the cafe, behind a row of over-filled bins and down a flight of steps. There they discovered a circular dirt track, a sign that read Driving School and a small open-top car.

'Doesn't look much, does she? But I tuned the engine and she goes like a bomb.'

After the driving lesson, Ben and Maisie had little left to trade. Maisie wanted to keep her pearl-handled pistol and couldn't give away the Mole's package, but was prepared to lose the tiny stiletto knife and one of her 'extra life' bonuses, which she gave to Felicity Freud for basic instruction in demon psychology.

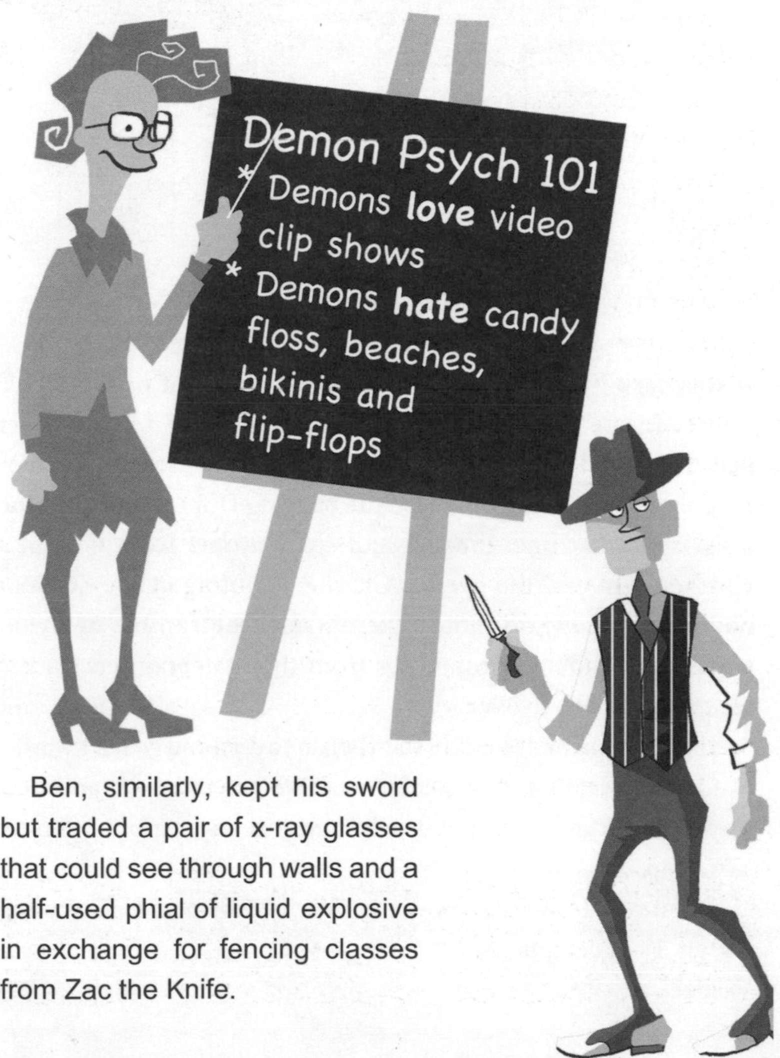

Ben, similarly, kept his sword but traded a pair of x-ray glasses that could see through walls and a half-used phial of liquid explosive in exchange for fencing classes from Zac the Knife.

Verity's Plan Goes a Bit Wrong

It was dark by the time the car drew up in front of the Fibbs' house. Inside the boot, Verity knew they were in her street because she'd recognised the sounds and smells of her neighbourhood – the pub with the barking Dobermann and the noisy quiz machine; the salt-and-spicy aroma from Charlie's Chicken Hut and the owner, Charlie, shouting at the delivery boy on his growling motorbike outside; the rumble of nylon wheels and shouted profanities from the skateboarders on the ramps under the flyover.

The car crunched to a halt, then began to turn and go backwards. Mud was reversing into the drive beside her mum's brand new tiny electric car. She'd had it delivered just days before the New York trip.

'Whatever I do from now on,' Verity whispered. 'Go along with it. I've got a plan. OK?'

'OK.'

Verity shivered with delight as Axel wriggled his arms up and squeezed her in a friendly hug. He was her willing accomplice.

They heard clunks, the groan of doors opening, then the car shuddered and the boot lid yawned above them.

'Oh, look, Axel! It's our mates, Sludge 'n' Drizzle!' said Verity sarcastically, before a large piece of carpet tape was slapped down over her mouth.

'Mmmmfffff,' she mumbled.

Sludge 'n' Drizzle lifted them out of the boot and dragged them stumbling up the steps to the front door.

'Key?' said Mud, looking at Rain, who had her talons fastened tightly around Verity's biceps.

'What key?'

'Don't tell me you don't have the key.'

'Bliss has the key,' said Rain. 'And the alarm code.'

Mud groaned and rolled his black-rimmed eyes. Then he looked at Verity.

'Mmmfff?'

'OK,' said Mud. 'If I remove the tape and you scream, I stick this between your ribs.'

Verity felt something sharp jab into her side and looked down. Mud had a huge knife in his hand. She gulped then nodded and Rain peeled the tape off her mouth.

'Owwwwerrrrrrr! That hurt.' She scowled.

Mud jabbed the knife.

Verity grimaced but continued. 'Duh! What complete incompetent morons you two are! Didn't bring keys, didn't get the code from Bli—'

Rain slapped the tape back again.

'Mmmmfff.'

'Give it a rest, kid.'

Mud held the knife in front of Verity's face then changed his mind and grabbed Axel's hair. He brought the blade up to Axel's throat and grinned at Vee. 'Do what you're told, you annoying little pain, or your boyfriend gets gutted all over this nice clean step!'

Axel was breathing heavily behind the tape and his eyes were pleading with her.

'Mmmfff.' Perhaps impertinence hadn't been the ideal response, she decided. She was always cheeky when she was nervous, but this was clearly not the time for humour. She'd just made them angry. She felt sick again. *If I can't think of a more intelligent way to get out of this, I'll be staring into the eyes of the coolest boy I've ever met while he bleeds to death.* She gritted her teeth and looked at Rain.

'Let's try again,' said Rain, removing the tape.

'OK,' said Verity, calmly. 'The key is in my pocket and, if you release my hands, I'll do the alarm code for you.'

Rain drew Verity's front door key out of her pocket and put it in the lock.

'Now, you *tell* us the code,' said Mud. 'And if you lie, and the alarm goes off, then we spill your guts right here. Both of you. OK?'

'OK.'

The door swung open and all four of them shuffled into the dark hallway.

Beep, beep, beep, beep . . .

Mud found a light switch while Rain elbowed the door closed. They would have to key in the four-digit code within thirty seconds or the alarm would be triggered.

'Code?' said Mud.

'Six . . .'

Rain tapped the key pad.

Verity glanced around the hallway and spotted her sweatshirt, where she'd thrown it, at the bottom of the stairs.

'Two . . .'

The assorted keys in the bowl under the mirror.

'Five . . .'

And the debris from the party still littering every surface.

'Six.'

The beeping stopped and Mud pulled his knife away from Axel's throat.

They all sighed.

Rain replaced the tape over Verity's mouth (though it had now lost most of its adhesion) and walked further into the hallway, while Mud returned his blade to the pocket of his coat and flexed his hands.

Then Verity pinched Axel's bum. He jumped but said nothing. He'd understood her signal. She was about to do something and he had to be ready to go with her. Verity opened her mouth wide, pushed her tongue out and spat the tape away. She looked over at Mud then back at Axel. He nodded.

Wooooaaaaeeeeeee

eeeeeeeeeeeeeeeeeeeeee

The wailing sound of the alarm flooded the house.

'Now!'

Verity and Axel leapt together, pushing Mud with all their strength, face first, into the wall; his nose made a sickening crunching sound. Then, perfectly synchronised, as they had recently mastered in the underground car park, they darted across the room like a slightly clumsy, two-headed, four-legged creature. Vee reached out her tied hands behind Axel's back and scooped up a set of keys from the bowl as they passed, then they slammed into Rain at the bottom of the stairs, sending her sprawling on to the floor into the numerous half-empty bottles and glasses.

CRASH!

A glass shattered against Rain's knee and gouged into her flesh. She rolled over and her hand caught a broken bottle.

'Aaagh!'

Then Verity yelled, 'Bend down!'

Vee and Axel bent their knees so Verity could grab her balled-up sweatshirt from the bottom step.

'Studio!' she shouted.

They changed direction and sprinted back across to the stairs that led down to the basement. Mud was only just recovering his balance as they stumbled down, missing steps, almost losing their footing, and reached the studio door. By some miracle, they eee!

managed to stay in unison and make it to the bottom without falling and landing in a heap. Tumbling through the door, Axel kicked to slam it behind them. Then they leaned on it and Verity used her elbow to slap the bolt across just in time. On the other side, Rain and Mud pounded their fists against the flimsy panels. They didn't have long; the goths would only have to kick hard at the wood a few times and it would disintegrate.

'Over here.' Verity pulled Axel towards Mum's cutting table. 'Turn this way a bit, so I can reach.' They shuffled around and Verity lifted her arms behind Axel's back. The table was quite high but she was able to slide her hands across to a pair of dressmaking shears – the huge, sharp scissors that her mum used to cut fabric.

'You're DEAD!' Mud's muffled voice was almost inaudible under the wailing of the alarm.

BANG! BANG! SPLINTER!

They were hacking at the door with the knife and kicking through the panels.

Verity twisted the enormous scissors and got her fingers in to the holes in the handle, but it was really difficult with her wrists tightly fastened to turn them around and get the blades in the right position to cut the plastic tie.

'When we get in there, we're gonna make your deaths REALLY slow and painful!' yelled Rain.

At last, Vee felt the cold scissors slice through the plastic. She was free. She disentangled her arms from around Axel's waist, then cut his ties, too. Axel pulled the tape off his mouth and his face crumpled. He'd ripped out some of his top-lip fuzz by the roots and it had hurt. They stood in the middle of the studio and looked at each other, wide-eyed and startled, like two cornered animals. Now what?

BANG! SPLINTER!

'Up there!' Verity pointed at the narrow, high window at the far end of the room.

'You're joking! We won't squeeze through that!'

'What do you suggest, then?' Verity was distraught. She'd planned all of this in her head in the back of the car, and so far everything had worked as she'd predicted – the wrong code, the keys, the studio, the scissors – but, now that she looked at her proposed escape route, it *did* look far too small. *Have I miscalculated again? Have I put us both in more danger? Are we going to be stabbed and bleed to death in the middle of Mum's studio?*

'You want to die a horrible painful death?' Vee shouted at Axel. 'Because I don't! Come on! We've got to try.'

SPLINTER!

The goths were almost through.

Verity scrambled on to a stool, climbed up on to a book shelf – scattering papers and a jar of pins – then crawled across to the top of the massive materials cupboard. Her elbow knocked a large cardboard box and it toppled on to the floor. The lid exploded open on the edge of the cutting table and the contents, thousands of large mother-of-pearl buttons splashed across the studio, making a sound like rain and forming a huge, shimmering puddle. Verity reached the window and pulled at the dusty, cobweb-covered latch. It clicked and the window creaked open, tilting down towards her. Then it stopped. She pulled harder but it wouldn't budge. There was a gap, but was it big enough? She peered through. She could see the grass of the front garden and the rear wheel of Rain and Mud's car.

'I'll never get through that,' groaned Axel in her ear. He'd climbed up behind her.

CRASH!

The goths were inside . . . stomping towards them . . .

Verity threw herself through the gap and wriggled out on to the grass, then Axel put his arms, head and shoulders through. Verity grabbed his hands and pulled.

He wriggled . . .

. . . and kicked . . .

. . . and wriggled . . .

He's going to be caught!

Verity was waiting for Rain and Mud to grab his legs and start tugging him back inside. But they didn't.

He kicked again and wriggled and finally popped out.

Why didn't the goths grab Axel? Why can't we hear their thundering boots and chilling threats any more? She rolled over and looked back through the grimy window. *Ha! That's why!* Mud and Rain had tried to cross the pearl-button pond but had found it impossible to stay upright. It was like walking on ice, their feet skidding one way and another with each careful step. They now seemed to have given up and were retreating back through the studio. Axel and Verity lay on the damp lawn for a moment and got their breath back before they heard the sound of boots on the stairs and Vee yelled, 'Quick! Electric car!'

They sprinted across to the driveway and Vee used the key she'd grabbed from the bowl in the hall to unlock her mum's new car. Her brain was spinning. Had she really seen horns protruding from the goths' foreheads and forked tails trailing behind them when they ran? Axel reached the other side and they climbed in. Vee put the key in the ignition, started the car then shook her head. Mum was right. She spent far too much time playing *Demon Streets*. She was beginning to see demons everywhere!

The Bridge

Mum had said that her new electric car was the easiest car she'd ever driven. 'You just start it up then steer,' she had announced. 'A baby could drive it!' Well, when Mum got home, Verity decided, she'd have to inform her that she was totally incorrect. *No way would a baby be able to accelerate, brake, turn the wheel, find the headlights and keep in the correct lane, all at the same time! Perhaps she meant that only a baby was small enough to fit inside!*

Verity drove the minuscule car around the bend at the end of the street and one of the tyres clipped the edge of the kerb. They bounced in their tiny seats and their elbows slammed together.

'Oh!'

It was definitely the smallest vehicle she'd ever been in. There was barely room for two people and she was so close to Axel, she was jabbing him in the chest every time she turned the wheel. She thought of opening her window to give herself a little more space but hadn't a clue which of the various tiny illuminated buttons to press.

'Want to switch seats?' Axel asked.

'No. Just look behind us and tell me if you see them following.'

Axel turned to look out of the small, oddly-shaped back window into the dark. 'Can't see anything. I think we might have lost them. No, wait. That's them!'

'Oh, no!'

'Put your foot down!' he yelled. 'Won't this stupid toy car go any faster?'

'It's a city runabout, not a racing car! The accelerator is flat on the floor!'

The car was emitting a high-pitched whine but seemed to be travelling horribly slowly. Less than twenty metres behind, a large and terrifying black shape with glaring white eyes was in hot pursuit and gaining on them. They'd be bumper-to-bumper in a matter of seconds. Verity turned hard left down a side street. The black car squealed and turned left as well.

What had Steve Speed said? Brake into a corner then power out of it. Do something unexpected.

She pressed the brake, turned the wheel, took the next corner too fast for comfort, then, before she'd straightened up, rammed her foot on the accelerator again. Verity's heart thumped wildly. It was no use. They were still behind them. They'd never get away from Rain and Mud in this useless battery-powered contraption.

What was I thinking? We nearly got our throats cut and now we're in the slowest getaway car on the planet! This was a really stupid plan!

She was waiting for a little icon to appear in the corner of the car's tiny windscreen – a 'power boost' button or a 'switch vehicles' option. This should have been the moment that an escape route was offered. Perhaps if she did a few clever manoeuvres with the car and gained some extra points, she'd win another weapon, like a grenade to throw out of the window to blow up the goths' car . . . or a machine gun so they could spray their car with bullets.

EEEEEK!

Vee slammed her foot on the brake. The street ahead of them was jammed with cars returning from a family day out or Sunday lunch in the country or shopping in the West End. The traffic was crawling along, barely moving. They were doomed!

Then she had an idea. *Do something unexpected.* She turned the wheel, stamped on the accelerator again and mounted the pavement. The tiny car had no trouble at all weaving between the few pedestrians and shop signs and the cafe chairs outside a brasserie. It seemed designed for the sidewalk.

'Genius!' cried Axel, looking behind them, then, 'Oh, crap!'

'What?' Verity swerved the car around a topiary tree.

'Keep going and don't look in the mirror.' Axel's face had lost all its colour.

'Why? What's happening? Did I hit someone?'

'No. But *they* might.'

Verity ignored his advice and looked up at the rear-view mirror. The goths' car was still following, but now they were roaring down the pavement, not caring about the fate of cafe chairs or shop signs or pedestrians.

CRASH!

The topiary tree flew in the air and landed in the gutter.

Verity turned the wheel again and barrelled down another long, empty residential street. The black car did the same.

They were getting closer . . .

Do something unexpected.

. . . and closer . . .

Brake into a corner and power out of it.

Verity braked, flipped the wheel and the tiny electric car spun then nipped down a footpath between two bollards.

'They'll never get through there,' she said, looking into the mirror again. Sure enough, the

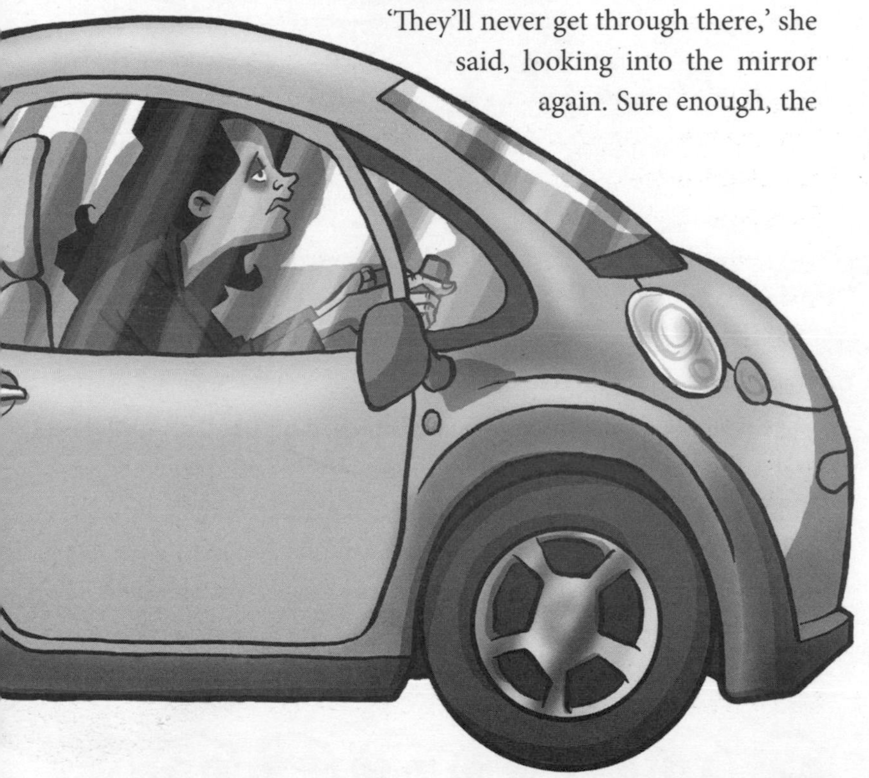

evil grin of the black car's chrome grill was now stationary *behind* the bollards!

'I did it!' She smiled at Axel. 'I lost them!'

'Phew! That was close!'

CRACK! THUMP!

His head jerked forward. 'What was that?'

Verity looked in the mirror again but couldn't see the car. There was something obscuring her view. The window had become a twinkling mosaic and there was a small, bright, starburst shape with a hole in the middle, like the halo around an eclipse. She realised, with a jolt, what it was. She wanted to throw up. It was a bullet hole!

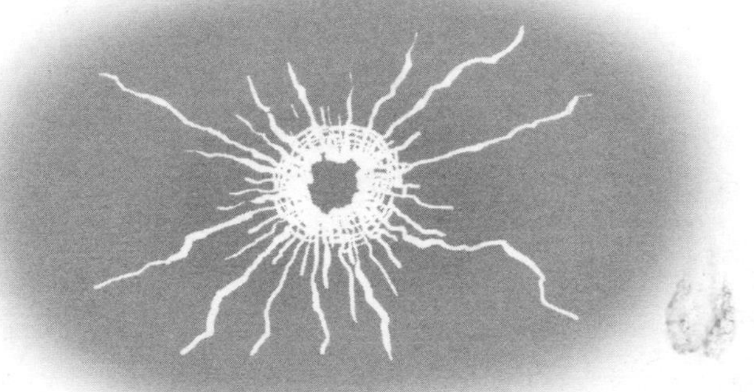

Axel guessed what it was, too, and reached his hand around the back of his headrest. His fingers found a hole with jagged edges punched in the spongy hi-tech fabric. He shivered as a horrific thought struck him – there must be a bullet lodged inside the headrest, probably just a few centimetres away from his skull!

'They're shooting at us!'

'I know!'

All of Verity's brain power was focused on one goal – remembering what Steve Speed had taught her so they could get as far away from the bullets as possible. They couldn't stop and they couldn't go back. She looked for every tiny gap in the traffic and plunged the electric car through it. They wound their way across the city, never convinced they had managed to lose their pursuers, getting totally lost and disorientated.

'Where are we?' Verity asked.

'I'm not sure, but I think I saw the London Eye between the buildings back there.'

'Really? Then we're not lost . . . except, you can see the London Eye from *everywhere*,' she remembered. 'And I don't recognise *anything*!' Her voice had become a terrified squeak. 'I don't even remember which side of the river we're on.'

'South, I think.' Then Axel had a horrible thought. 'How far can these electric cars go before running out of juice?' he asked.

'Dunno.' Verity looked briefly at him, her eyes wide with panic. 'Hope we can make it before that.'

'Make it where?'

'Dunnowww!' she wailed again. 'No point in going to Mum's office because Callista won't believe us and we can't go to Pye's house because it's back the way we came and—' She stopped. 'Oh, Pye! We've got to warn—'

CRUNCH!

An evil chrome grill leered down at them through the back window.

Verity screamed.

Oh my God! They're still behind us. They're going to squash this puny plastic car, drag us out, tie us up again, fasten weights to our feet, push us over the railings of a bridge and we'll drown in dirty, cold Thames water. It's going to be really horrible and Mum is going to be SO upset when she gets the fake suicide note! She'll be furious!

Imagining their deaths and watching it play through her mind like a cheesy horror movie gave Verity a new idea. She braked, turned the wheel – jabbing Axel in the eye because he was now curled down in his seat to avoid the next bullet – spun the tiny car around and headed in the other direction.

Do something unexpected.

'W-where you going?'

'I think I know where we are. G-gonna try something,' said Verity, her voice wobbling.

She slammed her foot on the accelerator again and turned off the main road, steering the car down a narrow lane, then left and right and under an archway.

Uhhh, I hope this is the right way! Yes, there's the . . . and if I go down here . . . there it is!

She looked for a gap in a row of metal posts, spotted one and drove on to the pavement, pedestrians jumping out of their way again. She squeezed the micro-car between the posts, past the *no entry* sign and accelerated down a walkway, weaving in and out of groups of tourists, strolling families and smooching couples. Up ahead, the walkway became a wide ramp and then separated, offering alternate paths either around the building or down into its basement. Vee took the path around, which opened out into a plaza with lawns and white birch trees and broad gravel paths. High above them, to their right, was the gigantic, floodlit red-brick façade of the Tate Modern gallery and, to the left, just visible through the trees, the bridge that Verity had been searching for.

I knew *remembering all the bridges would be useful some day!*

Suddenly, two powerful headlight beams swung around in front of them, flooding their car with eye-piercing light and cutting off their route. The goths were driving straight towards them! Verity swerved right into a wide circle and drove away from the river, between the trees lit from below with an eerie glow, towards the gallery building. Axel looked back. They had turned, too, and were right behind them, their engine roaring like a ferocious animal. At the gallery entrance, Vee spun the wheel again – Axel having learned, at last, how to keep out of the way – and began a circuit along the edge of the plaza. The car swerved and skidded on the gravel all the way around until they reached another path and another rectangular lawn fringed with densely planted birches. They were heading back towards the river. Verity's stomach clenched with horror when she saw what was up ahead. Their route was, once again, blocked by metal posts. Just before the end of the path, she spotted a small gap between the trees and turned towards it. Then she pressed her foot down and closed her eyes.

The gap's too small. We'll not get through.

THUMP!

The leaves in the canopy above shuddered as the tiny plastic car squeezed through the gap and twanged out the other side on to the ramp that led to the Millennium Footbridge.

'I must be completely mental. This'll never work,' she said, manoeuvring carefully between the glass and metal handrails on to the end of the bridge's central ramp.

CRUNCH!

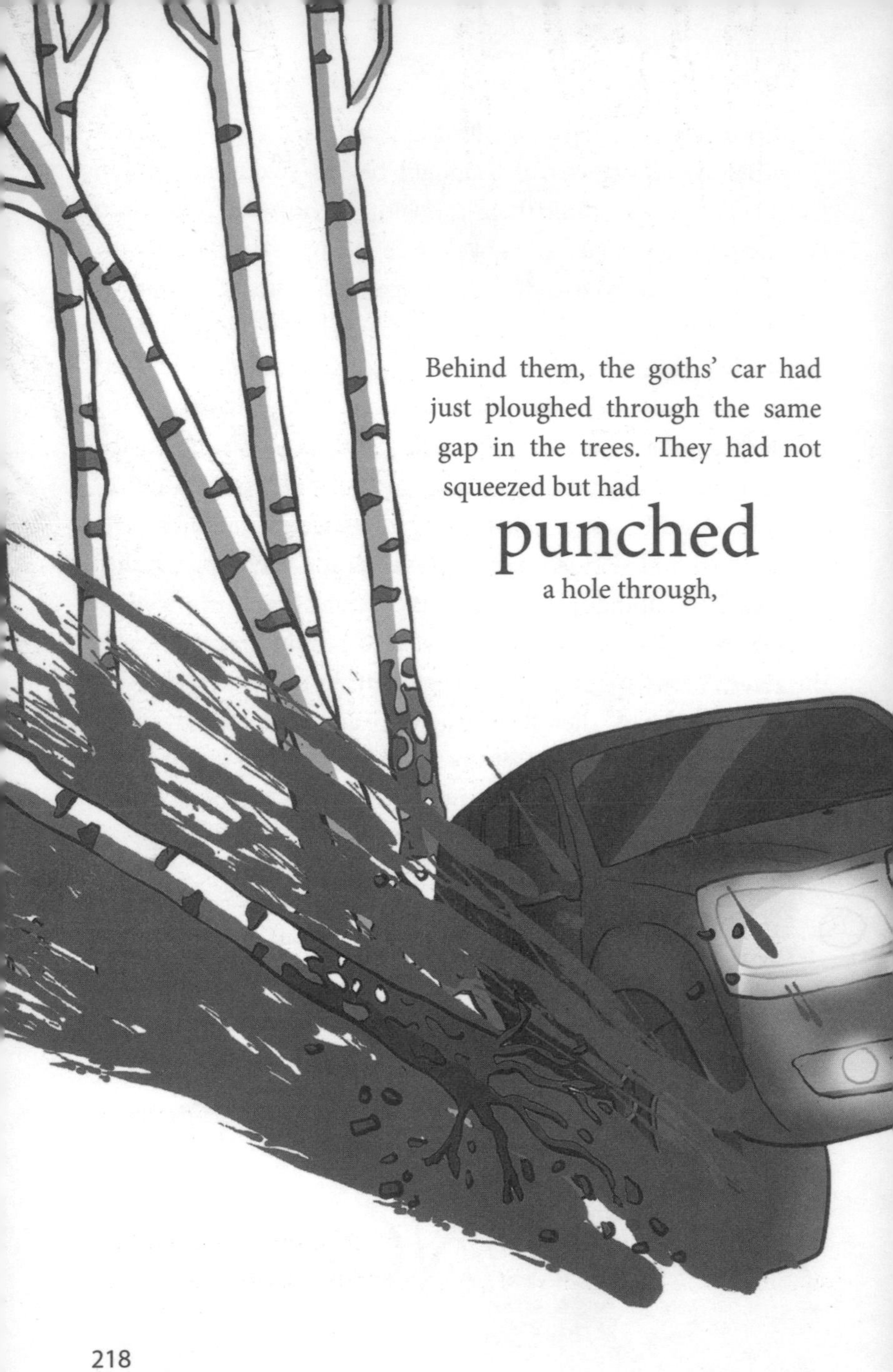

Behind them, the goths' car had just ploughed through the same gap in the trees. They had not squeezed but had

punched

a hole through,

ripping the pale, emaciated limbs out of the ground and sending shattered branches, shards of bark and clods of earth into the air.

Vee and Axel jerked forward as the chrome smile rammed into them again.

RROOOAAARRR!

The monstrous engine snarled, bumped them sideways up the ramp . . . then stopped.

RROOOAAARRR!

The beast growled again but didn't move. It was stuck. The goths were wedged in the gap between a *Cyclists Dismount* sign and a dented handrail.

The tiny plastic car whizzed up the central ramp, turned carefully at the narrow elbow, whizzed up the next ramp, over the top of the goths' car, then zoomed off along the glittering bridge, which stretched like a fragile cobweb across the starlit river.

+ 1,000 points
score: 11,450

The Skinny Model and the Secret Package

'Vincent! Vince! Are you there? Let us in. It's an emergency!' Verity jabbed again at the button on the intercom.

BZZZZ! BZZZZZZZZZZZZZZZZ!

She turned to Axel. 'D'you think he's already outside a club, stalking celebs?'

Axel shrugged.

'He must be here! He *must*!'

BZZZZZZZZZZZZZZZ!

CRACKLE!

'Wha'?' A voice barked out of the intercom speaker.

Verity jumped. 'Vince?'

'What d'you want?'

'Vince, it's Verity.'

'Hey, Vee! What's up?'

'It's an emergency! We need somewhere to hide! Let us in!'

'I-I'm busy.'

'I don't care. Press the stupid door button! It's a matter of life and death!'

BRRRRRRRRR! CLICK!

The door popped open.

Inside, their footsteps echoed up through the stairwell of the converted warehouse. Above them, they heard the sound of another door opening and the soft slap of bare feet, then a voice: 'I've got a guest, so you can't stay long.'

Vee looked up and continued to climb. Vincent was leaning over the banister rail. He wore a pair of jeans but no shirt.

'We need somewhere to hide. Can we stay in the studio? We won't be any trouble. You won't even know we're here.' Verity reached the top of the stairs.

'Uuuhh . . .' Vince began. Then a tall, skinny girl with cropped blond hair and jangling bracelets up both arms appeared in the doorway behind him.

'It's OK; I'm going. I've got an early flight tomorrow, Vince,' said the girl.

Probably a model, Verity thought.

'See ya, babe.' The model grabbed the top of Vince's jeans, gave him a long, noisy open-mouthed kiss, then released him and jangled past them down the stairs.

'Yeah. I'll call you,' said Vince, with a sigh.

'Whatever.' The girl disappeared and they heard the outside door slam.

Vince frowned. He looked really annoyed. 'S'pose you can stay, now.' He raised his arm and waved them inside.

The dockside photographic studio was a huge white cube with a massive, double-height ceiling and two large, arched windows punched through its painted brick walls. The view through the windows was stunning – a panorama of London that included the far-off floodlit dome of St Paul's Cathedral to the right, the shimmering river snaking through the middle, the stretched egg of the Gherkin and, over to the left, in the distance, the idiosyncratic jagged shape of Tower Bridge. It was probably one of the most impressive views in the city and it was Vince's reward for being a very low-paid studio assistant. He lived in a tiny cupboard-sized bedroom behind the kitchen but, when the studio wasn't

in use (which was rare), he was able to treat the space as his own impressive bachelor pad.

'So, can I ask what the emergency is?' asked Vince.

'You wouldn't believe me if I told you.'

'Huh. You've got that right. Actually, I've decided never to believe anything that comes out of your mouth ever again.'

'OK. How about, we're being chased by two goths who shot at us and nearly sliced out Axel's internal organs and wanted to chuck us off a bridge and pretend it was a tragic teen suicide pact?'

'See what I mean?' Vince looked at Axel and chuckled.

'No, I wouldn't believe her if she told me that, either,' said Axel with a nervous smile.

Verity slumped down on one of the large, shabby sofas while Axel stared out of the windows. Vincent walked through a side door and emerged a few minutes later, fully dressed and carrying several cameras.

'Help yourself to leftovers. I'm goin' out.'

'OK. Thanks,' said Verity with a smile, kicking off Mum's uncomfortable high-heeled boots at last.

'You can sleep on the sofas. But you've got to be out by eight tomorrow. There's a *Vogue* fashion shoot booked.'

'No probs. Thanks, Vince'

'Stay out of my room,' said Vincent.

'Sorry we ruined your date,' said Axel.

Vince was already out the door.

Verity looked down at the remnants of Vince's romantic meal with the skinny model – cardboard Chinese takeaway boxes scattered over a low, square coffee table. *No wonder she left*, Vee thought. 'Want a cold dumpling?' she asked Axel, prodding one of the boxes with a chopstick. She waved a skewered dumpling in the air.

'Not really. No appetite.' He dragged his gaze from the gorgeous view and sat on the other, equally shabby sofa opposite her. 'Do you think you should call Pye?'

'S'pose so,' said Verity.

Axel's eyes popped open in surprise. 'Don't you care if she's murdered, if they're all murdered?'

'Don't be stupid. Of course I do.' Verity was annoyed.

'Well, you don't sound like you care. I mean, have you been asleep for the last two hours or something?'

'What do you mean?' Verity couldn't understand why Axel was being all moody and angry all of a sudden.

'She's in danger! We're all in danger! You just told Vince that it was an emergency, didn't you?'

'That was just so he'd let us in.'

'But it IS an emergency! We were just shot at!'

Verity bit her lip and stared at Axel for a second. Then she shuddered and swallowed. His words had hit her like a slap. She clasped her hand to her mouth and stared at the dumpling that now resembled a flabby dead body on a stick.

Don't be sick!

She looked away but her eyes landed on a cardboard cup of glistening, blood-like sauce.

Don't be sick!

Until that moment, she hadn't really felt fear. She'd been full of adrenalin and excited like when she played *Demon Streets.* But now there was a prickle of sweat on her forehead as she rubbed at the *real* red marks on her wrist from the plastic ties and recalled the pressure of Mud's *real* knife under her ribs. She remembered the thud behind her ear as the *real* bullet had pierced the headrest.

This isn't a game! It's real life! Real cars, real villains, real knives and real bullets!

She threw the congealed dumpling on the table and stuck her hand in the pocket of her sweatshirt. The iPhone was still there, as was the credit card and the remaining emergency cash. She scrolled to Pye's number and pressed 'call'. Her hand was shaking.

Brr-brr . . . brr-brr . . . brr-brr . . . brr-brr . . . brr-brr . . . brr-brr . . .

Pye wasn't answering.

Brr-brr . . . brr-brr . . . brr-brr . . . brr-brr . . . brr-brr . . . brr-brr . . .

Verity's heart began to pound in her chest again.

What if she's dead already? What if Rain and Mud are right now arranging her lifeless body on that park bench next to Koshi? Ooo, Pye! I'm so sorry!

She tapped the menu button and selected 'text'.

P
V imprtnt U dnt go out!
STAY HOME!
U R in DANGER!
Pls call Koshi + co
tll thm beware of goths!
NOT JOKE! Vxxx

Her hand shuddered as she pressed 'send'. She returned her phone to the pocket then leaned back on the sofa. She felt a horrible tightness at the back of her throat and closed her eyes, hoping that would make it go away. She prayed that Axel wouldn't say anything because she knew that the smallest word or sigh or cough – even a grunt – would now make her want to cry. She crossed her arms and clasped her armpits, trying to hold back the sob that was building in her chest. The drizzle outside became heavy raindrops and began to clatter against the window panes. A cold draft whistled through the studio and across the wooden floorboards. Verity opened her eyes again and looked for something to pull around her. She spotted a grey blanket thrown over an armchair and flipped it over her shoulders. She tried not to look at Axel.

They were silent.

Verity closed her eyes again.

What do we do now? I can't . . . my brain won't . . . just want to . . . curl up . . . sleep . . .

But instead of shutting down, her exhausted brain was tormenting her with images of their escape. She saw *real* squealing tyres, *real* bone-crunching car crashes, *real* flesh-tearing bullets. A game was being projected on the inside of her eyelids. A game where there were no 'extra lives', no 'power ups' and no 'pause' button. Then eight bold capital letters appeared.

GAME OVER

'Urgh!' she groaned. She opened her eyes and looked at Axel. He was staring out of the window at the downpour, his forehead creased into a worried frown.

'Um, Vee?'

'Yeah?'

'You don't think they'll go after our f-families, do you?'

'I don't know.' Her stomach turned over and she felt like she was going to be sick again. She hadn't considered what Mud and Rain would do *after* they'd completed their mass teen-murder rampage. Who else was a threat to Eden's megalomaniac plans? Families? Mum? Her Aunt Tamsin? Her bio-dad in Devon? No, surely they wouldn't . . .

Axel shifted nervously, leaned forward, his elbows on his knees, and began to pick at the corner of his thumb nail. She watched as he tore at the edge of his finger then brought his hand up to rub his eyes. His pale face was creased into a horrible mask of fear making him look years older. As he dropped his hand down again, Verity felt a jolt, a stab straight through her heart. He was really scared and the thought of his suffering was so horrible that it somehow multiplied her own. Was it possible that caring about Axel was actually making her feel worse? She wanted to leap over the table and wrap her arms around him. She wanted to hug him until the fear went away. She wanted to hold him and whisper that everything was going to be all right.

'I want to . . .' he began, still looking down at his hands.

'What?' Verity's heart skipped a beat.

'I lied about a few things.' His voice warbled.

'I know. It's fine.' She sniffed. 'So did I.'

'No. I want to . . . I want to tell you the truth.' There was a catch in his voice that made Vee shiver.

She nodded and watched as he briefly closed his soft, tired eyes. Even the slow blink of his eyelashes was sad. She looked away and bit her lip. It had gone very cold. The rain seemed to have brought a black cloud of depression right inside the room.

If he tells the truth, she thought, *about who he is, where he's from, might it mean the end of . . . of what? . . . our adventure? . . . our friendship? Or just the end of the lying?*

'I should go home but . . . I'm afraid I'll . . . I'll lead them to—'

Where was his home? She hadn't thought about *his* home, *his* family. He'd made her think that he lived alone, but that was probably a lie, too.

'I bunked off school a week ago . . . eight days ago . . . took a few clothes . . . took a credit card . . . my mum's credit card . . .'

She'd guessed right, at the airport: shoplifter, pickpocket, thief.

'. . . and I took some cash . . . from her handbag.' He rubbed his eyes, obviously ashamed. 'But she probably won't cancel the card or call the police. I've been in trouble before . . . arrested and that. She knows it could be serious for me this time if the police get involved.'

He was silent for a moment but Vee said nothing. She didn't know what to say.

'I lied about the hotel, too.'

She smiled and nodded. Yes, she knew. She'd known, deep down, that most of what he'd told her had been lies, but it didn't matter. None of it mattered.

'Well, it was a sort-of lie. I mean, I got a hotel room and was going to pay with the card but I was sure they'd guess it wasn't mine, so I sneaked out without paying and nearly got caught. That's why I needed a room at your place.' He paused again, then looked up and took a deep breath. 'I live in Berkshire with my mum; I'm doing my A-levels at Parkside College and my name is Mikko. Mikko McKenzie.'

Verity reacted without thinking. She sniggered. It was a small, embarrassing grunt, a pig noise, and it burst out of her before she had a chance to stop it. She slapped her hands over her mouth but it was too late. Heat rushed into her cheeks. 'Sorry,' she said through her fingers. 'I didn't mean to laugh. It . . . It was a surprise. That's all.'

She looked down at the floor. Their tournament of tall tales was over.

'Mikko?' she whispered, trying out his real name for the first time.

'Mmm?'

'Would you . . . ?'

'What?'

'Would you come and sit . . .' She hesitated, nervous of what his answer would be. 'I . . . I kinda need a hug.'

'Yeah,' he said, softly. 'I was just thinking that.'

'You were?' Her stomach did a joyful backflip.

'Uh-huh.' Mikko McKenzie stood up and shuffled around the takeaway boxes. He lowered himself down beside her then opened his arms and enveloped her in a warm, reassuring embrace.

'Mmmm,' Verity swallowed. 'Th-that's better.'

'Better than being tied together in the back of a car?'

'Mmm.' She nodded and shut her eyes. She could no longer hold back the tears and two giant drops rolled down her cheeks into the folds of his jacket.

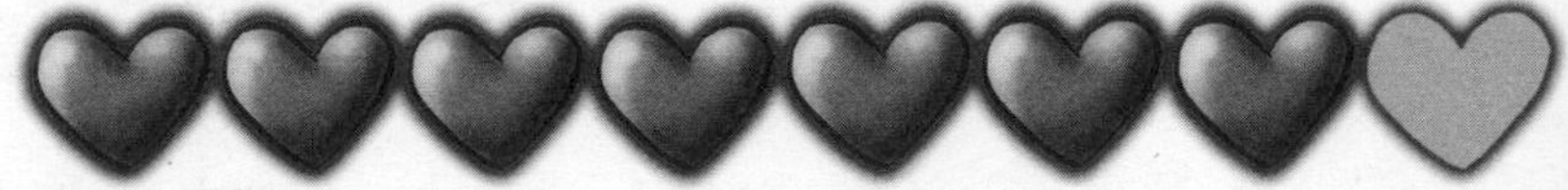

Maisie Malone and Ben Blades crouched in the shadows at the base of an immense stone wall – a wall that dripped with slime and seemed infinite in its enormity, soaring into the night sky above them. They had arrived at the boundary of the Boss's lair – the menacing, windowless fortress with its gravestone-shaped tower that seemed to radiate evil and misery while sucking in all the surrounding light and hope like a black hole. Their next task was to get safely across the Bridge of Death and inside the fortress without confronting any more demons, so Maisie had decided that now was a good time to open the package she'd thrust into her pocket back in Murder Alley. The package held the ultimate secret weapon. The Mole had assured her that its contents were the means to defeat the Boss.

Maisie dug her nails into the brown paper and ripped off a corner. Would it be a phial of lethal neurotoxin, or perhaps a special firearm – a pistol loaded with platinum bullets or something? It would have to be a small pistol, because the package was hardly bigger than her palm and extremely light. She pulled the remaining paper away and looked down at the cardboard box. She'd been expecting something a little more impressive – a jewellery box or, at the very least, something pretty you might buy to put a small birthday present in. This was awfully modest, even shabby.

She shook it and it rattled. It clearly wasn't a pistol. How could the contents of this ordinary cardboard box be a secret weapon that could destroy the most powerful demon of all? She eased off the lid and tipped the contents into her hand.

Something shimmered in the gloom.

A mother-of-pearl button.

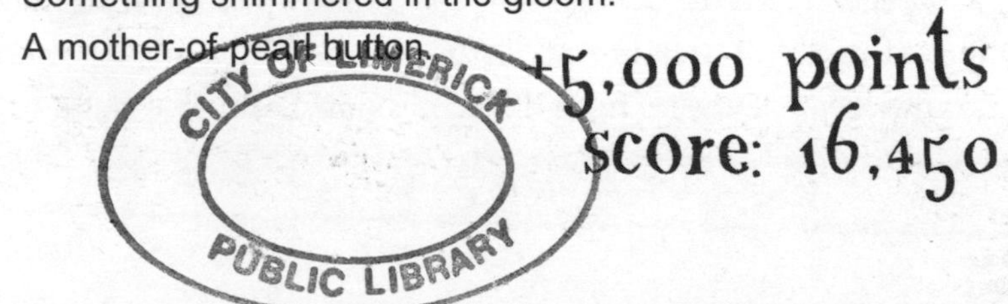

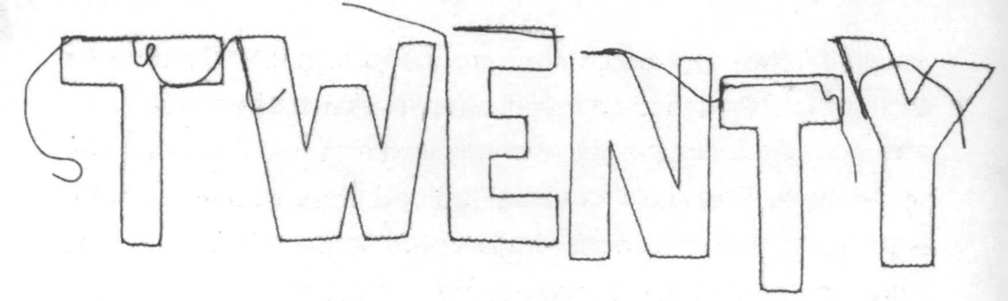

The Clips and the Shocking Phone Call

Verity couldn't sleep and didn't quite understand how Mikko McKenzie was able to. Not only were they still in deadly peril, but a storm was raging outside and slapping against the studio windows like a malevolent creature. She tapped 'call' on her phone again. There was still no answer from Pye. Was she dead already or was her phone out of juice? Her friend was notorious for failing to charge her phone and now she would probably not bother to do so until the morning.

This is unbearable! My best friend will be murdered because she didn't recharge her phone! Argh!

Vee groaned and uncurled herself from the cosy corner of the sofa into which she had tucked herself. She looked over at Mikko, his arms and legs sprawled carelessly. After their deliciously long hug several hours before, he had retreated to the other end of the sofa and fallen into a deep sleep. Still no snog, but that reassuring hug had been pretty intense. Her stomach rumbled. She was starving. She picked up the blanket, wrapped it around her shoulders again and padded over to the kitchen. She pulled open the fridge and looked inside. It was full of plastic-wrapped trays of half-eaten sandwiches – leftovers from a recent shoot. She pulled out a tray that didn't look too dried out or curly edged, grabbed a bottle of water from a shelf in the door and crept back into the studio.

She perched on the narrow windowsill and unscrewed the bottle. The water was ice cold and sent a shiver through her body as it slid down her throat. She gazed out at the rain-lashed city, pulled the blanket tighter and got out her phone.

'P,' she typed.

Pls txt me U R safe
U + Koshi + uthrs in GRAVE DANGER
dnt go 2 cffee shp or ride bikes
+ dnt take N E pills!
speshly frm GOTHS!
Vxxxxxxx

She jabbed 'send'. That was the tenth message. What more could she do?

Will I have to run away with Mikko and sleep rough and scam hotels and be a criminal fugitive for the rest of my life? If they're not dead already, will Pye and the supergeeks have to go into hiding for ever, too?

Then she wondered about going to the police.

What if we call them and they don't believe us? Vince didn't believe our story . . . and neither did Callista. Nobody believes me any more. But they'd have to if we show them the bullet holes in Mum's car. Sludge 'n' Drizzle will still be prowling the streets looking for us, so how can we get the car safely to a police station?

She'd parked the tiny electric car in a secluded courtyard beneath the warehouse, well hidden behind some wheelie bins and a skip.

Best not move the car but, as soon as it gets light, we'll put on disguises, walk to the nearest police station and show them a photo *of the bullet hole.*

She wasn't at all sure that a photo would be enough to convince the cops that their story was true, but she didn't have a better plan. She began to scroll through the iPhone's apps. She found one called 'camera' but next to it was an app named 'video'. *A video of the bullet hole might be more convincing.* She tapped the screen.

It wasn't the video-camera function after all, but a library of movie files, mostly stuff Mum had shot while visiting clothing factories when she was investigating poor working conditions. Verity sighed. She missed Mum so much. One of the videos had a name that made Verity's chest ache and caused a prickle at the back of her throat: 'V+ME'.

She gently touched the screen.

It was footage of a rare day they'd spent together at a theme park. Vee sometimes hated that her mum worked long hours at her office, often at weekends, brought a lot of work home and didn't take holidays. But that Saturday she'd suggested they get out of London for the day. Vee had been in one of her 'moods' and had insisted that Saturday was reserved for shopping with Pye and that she was too old for that 'lame kids' stuff' anyway. In the end, she'd agreed to go – she couldn't remember why – and they'd had a brilliant time. Vee tapped the screen and watched the three minutes of video again. Mum had handed the phone to a man selling balloons and asked him to film them. It was a bit shaky but the man had got the hang of it and framed the two of them with the water ride behind. There she was, her arm around Mum's shoulder, like they were twins instead of mother and daughter. They were both grinning and laughing. Verity smiled. *It's so cool how similar we look. Most people can't tell us apart when I'm dressed in Mum's clothes.*

She closed the theme park file and looked at the other titles. 'Fire Damage – Estonia Factory', 'New Mumbai Factory', 'UK factories – Leicester', 'Aborted Road Scheme – Mexico', 'River Pollution – China'. Then she slapped her hand over her mouth. *Oh my God!* Verity felt her body shudder with shock. *I've been so stupid! These video files are what Bliss and the goths were looking for. This phone is what Eden wants. There's something here, in one of these clips, that could damage him enough that he wants us dead.*

She tapped her finger on the first video and began to watch the entire library.

Mikko McKenzie touched the screen and played the clips again. He'd watched all the videos several times since dawn, when Verity had woken him. There was 'New Mumbai Factory': a journey around a brand new building full of smiling faces –beautiful, contemporary air-conditioned offices, rows of state-of-the-art sewing machines and glittering canteen facilities. There was 'River Pollution – China': a building beside a dark-brown river with lots of dead vegetation and a scum of dirty beige foam clinging to the banks. In the distance, men wearing masks and yellow overalls were cleaning up the site and a group of businessmen were standing beside a white Jeep. Then two hunched, black-clothed figures (whom they had immediately identified as Mud and Rain) climbed out of the Jeep just before the video ended. The other clips were similar – inside factories (some modern, some dark and filthy) or outside at polluted sites and in run-down, empty villages. One clip, 'Aborted Road Scheme – Mexico', was shot

from a moving vehicle and showed five or six large, expensive cars parked inside a vast, fenced-off compound. The cars had the same logos on the side as the white Jeep at the river clean-up and there were the goths again, emerging from a similar vehicle. It was a fuzzy picture but it was definitely them.

'You're right. This is what they were after,' said Mikko.

'I'm not sure how it's incriminating or worth killing for, though,' said Vee, exasperated. 'It can't just be that Mud and Rain were at a couple of textile factories. That's not enough!'

Poo-pi-pi-di-da-da-di-poo-pi-pi-di-da!

'Urgh!' Mikko almost dropped the phone.

Verity knew it had to be her friend and snatched it from him. 'Pye? You all right?'

'What's up?' said Pye's worried voice. 'Your texts freaked me out, Vee. Are you completely demented?'

'Pye, you've got to listen to me. I'm being serious. And I mean DEADLY serious! OK?'

'OK.'

'Something terrible happened to us at TRULY Towers and you've GOT to remember you're my best friend and that I'd do anything to keep you safe from harm and believe me when I say I'm telling you the absolute TRUTH about this.'

'For a change?'

'Yeah. I know I lie all the time, but I'm not lying now. PLEASE, Pyewacket! We're all in terrible danger. You and Koshi and all the others, too.'

'Koshi?'

'Yeah. Please say you believe me.'

'All right. I believe you. What do you want me to do?'

Verity told Pye to stay at home, keep an eye out for the goths, phone the others and tell them to do the same, then wait for instructions.

Verity couldn't hear Pye's reply because a load of noisy people had just walked into the studio. The photographer and the stylist for the *Vogue* shoot had arrived. When they disappeared for a moment into the kitchen, Verity pressed the phone to her ear, but there was only a disconnected tone. Pye had gone. Then she jumped.

Poo-pi-pi-di-da-da-di-poo-pi-pi-di-da!

Vee held the phone to her ear again and could just make out the familiar voice.

'Verity?' Mum sounded out of breath.

'Hi, Mum! Is something wrong? You sound strange.'

'Oh, darling! Thank goodness you're in Brighton. How's my sis?'

Verity grimaced. Mum didn't know she was still in London. 'Fine. Umm, we're having breakfast.' She hoped Mum wouldn't ask to speak to Tam.

'I don't want to worry you, but Callista called me last night. She's been at our house with the police. Apparently, there was a break-in. I'm SO relieved that you weren't there!'

'A break-in? Really?' Verity's stomach clenched with shame. So much for her new determination not to lie any more.

'Yes, sweetie. But you mustn't get upset. Callista is taking care of everything – changing the locks and things. She said there was a bit of damage but I don't think the burglars went upstairs to your room. I'm getting an earlier flight ho—'

'You don't need to do that.' Verity stood up and walked over to the window. The make-up girl for the shoot had arrived with several other members of the *Vogue* team. They were all chattering loudly about a club they'd been to the previous night.

'I've practically finished here, anyway,' said Mum. 'So I decided to check out and come home, prepare for Fashion Week.'

'When's your flight?'

'Now.'

'I can't hear you. Did you say—?'

Someone had switched the sound system on and Jimmy Hendrix was blasting out of the speakers.

'I'm calling from the plane,' said Mum. 'We land in about two hours. Eden very kindly offered to meet me at the airpo—'

'No, you can't . . . ! Mum?'

Brrrrrrrrrrrrrrrrrrrrr . . .

The line was dead. They'd been cut off.

'What's wrong?' Mikko was shocked at the look on Verity's face. She was obviously terrified and it scared him.

'Sh-she's on a flight!'

'Home?' He frowned but relaxed slightly. That was good, wasn't it?

'And if Eden gets there first—'

'Eden?'

'If Eden meets her off the plane—'

'At the arrivals gate?' He was starting to understand her panic.

'Oh!' she gasped and grabbed the lapels of Mikko's jacket. 'Everyone will think it's all romantic and cute, him being there to welcome her home.' She stared at him with wild eyes.

'But actually he's not—'

'Not romantic at all.'

'He's an evil . . . kidnapper!'

'Or worse!'

The Code Word and the Scary Text

Verity bit nervously at her lip as she typed another message. Then she pressed 'send' and looked up. Once again, she and Mikko were in the back of James's limousine at the airport.

'When do you think she'll check her phone?'

'Don't worry, Vee,' said Mikko, reassuringly. 'She'll get your message.'

'But what if she doesn't read it until she's past baggage reclaim and through customs and running into the arms of Eden Greenfield and he . . .' Verity began to jiggle her left leg up and down. 'Or if she reads my messages but just doesn't believe me?'

'James will convince her.'

'Yeah,' Verity sneered. 'James the chauffeur, who foolishly gave you his card and who thinks we are both wizzed-up, juvenile delinquent liars who deserve ASBOs. He's probably gone to the nearest police station to turn us in for scamming him last week.'

'He won't do that.' Mikko looked worried. 'I mean, he wouldn't . . . We paid him double what he usually gets.'

'With Mum's "emergency only" credit card, which she is going to be SO annoyed about!' Verity was now howling.

'But this IS an emergency, you idiot! Chill out! Your mum will be fine when you explain everything to her.'

Verity's leg continued to jiggle. She wasn't looking forward to explaining and no way did she intend to tell Mum *everything*! 'But I wish we were in there ourselves.' She stared out of the window at the rows of vehicles in the short-stay airport car park. 'We should have put on disguises, wigs or something, and gone to meet her.'

'We decided not to risk it, remember? Just like we decided that it would be safer not to go and get Pye.' Then he thought of something else. 'He'll use the code word you gave him, then she'll know he's genuine, won't she?'

'I suppose so.' She wasn't thinking about James any more, but imagining Pye ignoring her warnings and going down to the shops for some milk or something and getting kidnapped and tortured and . . .

'They're coming!' said Mikko.

Verity jumped in her seat and anxiously pressed her nose against the window. Mikko was right. Mum was walking towards them through the car park with James the chauffeur at her heels pulling her wheelie suitcase. She was striding and swinging her hips like she was on a fashion runway, but her face was creased into an unattractive, anxious scowl. As they approached the limo, James jogged around her and reached for the door handle.

'Darling! It IS you!' said Mum, peering into the back of the limo, her anxious scowl replaced by relief. 'What's all this intrigue? Why was I not to go with Eden? He was awfully insulted, you know. And the paparazzi were *so* confused. When the chauffeur said the word Mannequin I knew he was genuine and that it was you that sent him, but what on earth is going on, Vee? Oh, hello. I don't think we've met.' Mum smiled at Mikko and offered her hand.

'Hi, I'm Mikko,' he said accepting the handshake.

'Get in, Mum,' said Verity, shifting along the seat closer to Mikko and making a gap for Mum. 'We'll explain on the way home.'

James had stowed the suitcase and was already in the driver's seat, turning the key in the ignition.

'All right,' said Mum.

The limo pulled out of the car park, joined the traffic leaving the airport and headed for the city.

'So?'

'Right.' Verity took a deep breath then felt Mikko give her hand a tiny reassuring nudge. 'Well, the reason we did all this was because of the break-in.'

'The break-in?'

'Um, yeah. I didn't go to Brighton and I sort of lied to Tamsin about needing to stay in London because Pye had an accident, so we were there when they broke in.'

Mum's face contorted into a look of horror. 'Pye had an accident?'

'No.'

'She didn't have an accident, but you were at the house, our house . . . with Mikko?' She looked at Mikko and frowned.

'Yeah. It's quite complicated, but we saw who broke in and we know what they were looking for.'

It took the entire journey back to the house to explain about Bliss and the break-ins and how they had spotted her at TRULY Towers then confronted Eden and discovered *he* had sent her. Then her story had jumped forward to finding the videos on the iPhone and how these were probably what Bliss had been searching for. Verity tried to ignore the dark lump in the pit of her stomach as she left out all the scary stuff about the goths, the guns, the knives, the mass teen-murder plan and the car chase.

'Hmm,' said Mum, who had been sitting in angry silence for the previous half hour, the flesh between her eyebrows forming deep furrows.

I've given her premature wrinkles, Vee thought. *She'll need Botox and plastic surgery now and it's all my fault.*

'That man always made me uncomfortable,' said Mum at last.

'Eden?'

'Yeah.'

'But you had a date with him.' Vee was shocked. 'I thought—'

'It was hardly a date,' said Mum. 'Why does everyone assume it's a date if a man and a woman have dinner together?'

'But I thought you—?'

'Liked him?' said Mum. 'Not my type, Vee. You know that.' She smiled.

Verity thought for a moment. Mum was right. Eden was everything Mum disliked – too obvious, too arrogant, too much of a celebrity. Vee had been swept along by the gossip and hadn't trusted her own instincts, her own gut feelings 'So it wasn't really a date, then?'

Mum shook her head. 'It was actually a meeting about my factory visits. Now I guess I know why he was interested in the videos. We'll have to look at them again, see if we can work out why he was so eager to get his hands on them.' Mum paused and looked at Vee. 'And you lied to my sister. I'm not at all happy about that, Vee.'

Verity groaned. 'I know.' She thought she'd got away with it, that Mum would forget her aunt Tamsin amid all the excitement of the burglary and the Eden revelations. But this time, she now admitted, she'd gone too far. She'd lied so often in the past and had never felt bad about it before. She'd never had a knot of guilt in her stomach when she'd cut school or lied about homework or promised to phone her bio-dad on his birthday when she knew she'd probably forget.

'I'm really sorry. I just wanted to take Mikko to the party on the boat. You weren't going to use the invitations so I made up this story about Pye having an accident and staying at her house.'

'But there was no accident.'

Verity shook her head.

'And Pye's OK, she's not injured?'

Verity bit her lip. 'No.' *Oh God! I hope not!*

'So you were alone in our house with . . .' She glanced at Mikko again then stopped.

Beep!

Verity's phone vibrated in her pocket so she slipped her hand inside. The conversation was starting to turn bad and she could tell Mum was about to lecture her on respect, honesty and probably safe sex and annoying stuff like that. Vee pulled out the phone and looked at the screen.

WARNING
Do not make mistake of
thinking you are now safe . . .

Her heart skipped, then, as she scrolled down, her blood turned to ice in her veins.

> . . . if events of past 24hrs reach
> police or Twitter or ANYWHERE
> YOU WILL REGRET IT!

She managed to smile at Mum and waggled the phone to make her think it was a message from a friend. Then she turned the screen away and read on, a lump in her throat.

> i can destroy your mum's business
> with very little effort
> close all stores
> put all staff out of work
> Jiggery-Pokery RUINED
> if necessary, can arrange
> TRAGIC ACCIDENT for her too
> would be painful and messy
> many lives now in your hands, Verity
> and remember,
> NOBODY BELIEVES YOU

There was no name at the end, but she knew who it was from: Eden Greenfield.

'Vee? Vee, you all right?'

'Mmm?' Verity looked up. 'Oh, yeah. No problem. Just a text from . . . Pye.' She tried to smile again.

'You're not car sick are you? You look very pale.'

Verity shook her head.

'You were car sick all the time when you were small.' Mum began to shift forward in her seat. The limo was pulling up at their house. Mum looked out of the window at the empty driveway. 'Vee?'

'Yeah?'

'Where's my car?'

Apologies and Inspiration

Two hooded visitors crept silently up the steps, rang the bell and, a few seconds later, Saffron Fibbs let them into the dark house. She led the pair downstairs, where a weak light glowed softly in the basement design studio.

'The last of your friends are here, Vee.'

'Thanks, Mum.'

'Hamish! Ollie!' Seven voices sang out a greeting to the last arrivals. Hamish and Ollie peeled off their enveloping disguises and took their places with the others on the high stools around the cutting table. They had all arrived safely and Verity felt she could now breathe again. She looked around the table at the anxious and confused faces and couldn't quite believe that the school's misfits, the fashion-free supergeeks, were actually in her mum's uber stylish design studio.

'Can I get anyone a drink?' Mum asked from the doorway.

'No, Mum. We're cool, thanks,' said Verity.

'Tea? Smoothies? Chocolate bickies?'

'Large Jack Daniels?' said Mikko with a nervous laugh.

'Valium?' said Pye, giggling.

Mum smiled.

'Maybe later,' said Verity.

'The Valium or the chocolate bickies?' Mum laughed as she closed the new studio door behind her and went back upstairs.

Everyone turned their expectant gaze on Verity.

'What's going on?' said Hamish.

'Yeah, what we doin' here?' asked Ollie. 'I'm hungry.'

'All you ever think about is food,' said Hamish. 'Or your feet.'

'You can worry about food and feet later,' said Verity.

'Yeah. Shut up about your feet,' said Hamish.

'I never mentioned them. You did.'

'Shut up!' all the others groaned.

When there was silence again, Verity coughed and began. 'Well, first I want to apologise.' Mikko grabbed her hand under the table and squeezed it. She looked down in an attempt to hide the sudden flush in her cheeks. Every time he touched her or even looked at her, she felt confused and flustered. 'I'm . . . I'm s-sorry I didn't believe you. And I'm sorry I called you a beardy moron, Koshi.' She glanced up at Koshi.

'That's OK. I am a bit – the beardy bit.'

They all laughed and Jelly slapped him on the back, then, when the giggling had subsided, Mikko nudged Verity to continue.

'So, anyway, we totally believe you now.'

'You do?' said Pye. 'What changed your mind?'

'You know I told you we had a break-in here?'

Pye nodded.

'Well, there was slightly more to it than that. Basically, it was this girl called Bliss Meadows who got a job as a designer for my mum. She was really working for Eden Greenfield and he hired her to steal something.'

'Oh, is that what you found out at TRULY Towers?'

'Yep. Something else happened there, too, but . . .' Verity shivered at the image that had just flashed into her mind of Mikko getting punched in the face.

'We found out what the burglars were looking for,' Mikko interrupted. He glanced at Verity but she nodded for him to continue. She wasn't sure she was calm enough to tell the story properly. 'They were looking for videos and we think they might kinda prove you were right all along about Eden.'

A sigh of pleasure and satisfaction rose from the group. 'Yesssss!'

'You all suspected that Eden wasn't entirely truthful about his TRULY fashion label,' said Verity, 'and had found ways to hide the fact that he exploits people and swindles and cheats to make more profit. Well, we think these videos might contain evidence of foul play, but we can't find it. We thought you might.'

'There's something else, isn't there?' said Pye, her brow creased with confusion. 'You said we were in danger.'

Verity grimaced. This was the moment she had worried about. They were about to inform the supergeeks that there was a chance they might die horrible deaths at the hands of two psychopathic goths who'd been hired by one of the most powerful men on the planet – a man who'd probably stop at nothing to save his own reputation. How would they take it?

'There wasn't just one break-in and Bliss wasn't working alone,' said Verity. 'There are a couple of people who have been given this . . . um . . . this other assignment by Eden.'

'What sort of assignment?' asked Hamish.

'To keep us all quiet . . . permanently.'

'W-what do you mean?'

'We all know too much so they're planning to kill us,' said Mikko.

The room fell silent.

Verity looked at their faces. Would they believe her? Or would they assume that Verity the Liar was simply lost in an elaborate fantasy again, confusing real life with some role she was playing in an online game.

'We should just show you the videos,' she said. She opened the laptop on the table beside her and turned the screen so the others could see. Then she tapped the space bar.

The fashionably-challenged supergeeks watched, without a word, as Verity played each of the videos.

'What do you think?' Mikko asked. 'Is there something incriminating?'

'I'm not sure,' said Koshi. 'Let's watch them again.'

Verity clicked back and the clips repeated.

‘Those are the people that tried to kill us,’ said Verity, pointing at the fuzzy clip of Mud and Rain beside the car.

‘Urgh!’ said Pye. She clutched the front of her top with both hands. ‘They’re those creepy goths who were lurking outside your house before your party.’

‘And they were at the coffee shop yesterday,’ said Grace, looking at Jelly for confirmation. Jelly peered at the screen.

‘That tall one asked me where I got my cycle helmet,’ said Ollie.

‘Yeah,’ said Hamish. ‘We came out of the cafe—’

‘With our bacon and egg butties,’ said Ollie.

‘With our bacon and egg butties,’ Hamish continued. ‘And they were hanging around our bikes. I told you they were tampering with the tyres, didn’t I?’ Hamish punched Ollie’s arm, delighted that he’d been proved right about the black-clad figures.

‘They were at our school last week, too,’ said Chen. ‘Lurking outside the Science Block.’

Verity felt sick again. It was becoming a very familiar feeling.

'I think I might know what it is,' said Koshi quietly.

'The logo, right?' said Pye, taking hold of Koshi's elbow.

'Yeah. You think it might be that, too?'

'Mmm.' Pye leaned forward. 'It's weird, because we were talking about it just yesterday.'

'Subcontractors?' Koshi asked.

'Subcontractors,' Pye confirmed.

'What's "sub-contractors"?' said Mikko.

'Well, we couldn't find any proof that Eden was getting the TRULY collection made in unsafe factories or that he was exploiting his workers,' said Koshi.

'Like the factories in the videos,' said Pye. 'The ones that don't have fire exits and employ kids and pay terrible wages.'

Vee nodded. 'My mum makes sure none of her stuff is made in places like that. She only uses factories that are checked and monitored all the time.'

'Well, Eden has always been able to prove that he does the same. Your mum didn't find any of his garments in the factories she visited, did she?'

'No. She would have checked the labels and the order books and stuff.'

'Right,' said Koshi. 'But if he has another company, several other companies, subcontractors, doing all the illegal and unethical stuff, he can keep his own hands clean.'

'It's easy enough to sew in new labels in secret,' said Jelly.

'And the subcontractors can be blamed for pollution or industrial accidents too.'

'So those logos on the cars and the labels in the factories, they're Eden's subcontractors?'

'Yep!' said Koshi with a grin.

Verity's heart was beating faster. Could they have found the answer?

'Right,' said Mikko. 'So what do we do now?'

'First, I'm going to tell Mum,' said Verity. 'Then we'll have something to eat.'

'Excellent!' said Ollie, rubbing his hands up and down on his concave gut.

11

The kitchen telly was on with the sound turned down low and Mum was taking a pizza out of the oven.

'If you cut this up,' said Mum, 'I'll make a pot of tea. Did anyone want hot chocolate?'

'No, just tea and coffee, thanks.'

'So, now that we have incriminating evidence,' said Mum 'and we've discovered how he was fooling us all, what shall we do about it?'

Verity shook her head. She didn't know. She needed time to think. Should she tell Mum about the goth assassins and what Eden had threatened to do to her? She didn't want to. Telling Mum the whole truth would reveal the extent of all her lying and it would probably freak her out!

And would the subcontractor theory be enough? She suspected it wouldn't. If they went to the police or published the information online without significant, watertight evidence, then Eden was sure to refute it. He'd hire lawyers and PR experts and completely demolish their claims. She remembered the warning text. It had been chilling and utterly convincing. He *would* destroy her mum and murder nine teenagers to save his own skin. There had to be another way to expose him and they couldn't just give up, hand over the iPhone and hope he'd call off the goths. They all knew too much. They might never be safe.

'He's a very powerful man,' said Mum, as if she had been reading her daughter's mind.

'I know.' Vee stepped over to the kitchen window, opened a tiny gap between the blinds with her fingers and scanned the dark street outside. She couldn't see Mud and Rain or their car, but she knew they were out there, somewhere.

Mum put the steaming teapot on a tray next to a pot of coffee, then added a packet of biscuits. Verity sighed. They couldn't all stay in this house for ever. Eventually they would have to leave, go home, go back to school. She selected a large knife from the knife block and began to halve then quarter the pizza.

. . . this amazing sight . . .

There was a chuckling male voice on the telly, hardly audible.

. . . Millennium Bridge . . .

Vee looked up and almost sliced through her finger. On the TV screen, a tiny green shape was whizzing over the Millennium Bridge. Verity glanced at Mum. She was looking the other way, but Vee moved sideways and stood in front of the telly, just in case. They were ending the evening news with an amusing story – an astonishing mobile-phone video of an electric car darting across the famous footbridge.

'Police are seeking the drivers,' said the newsreader with a smile.

Then Vee shuddered. Eden's grinning face had appeared on the screen. The very last item was a celeb story. Eden Greenfield was announcing a Perfect Eden project aimed at teenagers. He had recruited three celebrities to promote three new initiatives.

Tom Wilde was heading an anti-knife project, Flash Campbell was starting a road-safety scheme and Bethany London would be working with police to stamp out cyber bullying. There was a clip from a noisy and chaotic press conference, with journalists shouting questions and flash bulbs popping. But Verity didn't notice the noise or the flickering lights. She was staring at their faces – Tom, Flash and Bethany.

She dropped the knife and threw the pizza on to the tray then ran all the way down to the basement with it. The coffee pot wobbled dangerously and tea sloshed from the teapot spout as she slammed the tray down on the work table.

'I've got it!' she yelled.

They all gaped at her, eyes wide with anticipation. They could hear footsteps on the stairs; Mum had followed her down.

'I think I know how we can expose him,' Verity went on. 'It might mean putting ourselves in more danger,' she warned, then turned to her mum. 'And we'll all have to do a bit of acting, y'know, like role play.'

'That's no problem,' said Mikko, speaking for the others.

'Does that mean I can dress up?' asked Mum, smiling.

'Well, yeah, if you're up for it,' said Verity.

'Bring it on!' said Mum.

The Bridge of Death and the Fashion Show

Maisie Malone and Ben Blades crouched in the shadows and stared down at the Bridge of Death. It was their last obstacle before entering the tower. Instead of being heavily fortified, as they'd assumed, the bridge appeared empty – a clear, moonlit cobbled path over the river. For a moment Maisie was elated. This was going to be easy, she thought. Then, as they waited, recovering from the effort of avoiding all demon contact through the narrow streets of the city, a figure approached the bridge. The figure was very thin, had a white, goat-like beard and wore a long coat. He walked slowly to the end of the road, put out his foot, lowered his heel on to the first cobble of the bridge and a roar of anguish ripped through the air. A tiny angry troll leapt from beneath the bridge, landed with a crash in front of the stunned figure and looked up at him.

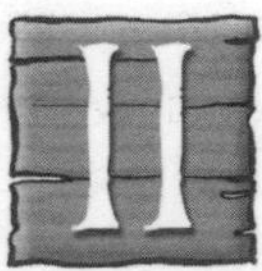

'What d'ya want?' demanded the troll. He was fat and hunched and looked a little like a character from a fairy story, Maisie thought. It seemed that trolls guarded bridges in Demon Streets, too.

'To cross the bridge,' said Goat-beard.

'Girls only,' said the troll, picking his nose. 'You're a boy, so you can't.'

'But, I—'

'My bridge, my rules!' sang the troll with a smug grin. 'If you don't like it, you can just hoof it!'

'So, you're saying, if I was a girl, I could cross?'

'Only in the next ten minutes.'

'What?'

'Then it might be boys only . . . or boys and girls, but only those with blue hair . . . or just dogs with three legs.'

'But that—'

'Told you. My bridge, my rules!' The troll folded his meaty arms and smirked.

The thin figure backed away, clearly defeated by the troll's arbitrary criteria, and began to walk towards the alley where Maisie and Ben were hiding.

Then two icons appeared.

Maisie smiled. She had wondered if they might be offered another weapon before entering the tower, but she hadn't expected this. These were red action icons, not weapons. The first icon was a silhouette with a question mark, and the second – two arrows chasing each other in a circle.

'Shape-shifter or Body-switch?' said Ben.

Maisie had chosen the Shape-shifter option once, back on one of the early levels, and it had been fun prowling Demon Streets as a panther for a while. But the Body-switch option had seemed pointless then. It still did. Maisie was already a girl and the switch wasn't being offered to Ben, only to her. How would this help them to cross the bridge? Then Maisie had an idea. Perhaps Goat-beard would give them something really valuable, something that would be useful inside the tower, if Maisie offered to switch bodies with him long enough for him to cross?

'Body-switch, I think,' said Maisie.

'You sure?'

'Yeah.' She pointed at Goat-beard. 'If he crosses the bridge as me, we find out how to get past the troll and make sure it's safe.'

'Genius!'

score: 16,450
options
play
II

Maisie and Ben stepped out of the shadows and Goat-beard stopped.

'Hi. Wanna be a girl for ten minutes?' Maisie asked.

'Body-switch with you, you mean? Ummm, OK.'

'What can you trade?'

'Er, how about one of these?' Goat-beard flapped open his coat to reveal dozens of assorted weapons hanging from the coat's lining. There were pistols and revolvers, long blades and short, even a hammer and a hand grenade. But Maisie was disappointed. There were no buttons. Nothing was button-shaped or button-decorated or even had a button etched on its handle. Surely, the Mole's package was supposed to help them with their selection.

A pretty knife with a shimmering handle caught her eye. It was small, pocket sized, and would match her pistol. Without an obvious clue, Maisie decided, matching her pistol was as good a reason as any.

'OK,' said Maisie. 'The pearl-handled blade for a ten minute switch.'

Ben Blades and Goat-beard crouched back in the shadows and watched Maisie Malone approach the bridge. It wasn't really Maisie, but Goat-beard in Maisie's body, making a second attempt to cross. Ben looked at the bearded figure beside him – Maisie in Goat-beard's body. Weird. As before, as soon as a foot touched the first cobblestone of the bridge, the troll leapt from beneath it.

'What d'ya want?' The troll vigorously scratched his bum.

'Um, to cross the bridge,' said Goat-beard as Maisie.

'Gerrr-off!'

'But, I—'

'You can cross if you say "please".'

'OK. Please.'

The trolled grunted, stepped back and waved Maisie through.

'Thanks,' said Maisie and began to walk across.

The troll then leaned over the side of the bridge revealing a hairy back and the crack of a similarly hairy arse. When he stood up straight again, there was a giant club in his hands – an evil-looking club, almost as large as he was and studded with nails. With one swing at her legs, he knocked Maisie to the ground and proceeded to pound at her head with the club. As he smashed away, the troll yelled, 'I said, "say 'please'", not "OKpleasethanks"!'

Even from their hiding place some distance away, Ben and the bearded Maisie could tell from the grisly crunching sound and the pool of blood spreading across the bridge that Goat-beard had had it.

'Eargh!' said bearded Maisie. 'I hope I don't get my body back in that state.'

'That might have been you,' said Ben. 'Or me.'

'I think we might have to cross the river some other way.'

– 1,300 points
score: 15,150

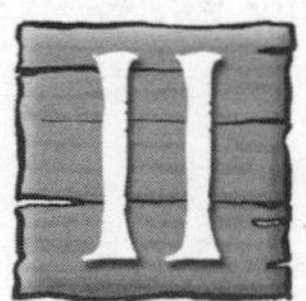

Verity came up the stairs from the studio carrying the last of the props and costumes and almost tripped over a stack of computer boxes. Deliveries had been arriving all morning – costumes and wigs from a theatrical agency, t-shirts in assorted colours from a local printer, numerous goodies from a computer store and, just minutes before, a tiny package from a shop in central London called SpyStuff. In the last twenty-four hours, they had brought Verity's elaborate plan together with astonishing speed.

Being under siege in the house had turned out to be less of a problem than they'd thought. Everything they needed could be ordered and delivered and, as it was still half term break, there were few objections to Pye and Koshi and the other supergeeks staying over. Mum had called the parents that had needed reassuring and used her influence to change schedules and relocate the Jiggery-Pokery staff to the house. The Jiggery-Pokery London Fashion Week show would go ahead as planned, but with a few alterations. Mum and Callista had been going through the final schedule over breakfast but now Callista was leaving. Verity ran to catch her at the front door.

'Callista.'

'Mmm?' Callista turned and coldly raised an eyebrows. As always, she was a grey-suited picture of frosty efficiency. Verity imagined her with snakes for hair. *That look of hers could definitely turn you to stone*, she thought.

'Um, thanks for cleaning up the house and, um, not telling Mum about the bullet in the car.'

The car had been returned, good as new and bullet-free, that morning.

Callista flashed a lopsided grin – the closest she could get to a smile. 'As you know, I don't approve of lying, but, in this case,

I thought it best not to cause your mother any further distress. I think this past week has been quite scary enough for her. Mmm?'

Verity nodded.

Callista stepped out of the door.

'Be careful,' said Vee.

'Don't worry about me. I suggest you go and have a quick chat with your Mum before this whole thing kicks off.' Callista walked down the drive and got into a taxi.

Verity bristled. It was so irritating when adults told you to do something you were already going to do. *I don't need stupid Callista the stupid Medusa to say when I should talk to my mum.* She slouched angrily back across the hall. The hallway was quite a large space, but today it felt overcrowded. There was pandemonium in the house. Everyone was now rushing about and talking far too loudly.

'Here,' said Mikko. 'You'd better take this.' He held out the small plastic box from SpyStuff.

They stood in the middle of the hall while the others seemed to spin like a whirlpool around them. Verity nodded and tried to smile but she was too nervous and her smile muscles seemed not to be working. *I bet he regrets ever having met me*, she thought. *If he hadn't come to the boat party with me, he would never have been at TRULY Towers, or been on Mud and Rain's hit list and he'd probably be safe at home, far away from the crazy girl who plays lame role-play games and talks to herself.*

'This is gonna be awesome!' said Mikko, his own smile muscles working fine and at maximum stretch.

Verity frowned. 'Aren't you even a bit scared?'

'I hiv no fear. Vee are Christoph *und* Lottie Schnitzehoff,

Masters *von* Illooooosion! Remember? Zis vil be our finest trrrrick.' He tugged at his cuffs in a theatrical way and opened his palms like an old-fashioned stage magician. Verity tried again to smile. 'Or d'you wanna be my wife with the bad Scottish accent again? Eh, hen?'

'It was a great accent. Better than yours.' Verity remembered how she'd felt being the fake Mrs Butterworth at the airport – the thrill of applying the lipstick, stepping into the crowd then taking Mikko's arm. It had been a moment of both terror and triumph. She'd been scared but thrilled at the same time. In fact, except for the punching, the knives and the death threats, their whole week together – lying, cheating and risk-taking – had been pretty amazing. Maybe Mikko didn't blame her for how it had all gone horribly wrong. Maybe he had actually enjoyed her company, their camaraderie, their friendship. Was there a bond between them other than their being hunted by the same assassins?

She looked down at the plastic box and prised open the lid. Inside, under a thin foam cover, sat a tiny mother-of-pearl button. Verity pushed it slightly further into its button-shaped foam bed, then closed the box and slid it into her pocket. *We certainly are Masters of Illusion*, she thought. *I really hope the trick works.*

It was quieter in the kitchen. Vee climbed on to the stool beside Mum at the counter. Mum looked up from tapping on her Blackberry, wrapped her arm around Vee and squeezed.

'Did Mikko call home again?'

'Uh-huh.' Verity nodded.

'Good. I expect his mum was awfully worried.'

'Mmm. I expect so.'

'You all right, sweetie?'

‘Fine.’ She didn’t sound fine.

‘I don’t mean about him going home when this is over, although I’m sad about that, too. I’ve grown quite fond of him. He’s a nice boy. What I mean is, are you OK about today? We could call it off, you know. It’s not too late.’

‘No, we have to do it. Eden’s got to be stopped. People have to know the truth.’

Mum nodded. ‘I’m just concerned about you, darling, and how much this whole thing has affected you.’

‘I’m fine, Mum. Really.’ She bit her lip.

‘I’d give it all up in a heartbeat – my career, the company – if it was hurting you. You know that, don’t you? I could call Eden now and tell him he’s won and that we’ll give him the videos. I’d even offer him ownership of Jiggery-Pokery if he’d guarantee our safety.’ Mum squeezed again. ‘And, just so you know, I can tell you’re lying when you bite your lip.’

Verity stopped biting.

‘Wanna try telling me you’re fine again?’ Mum asked with a smile.

‘Shut up!’ said Verity. ‘I AM fine, but let’s go and do it before I change my mind.’

The enormous black car pulled up at the kerb and two black-clothed figures got out of the front, checked the crowd like secret agents, then opened the rear door for their boss. Jelly, who’d been waiting in the lobby to give her friends the signal, was shocked at the tycoon’s arrogance. Verity had been right. He didn’t care any more about being seen with those thugs. He was so confident about his stain-resistant reputation that he believed even the intimidating appearance of Mud and Rain couldn't tarnish his image. The paparazzi cameras flashed and whirred. Eden smiled and waved while his fans screamed. Bliss was last out of the car and trotted to catch up with Eden, who had reached the end of the red carpet and was entering the 'London Fashion Week' venue.

'The Boss is in the building,' whispered Jelly, into her phone. 'Repeat: the Boss and Bliss are in the building. Goths are parking.'

Eden strode past late-arriving magazine editors and fashion journalists who were having to queue despite their importance and allocated front-row seats. Verity, Pye, Mikko and the others had seats, too, and had been waiting in them, nervously, for the last hour. They had decided that it was essential, in this part of their plan, for them all to stick together. – They'd travelled in a convoy of three cars from the house and were now sitting in the same row in the audience. Only Mum had gone backstage to oversee the show. She should be safe, for now, surrounded by models, dressers, make-up artists and hair stylists.

Eden worked his way through the crowd, greeting friends and editors with his usual elbow-grab handshake. He took his seat, the last of the audience found their places and the final stragglers squeezed in at the back. The excited chatter had to compete with pounding music, but suddenly the sound faded and the lights dimmed. Verity used the momentary gloom to twist in her seat and scan the back of the room. There was Bliss's bright red hair. A new track began with a rhythmic beat. Verity snapped her head back to face the front. The Jiggery-Pokery autumn/winter show was about to begin. The audience fell silent.

The pack of photographers at the end of the runway raised their cameras or adjusted their long lenses on their monopods. Most of them had taped out their precious metre of floor space hours ago or sent an assistant to hold their spot. Now they were ready to capture every garment in the new Jiggery-Pokery collection – full length, half crop at mid-thigh, lower-leg footwear shot or zoom in for a hair or make-up head shot. The photographers were like strange cyborg creatures, connected to their cameras and equipment by umbilical cables, ready to collate their pictures on their laptops and send them to picture editors' desks within minutes of the show's finale.

A golden glow grew at the far end of the catwalk, illuminating the name in metre-high letters on the back wall:

Jiggery-Pokery

Then the first model appeared from the wings. A ripple of applause filled the room and the cameras whirred and flashed.

Verity couldn't concentrate. She stared at the procession of gorgeous models in gorgeous clothes but she saw nothing but a blur. She knew most of the collection already, having seen sketches and toiles or the final garments being fitted on each model in Mum's basement studio. And she knew this was her last chance to go over her part in the plan – to rehearse the timings and the running order in her head. *It's just like being in the school play*, she told herself. It would be fine as long as she didn't miss a cue or forget her lines. Her left knee began to jiggle nervously. There could be no mistakes.

To her right, Pye perched on the edge of her gold-painted chair. Her face was white with anxiety. Verity put out her hand and Pye took it. They smiled at each other. On the other side, Vee felt for Mikko's hand, too. He flinched at her touch but then

slipped his sweaty hand into her hers and squeezed.

It will be OK. As long as we stay together and the plan works, we'll be OK.

After the Show and Red Lipstick

Saffron Fibbs stepped out of the wings and took a modest bow. The audience rose to their feet and cheered. As the roar subsided, but before Saffron and her applauding models had filed off the runway, journalists and fashionistas with backstage passes were flooding through a curtained doorway into the enormous changing room. Verity, Mikko and the others joined the throng. In the overexcited crush, Bliss Meadows felt something slipping into her pocket. She slapped her hand to her hip and felt a hard shape, a small plastic box.

When Verity and the others had made it through the doorway bottleneck and were close enough to see Saffron, she was already surrounded by air-kissing editors who were all telling her how 'simply divine' and 'utterly miraculous' her show had been.

'Marvellous, daaarling! We'll have those diviiiine silk dresses in our September issue.'

Verity was being jostled sideways. Someone behind her was pushing through. It was a TV crew, the cameraman walking backwards.

'Eden! Eden!' said the female journalist, waving her microphone. 'Eden? What did you think of the collection?'

The cameraman jabbed Verity in the ear as he passed.

'A work of genius, as usual,' said Eden, smiling.

'Are you and Saffron dating?'

Eden continued to smile as if he hadn't heard the question. He had now reached Saffron Fibbs and her flapping circle of editors. The circle parted and Eden manoeuvred in beside her where he kissed her cheek, posed for more pictures and smiled some more.

'Eden! Eden?' said a young male voice.

Eden tilted his head but his grin remained fixed.

'Eden, is it true that you are a crook and a cheat and have been lying to your customers for years?'

Eden raised an eyebrow but continued to smile. 'I thought we were here to celebrate Saffron's wonderful collection,' Eden laughed, 'not throw mud at me.'

Koshi glanced quickly at his notes and went on. 'Eden, are your ethical credentials a complete sham?'

Eden said nothing.

'Did you, or did you not, hire a company called KleenaPlanet International to clean up, and subsequently to cover up, a serious river-pollution incident in a Southern African village last year, an incident for which toxic chemicals, dumped from your fabric-processing plant, had been responsible?'

Eden smiled. The telly journalist thrust her microphone at Koshi. This was an interesting story.

'And did you lie to the Pollution Investigation Committee about the extent of the damage to wildlife, topsoil and water supply, that resulted in the eventual ruin of the thriving local agriculture?'

Eden smirked as the journalist flipped her microphone away from Koshi and towards him. 'It's rather unfair of you, young man,' he said, 'to hijack the Jiggery-Pokery show like this.' He shrugged and gave a patronising chuckle. 'But it seems you have got hold of some apparently incriminating information – all of it completely false.' He casually brushed back his fringe. 'You have to understand that I run a hugely successful global corporation and, sad as it may seem to young, idealistic people like yourself, the world is a wicked place My less honourable competitors are not afraid to cheat and steal and libel me at every possible opportunity. I have been reacting to slanderous, so-called leaked documents, like the one you mention, for many years – sometimes as many as three or four a day.'

Koshi's hand shook as he turned the page. They had predicted that the confrontation would be tough and that Eden would know exactly what to say and how to say it, but he'd demolished Koshi's first question without pausing for breath or dropping his smile. Koshi looked down at his notes again. This would be excellent practice for when he became a barrister, he thought, and had a difficult witness to cross-examine.

'What would you say, then, to the accusation that agents of your hugely successful global corporation have ruthlessly and cynically exploited farmers in Central America, in India, Malaysia and Eastern Europe, by promising trade deals that never materialised, and guaranteeing to build roads, schools and community projects that were never built?'

'Once again, I fear you have been misled,' said Eden. 'While

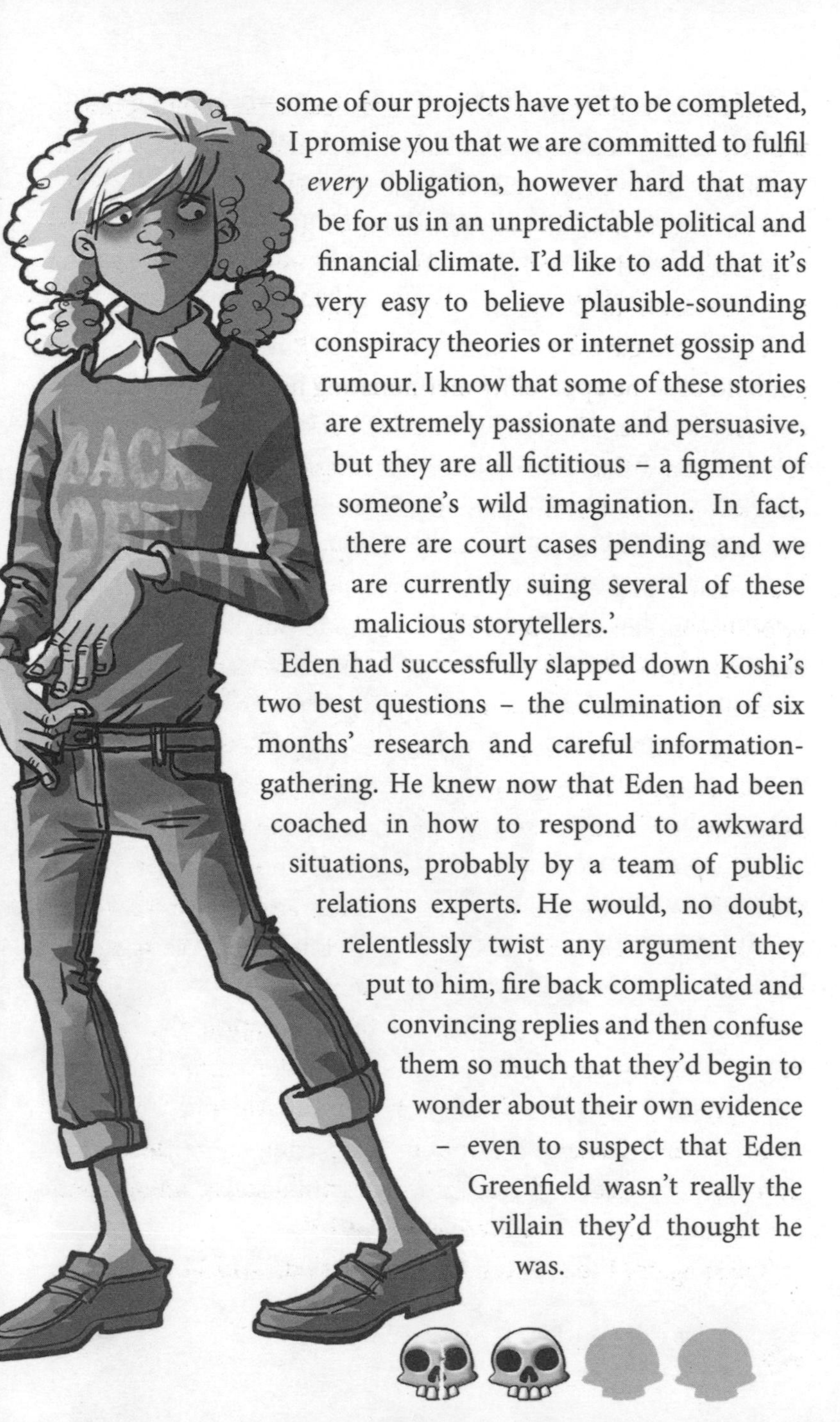

some of our projects have yet to be completed, I promise you that we are committed to fulfil *every* obligation, however hard that may be for us in an unpredictable political and financial climate. I'd like to add that it's very easy to believe plausible-sounding conspiracy theories or internet gossip and rumour. I know that some of these stories are extremely passionate and persuasive, but they are all fictitious – a figment of someone's wild imagination. In fact, there are court cases pending and we are currently suing several of these malicious storytellers.'

Eden had successfully slapped down Koshi's two best questions – the culmination of six months' research and careful information-gathering. He knew now that Eden had been coached in how to respond to awkward situations, probably by a team of public relations experts. He would, no doubt, relentlessly twist any argument they put to him, fire back complicated and convincing replies and then confuse them so much that they'd begin to wonder about their own evidence – even to suspect that Eden Greenfield wasn't really the villain they'd thought he was.

'Is it true there are videos that would prove what you just said is a lie?' squeaked Pye. Her body was rigid with fear.

'No, it's not!' Eden snapped. He tugged at his shirt cuffs and began to fiddle with the buttons. 'Now, if you'll excuse me, I have a tight schedule and must leave Saffron to her celebrations. Thank you, everyone.' He put up his hands, palms out, to indicate the interview was over.

'Wait!' yelled Pye. They couldn't let him leave yet. It had been over too quickly. He'd been rattled by that last question – she could tell from his sudden fidgeting – and they needed to press him further. The TV crew began to move away and the journalist was already pushing her microphone into the face of a stick-thin editor wearing giant shades who was announcing that she thought the Jiggery-Pokery show was the best she'd 'ever seen'. This was the news the fashion press wanted, not a load of geeky kids moaning about exploited farmers.

'Mr Greenfield? Wait! Mr Greenfield!' Pye elbowed her way through the crowd.

Eden glared at her then suddenly reached down, took her hand and dragged her backwards across the room. All eyes were now locked on the gushing editor and looking the other way as Eden pulled Pye behind a wall of mirrors. Verity and the others, trapped in the stampede, watched with horror as Pye's blond curls and Eden's floppy hair disappeared. Champagne was being served in another part of the room and people were now surging towards that, too. Vee prayed that Pye would remember their plan and wouldn't let Eden intimidate her.

Eden pushed Pye backwards behind the clothes racks and glared at a weedy youth who was sorting shoes, putting them back in the right boxes. The boy looked up and gawped at the tycoon.

'Why don't you go and get some champagne?' Eden said to the boy, his glare softening into a pleasant smile. 'You deserve a break after all your hard work.'

The boy dropped the purple suede boots he'd been clutching and scuttled away. Eden checked in all directions. No stylists, no models, no journalists with their microphones. They were alone. He'd grabbed the blonde girl because she looked like the weakest of the gang of teen 'irritations'. He'd had enough. He had decided that today was the day he would finally end this video fiasco – end it once and for all.

Eden bent over, grabbed her wrist again and whispered in her ear.

'Did you really imagine you could threaten me with your juvenile questions?' he hissed. 'Do you think I'm a moron? Did you and your stupid friends suppose I'd somehow incriminate myself in front of some TV cameras? You lot are pathetic amateurs!' He was squeezing her wrist so hard, digging in his fingernails, that Pye thought he might break the skin. She winced. 'Tell your mate,

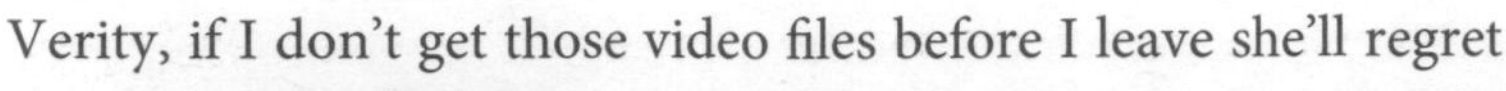

Verity, if I don't get those video files before I leave she'll regret it for the rest of her short, tragic life! You all will.'

Pye grimaced then replied, 'Your breath smells really repulsive. Makes me want to throw up.'

Koshi, red-faced, stumbled through the rack of clothes.

'Pye! You OK?'

'Yeah. Stinky-breath is just leaving.'

Still at the main entrance, Jelly relayed Eden's location back to her friends.

'Bliss is talking to the Boss. I think she's persuading him to do an interview on the red carpet . . .'

Back in the changing room, Verity, Mikko and the others gathered around Saffron in a curtained-off changing area.

'Right,' said Mum. 'We don't have much time.' She'd already begun to take off her clothes. Verity was removing hers, too.

Hamish coughed and looked the other way, embarrassed.

When he noticed that Ollie was staring at Verity, he put his hand over his friend's face. 'Oi! Give the birds a bit of privacy, mate!'

'Sorry,' said Ollie, sheepishly. He closed his eyes, then he and the other boys turned to face the wall.

When Jelly called again with an update three minutes later, Mum and Verity were almost ready. Mum, who'd wiped all her make-up off, was painting Vee's lips bright red.

'The Boss is nearly at the end of the carpet,' said Jelly.

'OK. Message received. Where are Mud and Rain?' Pye asked.

'They've brought the car already.'

'Don't let the Boss get in,' said Pye.

'How do I do that?' Jelly yelled, baffled. 'You want me to rugby tackle him to the ground or something?'

'I dunno!' said Pye, desperately. 'Vee, your mum has got to go *now!*'

Mum and Verity took a step back and looked at each other. It had been Mum's idea to switch places, but Verity had taken a lot of convincing. At first she'd thought it would be brilliant fun, then she'd remembered Goat-beard as Maisie Malone getting his head pounded to a bloody pulp by the troll. *Oh no! Mum would get her brains bashed out!*

But they'd finally decided that the best way to trap Eden was to confuse him with misdirection – a magician's trick. The switch was a great way to do it.

'I trust you to use some common sense,' said Verity.

Mum smiled. 'I'll be fine. I'm not a kid any more.' Mum perfectly mimicked Verity's voice. 'I learned how to walk and talk and dress myself, like, at least a week ago.'

'Don't talk to strangers,' said Vee. 'And put the dishwasher on when it's full.'

'Shuuut uuup!' said Mum, then enveloped her daughter in a hug.

'Be sensible,' Vee mumbled into Mum's shoulder. 'And pleeease be careful.'

'I will,' said Mum. 'Now, get out of my life, you controlling freak!'

'The taxi's here,' said Jelly's voice from the phone.

'Go!' said Verity.

Mum turned and dashed across the changing room.

The Red Van and the Bridge

Eden, who was about to get into the car, didn't spot the 'teenager' running out of a side entrance and into a waiting taxi, but Bliss did and so did Rain.

'There's that girl – the daughter,' said Bliss.

'She's trying to make a run for it,' said Rain from the front seat.

'She's got the phone. Look!' said Bliss.

She was right. The dark-haired girl was holding an iPhone in her hand and was pushing it into the pocket of her hooded sweatshirt.

'Stupid kid,' Eden growled. 'She must think I'm a fool. Follow that taxi.' IIe climbed into thc car.

'No, wait,' said Bliss. 'Send those two on their own. No point all of us chasing after her. It'll look odd if you don't turn up at the Perfect Eden shoot. I can get us another car.'

'Sometimes, Bliss, I'm glad I hired you,' said Eden, getting back out again. 'Not often, 'cause most of the time you're a waste of space.' He slammed the door then leaned through the front passenger window. 'Go get that phone. Don't muck it up this time and don't bother coming back until you've got it! Got it?'

Bliss got out a white business card, made a call, then stepped nervously from foot to foot as they waited for the limo to arrive. Eden tried not to look like he'd just been abandoned and smiled and waved at the paps and fans.

Minutes passed. Too many minutes. He was just beginning to lose his patience and had decided to threaten Bliss with sacking if the limo didn't come in the next thirty seconds, when a skinny youth with a dark fringe covering his eyes, dashed towards him down the red carpet. Eden recognised him. It was Verity's boyfriend – Axel, the driving instructor. The boy pushed something into Eden's hand.

'Verity thought she could trick you,' said the boy, his eyes wide with fear and glistening with tears. 'But I know you're serious. She's got a fake. The videos you were looking for –' he looked down at the iPhone in Eden's palm – 'are on that one. Will you leave us alone now?' He sniffed and wiped his nose with the back of his hand. Then he looked up and was confronted by Eden's famously perfect tombstone teeth, framed in a triumphant grin.

'I knew you'd see sense.'

The new limo pulled up to the kerb. Bliss blew out her cheeks with relief and reached for the door handle.

'But, you're not off the hook yet. None of you are.' Eden moved towards the car. 'You tell your girlfriend her scam was a really stupid mistake.'

The boy nodded and looked down at his shoes. Eden and Bliss got into the limo as the boy quickly wiped his damp cheek with his knuckle.

The back of the limo was vast, but Eden seemed to fill the back seat, spreading his knees wide and sliding his arms out across the leather trim. Bliss had pulled down a folding seat opposite him.

'Tell the driver to raise the screen,' Eden barked at her.

Bliss swivelled to face the uniformed chauffeur but, before she could open her mouth, Eden was barking again.

'Hey! Mate! Raise the screen!' Then, realising it was probably a mistake to drop his usual Mr Charming persona, he smiled and added, with a voice like honey, 'Not that we don't trust you, of course. Expect you're the soul of discretion. Just need a bit of peace, that's all.'

The chauffeur hunched forward, pressed a glowing button on the dash and the solid screen began to rise. As soon as the driver was no longer visible, Eden tapped the phone.

Bliss fastened her seatbelt and lifted her Blackberry again.

Eden chortled. 'I knew one of them would break . . . turn on his friends. Never imagined it would be the boyfriend. Ha! He was sobbing like a girl. Did you see?' He'd found the video files and was scrolling through them. 'This is the phone we were looking for.' He opened his hand and the phone dropped on to the carpeted floor. Then Eden raised his foot and brought his heel down on the screen with a crunch.

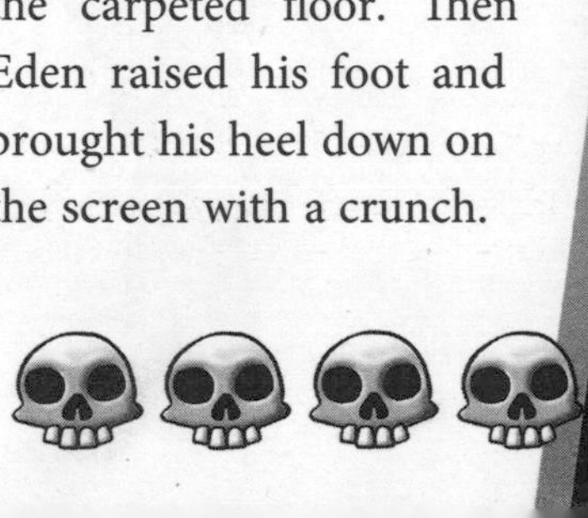

He stamped again. 'I'd told those idiots not to allow filming in the factories and when they said Saffron had been snooping and asking questions I couldn't believe it.' He screwed the heel of his shoe into the memory card, turning it to dust. 'Then the stupid woman told me she didn't make any copies or download it, so all it takes is my foot –' he laughed and stamped one final time – 'and it's gone for ever.' He looked up at Bliss. 'Call Mud and Rain. Tell 'em they can deal with Little Miss Fibbs another day.' He rubbed his fingers across his lips. 'She's more useful alive. I might use her to control her mother. I bet I could get Saffron to agree to anything now, eh? I'll own her little fashion brand in no time – get her working for me.'

Eden's chuckle made Bliss shiver. He was evil. Completely puppy-kicking, butterfly-squashing, sick-minded, black-hearted evil.

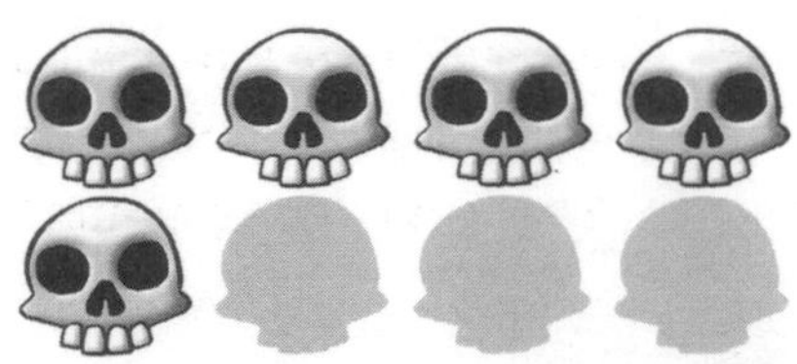

Mikko jumped through the side door of the red van and Hamish pulled and slammed it shut.

'Go! Go!' he yelled.

Ollie, who was in the driver's seat, looked over his shoulder, released the hand break and rammed his foot on the accelerator. The van darted out of the parking space, throwing all the passengers backwards with a jolt.

'Woah!' yelled Hamish. 'Watch it, Ollie! We want to get there with some of us still alive!'

Nobody laughed.

'Did he go for it?' Pye asked Mikko.

'Yeah. I think so.' Mikko slid on to one of the benches that ran down each side of the van.

'Did you look really upset?'

'Even managed a tear,' said Mikko.

Hamish slapped him on the back. 'Well done, mate. Vee said you were a brilliant actor.'

'Is she OK?'

'She was lovin' that after-show party,' said Ollie. 'Y'know, drinking champagne with male models and shmoozin' with all those glam fashionistas.'

'She does look exactly like her mum,' said Hamish.

'I know,' said Mikko. 'That's kinda what got us into this trouble in the first place.'

'Right, that's enough chatter,' said Pye, trying to sound businesslike. 'Vee and the others are safely on their way and we can't hang about either. We'd better change into our costumes.'

'Why's it taking so long?' Eden moaned. 'Is the driver lost or something?'

'No, I think it's just heavy traffic,' said Bliss.

'Is he stupid? Tell him to try a different route, then.' He tutted impatiently. 'I hate sitting in traffic. It's such a time-sucker.'

Smashing the iPhone had been exhilarating. Eden felt invincible. He had complete control, absolute power, could manipulate anyone to do his bidding, could crush his pathetic opponents under his heel. But this limitless confidence came with a bad temper and it was making Bliss nervous. She twisted in her seat again and tapped on the partition. With a sigh, the screen dropped a few centimetres.

'Yes, Miss?' said the driver.

'Um. W-what's the hold-up? C-can we try a different route?'

'I'm afraid not, Miss. We're stuck on a bridge, you see.'

'Oh, right. We're stuck on a bridge, Eden.'

'Well, tell him to get off it,' Eden spat.

'Can we get off it?' Bliss asked.

'That's the thing about bridges,' said the driver. 'All you can do is go forwards or backwards. Can't turn off, unless you wanna go for a swim.' He chuckled at his own joke.

'Then go friggin' forwards or backwards, then! It's not quantum physics!' Eden shouted, finally losing it. Being polite and charming didn't matter any more.

'Actually, sir.' The driver turned to face Eden. 'I think there's been an accident. Might take a while to clear.'

Eden slapped his hand down on the seat beside him then leaned forward and grabbed the door handle. 'I can't sit here any longer with a couple of hopeless idiots. I'm gonna go and sort this out.'

Bliss and the driver exchanged worried glances as Eden leapt from the limo and began to stride between the stationary cars. He'd only gone about ten paces when a young policeman stepped in front of him and barred his path.

'Sorry, sir. Can I ask you to return to you vehicle?'

'What's going on?' Eden looked down at the policeman's hand touching his lapel. He pushed it aside with disgust as if the officer's hand were a piece of putrid, worm-infested meat. 'I've got a very important photo shoot this afternoon. I'm already late because I'm surrounded by imbeciles. And now you are leaving grease stains on my rather expensive suit. Do you know who I am? Let my car through. Or are you an imbecile, too?'

'Not an imbecile, no, sir. But, even an imbecile would be able to tell you that you can't drive a car through a solid object. As you can see—' The policeman pointed up ahead at a red van parked at an angle across both lanes. 'There's a van . . . see? . . . and a girl knocked off her bike. We're waiting for the ambulance.'

Eden screwed up his face and raised his hand to shield his eyes. It had become a sunny spring day after several days of grey skies and rain. He could see a huddle of people – passing pedestrians, concerned bystanders and another police officer. At their feet was a crumpled bike and a body lying on the road. It was covered by a blanket but he could see the girl's hair. It was blond and frizzy, like that irritating kid at the fashion show. *Hope it is her*, he thought, and returned to the car with a smirk on his face.

The Other Van and the T-Shirts

Verity looked down at the new phone in her hand and the tube carriage tilted. She felt faint. Her head wasn't spinning because they had just run all the way from the Show venue to the tube station, but because she'd just noticed she had absolutely no signal because they were underground. She felt a horrible wave of nausea. They wouldn't be able to communicate with the others until they were out of the tunnels again. Whoever had suggested they take the tube to avoid the traffic chaos hadn't thought of that.

'Stupid, stupid,' she groaned and slapped her palm to her forehead. It didn't stop her head from spinning.

One by one, the cars, taxis and vans behind the limo backed up, turned, zigzagged backwards and forwards and unravelled themselves off the bridge like a piece of knitting.

‘Drive!’ Eden shouted as the chauffeur reversed gently away from the accident.

Back on the road and satisfied that they were again making progress, Eden jerked his hand to indicate that the screen be raised.

‘Don’t ever hire this limo again.’ Eden tapped his temple. ‘That driver is clearly a moron. And he thinks he’s a comedian. I hate comedians.’ He sneered and looked out of the window. ‘And foetus policemen.’

They were approaching another river crossing. The limo rounded the corner and got all four wheels on the next bridge before it rolled to a stop. Ahead, like a double strand of beads, were glowing red lights. Once again, all the traffic was stationary. Once again, Eden leapt from the car. This was unacceptable, intolerable.

Another van blocked their path. This one was small and silver, not much more than a cart. It had a flat rear tyre, had swerved on to a traffic island and come to rest wedged against a *keep left* sign. On the side of the silver van was a picture of a sausage stabbed by a fork and the words,

GUT BUCKET

EXTREME EATING TOURNAMENTS

Test your stomach against GUT BUCKET and win £££s

The back of the van was open, doors blown wide, as if its contents had burst out. Debris from the accident – a slick of jellied eels, rosettes of fire-red chillies and mounds of mashed potato – covered the road in a peculiar food carpet. A slim youth with ginger curls escaping from beneath a knitted cap was scooping shovels of jellied eels into buckets. *Surely this was not Gut Bucket*, thought Eden. *He was too puny. A stick insect. Any test of stomach capacity against this specimen would win you plenty of £s.* Eden chuckled at the bizarre scene, then noticed the bus tucked up behind his limo. They were trapped again. He slammed his fist down on the roof.

'Urgh!' he bellowed at Gut Bucket. 'Move your friggin' food out of my road, you skinny freak!'

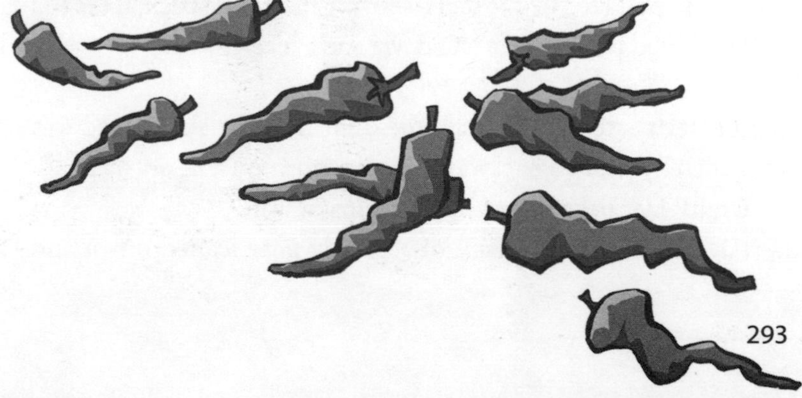

The paparazzi waiting outside the dockside studio had never seen a celebrity arrive on foot before. A limousine, a large posh car or, at the very least, a black taxi would be the norm. Bethany London and Flash Campbell had both arrived in limos with a bodyguard and an assistant five minutes ago, while Tom Wilde had climbed out of a cab with his publicist. But was that the famous fashion designer, Saffron Fibbs, followed by four geeky teenagers, jogging along the street? It looked exactly like her. Saffron waved and smiled. Saffron was dating Eden Greenfield, wasn't she? And this was a Perfect Eden photo shoot, so it must be her.

'Saffron! Saffron!' they shouted.

She paused very briefly to pose for a few shots, then pressed the buzzer.

'It's . . . it's us,' said Saffron, a little out of breath. 'Ver— I mean, Saffron Fibbs.'

The door clicked open and they all slipped inside.

Verity opened Mum's expensive leather handbag, extracted a cosmetics wipe and removed all her make-up. Then she took out the phone again. Still no message from Mum. Why had she not called? Or sent a text? Had their plan worked? Or was she . . . ?

The memory of the troll bashing Maisie Malone's head flashed into her mind. *Eugh!* She wobbled on the first step of the winding staircase and grasped the handrail to steady herself. Then she followed the others and pounded up the stairs, shoving the phone back in the bag as she ran and pulling out a blond wig and a black t-shirt.

Blond Verity stepped through the door into the studio and was immediately pushed backwards by an enormous, fleshy hand.

'Urgh!' Her back slammed up against a wall.

'ID.' A bald man the size of a grizzly bear leaned down and

breathed onions into her face. 

'I'm catering,' she explained, wrinkling her nose and trying not to inhale. 'From the catering company. Look.'

She pushed his hand away from the front of her t-shirt and pointed at the logo – a sausage on a fork and the words,

GUT BUCKET
LOCATION FOOD

'It's OK,' said Koshi, who was wearing a straight black wig and pointing at his own identical t-shirt. 'She's with us. Catering.'

The grizzly bear released her and Verity followed Jelly, Grace, Chen and Mikko across the studio. In the far corner, Vincent was setting up the shoot. He had already unfurled a new white paper backdrop that hung like a ski jump from a roll high on the wall. It almost covered the floor. He was now unscrewing a bolt to adjust the height of a floor light with a giant tent-like reflector.

'How's it going?' asked Vince.

'OK so far,' said Vee. 'What was all that about?' She nodded at the grizzly bear.

'Worried about stalkers, aren't they . . . these celebs,' said Vince. 'Can't go anywhere without a bodyguard. That one is Bethany's.'

It was another thing they hadn't really considered – the possibility that the celebs would bring bodyguards and assistants. After all, Verity's mum never had a bodyguard. *But I suppose Mum has Callista. Callista is like a whole army of bodyguards. Or a vampire bodyguard with poison fangs, snakes for hair and a petrifying stare.*

Vee took note of Flash's assistant and Tom's publicist, both talking into phones, perched at either end of the shabby sofa as she and Mikko had been just days before. She hoped they wouldn't be a problem.

'Any news from James?' she asked Vince.

'Last text, they were still with Mikko on the bridge, but I don't think they'll be there for long. He says Eden's really angry.'

Verity's mouth contorted into a lopsided grimace. She wished Mum would text to say she was safe and she wished Pye and Mikko would get there. She needed the support of her best friends. They probably only had a few minutes before Eden Greenfield arrived, so she had to go ahead now. The plan was risky and she had no idea if her hunch was correct. It might backfire or make everything worse. It could be a disaster! Eden was right about one thing: many lives were in her hands.

'They're over there,' said Vince looking over at an area that had been screened off by racks of clothes and one of the sofas. 'Your celebs.'

'OK,' said Vee. 'Let's get on with it.'

The boys headed for the kitchen, pulling laptops out of their backpacks, then Vee, Grace and Jelly walked around the racks of clothes. Sitting in three canvas chairs in front of three mirrors were Tom Wilde, Bethany London and Flash Campbell.

Verity and the others had all pulled on wigs and t-shirts as they came up the stairs and, while Vee's and the boys' said they were caterers, Jelly's and Grace's were white with a logo which read,

SAY CHEESE

studio styling

above a cartoon grin. When they'd begun making their plan, Jelly and Grace had automatically been allocated the stylists' roles until Koshi had argued that it was 'blatant gender stereotyping' for the girls to do hair and make-up while the boys were police officers and techies. Then Koshi, trying to prove his point, had made a disastrous attempt at applying liquid eye liner and Jelly had stunned them all with her mastery of hair-strengtheners and super-shine wax, so they'd agreed Koshi should stay out of harm's way – serve sandwiches or be Chen's assistant.

'OK,' said Verity, taking a deep breath. 'Wish me luck.'

'Nah!' Grace whispered. 'Actors always say "break a leg".'

*

'I won't have to tolerate drivers like that when I'm *Sir* Eden Greenfield.'

Bliss followed Eden up the echoing staircase.

'The police won't dare to let me sit in traffic jams when I have my knighthood. They'll wave me through.' He span around and glared at Bliss. 'You got confirmation yet? How long does it take to get confirmation?'

'I-I think I said before. Y-you can't just demand to be on the honours list. You have to be nominated and chosen,' said Bliss.

'Fine. So all you have to do is talk to the nominators and the choosers, give 'em a wad of cash and bingo! Honestly, Bliss. You really are dumb, aren't you?'

'Y-you can't pay for a knighthood, Eden.'

'Of course you can. Enough money and you can buy anything! Information, buildings, countries, people, celebrities to support your stupid charity . . . murder.' He grinned and raised his eyebrows at her.

They reached the top and pushed open the door into the bright dockside studio. The cheerful spring sunshine made the already impressive view into something completely breathtaking. Eden smiled with satisfaction. Bliss had suggested this relocation and, he decided, it was probably the only good idea she'd ever had. Perhaps he wouldn't sack her. Not today, anyway.

‘Hi, Mr Greenfield,’ said Vincent. ‘Welcome to Dockside Studios. We’re not quite ready for you in hair and make-up, but can I offer you some refreshment?’ Chen came towards them from the kitchen, carrying a tray of champagne glasses. His hands trembled slightly and the glasses clinked together.

Eden smiled benignly and Vince relaxed. James may have reported that the millionaire tycoon had been ‘like a volcano of anger’ in the limo, he thought, but he seemed to have calmed down now. Not even a bubble of lava.

‘Thank you.’ He took a glass with a gracious nod. ‘Are the others here?’

‘Just getting a spray and a retouch . . . in the paint shop.’ Vince laughed at his own lame joke, but Eden’s smile didn’t flicker or dim, even though he was now thoroughly sick of imbeciles and comedians.

Verity heard the low growl of male voices around the corner in the studio. She hoped it was just Vince talking to the assistants and not Eden arriving already. He would be far too early. She had only just begun talking to Flash, Tom and Bethany and she still wasn’t sure of her hunch. Verity closed her eyes. *I need more time. And I need Pye and Mikko to help me out!*

‘You mean . . .’ said Flash, pointing at the iPad that Koshi had put in his hands. A jerky video was playing – the one from YouTube of the electric car driving over the Millennium Bridge. ‘This is you?’ He looked up at Verity, eyes wide with astonishment. ‘Cool!’

‘Pah!’ Tom Wilde snorted with derision. ‘*You* were driving *that*?’

‘Yes. That was me . . . and my friend.’ She looked back at Flash

Campbell. 'Actually, it was you who taught me how to do it. You said "do something unexpected".'

Flash frowned. 'But, we've not met, have we? And I'm a Formula One champion, not a driving instructor.'

'In *Demon Streets*.'

Flash's mouth burst into a grin. 'You play *Demon Streets*?'

Verity's stomach flipped. She nodded.

'I met you in the game?' Flash was delighted. 'What's your avatar name?' He started bouncing in the canvas chair like an excited kid.

'Maisie Malone,' said Verity. 'You're Steve Speed.'

Flash whooped and nodded. 'Yeah! Wow! This is so cool! I've never met another online player in the flesh. I love *Demon Streets* but I'd kinda assumed most of the other players were, like, nine-year-olds in Korea or something. None of my mates play. They think it's nerdy.'

'I play,' said Tom Wilde.

Everyone looked at Tom and Verity's stomach flipped again. Her hunch was right.

'You're Zac the Knife,' said Vee. 'You taught my sidekick how to use his sword.'

Tom leaned over and shook Vee's hand. 'Excellent to meet you, Maisie.'

'Our mates, Ollie and Hamish, play too,' said Koshi. 'And we never knew.'

'I played once at Ollie's house,' said Grace. 'It's really addictive.'

Verity smirked then shivered as a blast of cold air hit her neck. Someone had entered the dressing area behind her. She felt the same ominous chill she'd had in Eden's office: the feeling of doom when Mud and Rain had walked in. She looked over at her friends, not wanting to turn around, in case he recognised her. She silently mouthed the word, 'Eden?'

Koshi, Grace and Jelly nodded, their faces now petrified by fear. It might only be a second or two before Eden guessed who they were. They hadn't even had the chance to show the celebs the factory videos yet or to explain their significance. Nor had they begun to present Koshi's additional research on the subcontractors or their theory that Eden had tricked the three celebs into supporting his charity. Verity had hoped to have them on her side and to have planted the seed of suspicion before he arrived.

'What's going on?' said Eden.

Verity scratched her itchy forehead and her blond wig shifted slightly. Then she felt it being ripped from her head.

GAME OVER

A fan-shaped spray of blood flew through the air as the troll's head tumbled across the cobbles and came to rest in the gutter. It joined his right arm which had been severed cleanly just below the shoulder, the hand still clutching the nail-encrusted club. Ben Blades grinned and wiped the troll blood from his sword with the cuff of his sleeve. He and Maisie, who now had her body back good as new, had decided it would be pointless to play the troll's puerile mind games. Better to simply behead the ugly, hairy slob and cross the bridge without fuss. Ben's sword lessons from Zac the Knife had been very handy.

Numbers flashed: 22,000 . . . 25,000 . . . 27,000. Killing a troll was a big win. Maisie had almost doubled her points. They would face the challenge of the Tower with fewer weapons but a seriously increased score.

You switched with your mum?' said Eden.

'Duh!' Verity resorted to sarcasm in the face of dread, as she'd done before, in his office. Her heart was now pounding. 'Of course I did, moron. And you fell for it again. You're not very bright, are you?'

'What's going on?' asked Bethany.

Eden threw Vee's blond wig to the floor 'Nothing to worry about. A small irritation, that's all. I'll deal with it . . . Just make a quick call.' He seized Verity's arm, dragging her from the make-up area and across the studio.

'Everything all right, sir?' asked the grizzly bear still guarding the door.

'Yes, yes . . . nothing.' Eden pulled her again. This time towards the window.

The assistants on the sofa shifted in their seats and Vincent stepped forward. But Vee held up her free hand and managed a smile. Vince backed away and the assistants sagged again.

'Bliss,' Eden hissed. 'Get over here.' Bliss reluctantly followed them to the window. Her face was white with panic. 'Get that pair on the phone,' he growled through gritted white teeth. 'Tell 'em they switched. And tell 'em the job's back on. And tell 'em I want multiple teen suicides to be tomorrow's headline!' He glanced at the assistants on the sofa to make sure they hadn't overheard. They were oblivious and hunched over their smart phones again.

'No!' said Bliss.

'What?'

'I said, "no".'

Eden grunted. 'You won't make the call?'

Bliss nodded.

'You *refuse*?'

'I w-won't call them for you and I won't tell them to murder people and I'm handing in my notice. I quit.'

'Keep your voice down. You can't quit,' he whispered. 'You're sacked. With no references. You'll never work in fashion again . . . or anywhere.' Then he grunted. He'd had an even better idea. 'In fact, you'll be having a little accident, too.' He smiled.

'Y-you don't scare me.' This was clearly untrue because Bliss was shaking.

'Gimme that,' Eden snatched the Blackberry out of Bliss's hand. 'I'll call them myself.' As he dialled, the three celebs, the 'stylists' and the 'caterers' moved silently into the studio. Eden waved at them. 'No probs, everyone. Go back to your hair gel and all that. The shoot's gonna go ahead as soon as . . .' He paused. 'Hey, why aren't the creative director and the team from the ad agency here? And who . . .?' Something else was odd. His mouth fell open. 'You?'

The friends looked at each other then back at Eden. They nodded and removed their wigs. Verity's stomach clenched. He'd taken a bit longer to work it out, but it was still happening too quickly. They weren't ready. Mum hadn't called to say she was safe yet.

'Good!' Eden's smile became a sinister leer. 'You're all in one place.' He tapped the Blackberry. 'Makes it easier. We won't have to round you all up. Where's your boyfriend, Verity? I don't see him. He dump you, then? Suppose he didn't tell you he gave me the videos behind your back, eh?' He scanned the young faces again. 'And that blonde mate of yours is missing. She dump you, too?' He chuckled. Perhaps she *had* been the body on the bridge.

'Eden, mate?' said Tom Wilde. 'These kids have been showing us some stuff.'

Eden looked at him, startled. 'Ignore them. They're – liars, con artists. They tried something similar at a fashion show earlier this afternoon. Quite pathetic, actually.' He waved the phone dismissively. 'It's a foolish attempt to discredit me. Don't worry. My lawyers are already on the case.' He held the phone to his ear and the room went silent. They waited. Everyone seemed to hold their breath. Was he calling Mud and Rain? Why weren't they answering? Eden's face was expressionless but Verity was close enough to notice a slight flicker in his left cheek. Then he straightened up and threw back his head.

'It's me. Where are you?' he spat impatiently into the phone. Then he stopped and nodded several times. Mud or Rain must have been answering. 'She had a what?' Eden continued. 'An accident? Saffron had an accident? That's terrible.' Eden's shoulders dropped and his face crumpled.

Verity felt her legs begin to buckle beneath her. Eden let go of her arm so she swayed and staggered backwards. *Mum has had an accident.* She recovered her balance and looked up at Eden. The troll's evil smirk looked back. *The switch backfired and Mum is . . .*

Then Eden brought his left hand up towards his wrist . . . and twiddled with his cuff button.

'Finish up there, then come over to the studio. I've got another job for you.' Eden ended the call but continued to play with the button. 'Verity. That was Rain. I'm afraid something awful . . .'

Verity felt dizzy. Mum's voice echoed inside her head. *Just so you know, I can tell you're lying when you bite your lip . . . you bite your lip . . . you're lying when you bite your lip . . .*

'You're lying,' she blurted.

'What?'

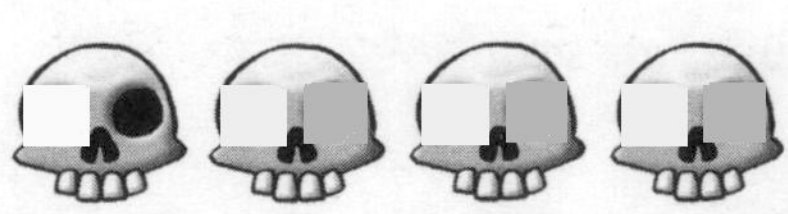

'You're lying. I know you're lying. It takes one to know one and I know you're a liar.'

'You're mistaken.' Eden continued to twiddle. 'There's been a terrible—'

'You play with your cuff button when you lie. I've noticed it before. So I know there hasn't been an accident. Mum's fine. Nobody answered that call. You were talking to their voicemail because they're probably in police custody by now.'

'I assure you they are not.' He twiddled the button again, then realised what he was doing and stopped.

'Chen,' Verity called out, keeping her eyes fixed on Eden. 'Are we ready to go live?'

Chen, who was clutching a laptop, stepped forward and nodded.

Verity took a deep breath. *I'm not ready,* she thought. *But here goes.* 'You're lying because you want to scare us. But you can't scare us or hurt us any more. We gave you that phone and allowed you to destroy it because we have something better than the videos.'

'Oh, yes?' Eden was unconvinced.

'Yes. You incriminated *yourself.*'

'Nonsense!' Eden again played with his cuff.

'We have footage of you, just now . . . in the limousine.' Vee could feel her whole body pulsating in time with her frantic heartbeat. In fact, the whole floor was vibrating. No, it wasn't her heart, it was . . . It was feet on the stairs! Footsteps were rumbling up the stairs. The door flew open and Mikko, Pye, Hamish and Ollie ran into the studio. They were still wearing their costumes. Hamish and Ollie wore police uniforms, Mikko a curly ginger wig and Pye had fake 'accident' blood on her face. In an instant,

Pye and Mikko were at Verity's side, wrapping her in a hug, just in time to stop her dropping to the floor.

'Urgh, I've never been so glad to see anyone in my life!' Verity sobbed.

'Thanks,' said Ollie. 'I'm quite pleased to see you, too.'

Vee, Pye and Mikko burst into laughter.

'She doesn't mean you,' said Hamish, pushing his friend sideways.

'Oh, OK,' said Ollie, confused. 'Any food left?'

Verity looked at her two best friends. Pye grinned and squeezed her arm. Mikko awkwardly patted her on the back 'You all right?' he asked. 'Got a message from your mum yet?'

'No,' said Vee. 'But, he tried to tell me she's de—' She couldn't finish.

Pye squeezed her friend harder.

'But I knew he was lying so we were just about to show him the stuff from the limo. The stuff we're about to post on—'

'This is ridiculous,' said Eden and turned to the grizzly bear. 'These kids have gained access to the studio under false pretences. They are dangerous activists . . . criminals . . . terrorists! They should be arrested.'

The grizzly, a little confused, took hold of Mikko's sleeve.

'Hey! Wait a minute!' Bethany London stepped forward. 'I want to hear what they have to say.'

'Bethany, I can assure you. It's not worth hearing.' Eden was starting to look worried.

'They may not be stylists or caterers,' said Bethany. 'But I'm pretty sure they're not terrorists either. They've been showing us videos and documents and I want to ask some questions about this charity of yours.'

Tom Wilde and Flash Campbell nodded in agreement.

'I'm not sure I want to be involved in Perfect Eden until I get some answers.' Bethany turned and smiled at Verity. 'I play *Demon Streets,* too.'

'Really?' Vee was astonished. She'd recognised Tom and Flash in the game, but not Bethany. *Have I met Bethany's avatar? That would be the most amazing coincidence.* Bethany nodded. Vee rapidly trawled back through her game memory. *A female character. The woman in the diner? Felicity Freud the demon psychologist? Pamela Pout? Yes! She must be the glamorous Pamela Pout.*

'Your sidekick cut off my head,' said Bethany.

'What?' Ben Blades hadn't cut Pamela's head off. Verity frowned 'You're not . . . You can't be . . . You're Veronica Vamp?'

'Yep!'

Of course, Vee thought. *Bethany is famous in Hollywood for playing villains. She's a villain expert. Don't know why it didn't occur to me.*

'Oops! Sorry!'

Something shuddered in Verity's jacket. She dipped her hand into the pocket and brought out her phone.

NEW EMAIL MESSAGE

It was from Mum with a jpeg attached.

Vee darling,

Switch a complete
success – eventually.
Sorry it took so long.
Once your two nasty
stalkers were inside
Jiggery-Pokery office
Callista's trap
worked perfectly. See
attached pic.
Text you are ok too,
please.
Love you, Mum
xxxxxxxxxx

Verity looked up at Eden and smiled. She had her confirmation, at last, that Mum was safe. They could go ahead.

'Your childish little threats are pathetic,' said Eden 'You DO know that, if you try to broadcast anything, I can have it stopped like that!' He clicked his fingers. 'I just have to make one call to someone who owes me a favour. And when I've done that, I'll arrange the painful deaths of each and every one of you . . . and your parents and brothers and sisters and sweet little grannies.' He seemed to have forgotten that Bethany, Tom and Flash were in the room.

'Don't listen to him,' said Bliss. 'He said all that to me, about hurting my family if I didn't do what he said, but I decided I'm not afraid of him any more.'

'Yeah, good for you! Go girl!' sang the others.

'Show him the button,' said Mikko.

'OK,' said Bliss and she began to unfasten a button from her shirt. It fell into her palm and she held it out to show her boss. It was the same button that Verity had slipped into Bliss's pocket at the fashion show. The button from the shop called SpyStuff.

'How's that gonna harm me?' Eden sneered.

'Everything you've said or done since leaving Mum's fashion show has been transmitted,' said Verity. Bliss took a small black box out of her pocket – the transmitter.

'To our computers,' said Chen.

'And we've edited it and downloaded it to YouTube,' said Koshi.

Chen swivelled his laptop so that Eden could see the screen.

'We're ready to go live,' said Verity.

'I don't believe you,' said Eden, folding his arms.

Chen tapped 'return' then turned up the volume. A jerky image appeared on the screen – a figure standing by a black car. There was the sound of rapid breathing then a voice:

Go get that phone. Don't muck it up this time and don't bother coming back until you've got it! Got it?

The image cut to inside, the same male figure, sprawled in the back of a car, legs spread wide. The sound of the car engine was almost inaudible under a loud heartbeat – Bliss's heartbeat.

This is the phone we were looking for.

The male figure dropped something out of his hand on to the carpet and stamped on it. *Crunch!*

I'd told those idiots not to allow filming in the factories and when they said Saffron had been snooping and asking questions I couldn't believe it . . . the stupid woman told me she didn't make any copies . . .

The man ground his heel down, turning the phone to dust.

. . . all it takes is my foot . . . and it's gone for ever.

He stamped again.

Call Mud and Rain. Tell 'em they can deal with Little Miss Fibbs another day.

On the screen the man rubbed his fingers across his lips.

Pye gave Verity another squeeze.

She's more useful alive. I might use her to control her mother. I bet I could get Saffron to agree to anything now, eh?

The man raised his eyebrows.

The image cut to another shot. The figure was outside the car, shouting.

Urgh! Move your friggin' food out of my road, you skinny freak!

Another cut to a dark lobby.

Y-you can't just demand to be on the honours list. You have to be nominated and chosen.

Fine. So all you have to do is talk to the nominators and the choosers, give 'em a wad of cash and bingo! Honestly, Bliss. You really are dumb, aren't you?

Y-you can't pay for a knighthood, Eden.

Of course you can. Enough money and you can buy anything! Information, buildings, countries, people, celebrities to support your stupid charity . . . murder.

Finally, the figure stood in front of a vast window and a breathtaking view.

Tell 'em the job's back on. And tell 'em I want multiple teen suicides to be tomorrow's headline!

'Go live, Verity,' said Flash Campbell, scowling. 'Press the button.'

'Yeah. Press it,' agreed Tom Wilde.

'Go live!' said Bethany.

'Go live!' said everyone.

Verity pressed 'return'.

EPILOGUE

The Tower

'YOU CAN'T DEFEAT ME WITH YOUR PUNY WEAPONS!'

The *demon* Boss leered down at them and stamped his foot.

The tower shook.

Ben Blades fell to the floor and began to pick up the shattered remains of his precious sword. All he'd done was swing it against the demon's massive thigh and it had broken into pieces like an icicle.

'That's one weapon down,' said Maisie. All she had left now were her matching pearl-handled knife and reloaded pistol. She pulled them out from under her coat.

The Boss shuddered.

Maisie looked down at her hands. *He flinched*, she thought. *Why did he flinch?* Then she smiled. Were all those weird clues finally making sense? *Demons avoid water, are allergic to seafood, they loathe the seaside . . . and what about the Mole's button . . .? The pearl button?*

'Mother-of-pearl!' yelled Maisie. 'It's made from shells . . . seashells.'

'What?' said Ben Blades.

'The Mole's clue: it's not buttons – it's mother-of-pearl that will defeat the Boss. I think he might be allergic to it. You know, like a vampire is to silver and sunlight.' She tossed the pearl-handled knife towards Ben, who caught it skilfully and jabbed it at the *demon*. The Boss took a step backwards.

'Attack!' cried Maisie.

'Die!' cried Ben.

'NOOOOOOOOOOOOO!' cried the Boss. 'NOT THE MOTHER-OF-PEARRRRRRLLLLL!'

Maisie Malone and Ben Blades rushed at the *demon*, firing and stabbing.

+100,000
bonus points
score: 127,000
options
play
II

Verity pushed her hand into Mikko's jeans pocket and tilted her head then pressed her lips harder against his. Mikko's tongue had been exploring her mouth for the last three and a half minutes and Verity wondered if it had found what it was searching for. She sent her own tongue in to help out and ran the tip along his teeth. His mouth was somehow cool but warm at the same time and tasted delicious.

'Mmm,' she moaned. She smiled and began to pull away, even though she wanted to do this for ever. But she'd been standing there, wrapped in his arms, snogging for what felt like days and her cheeks ached. Mikko ended the kiss with a series of tiny, fluttering pecks across her now-tingling lips. She sighed. That was nice. It had been one of the best yet. She'd probably put it in her top five snogs of all time.

All five had been with Mikko, of course. The other boys from school didn't feature on the list any more. The best one – their All-time Greatest Snog – had been their first. The day they had defeated Eden, when they had realised that they were safe and it was all over, Mikko had grabbed her and they had kissed so hard that she had thought her head might explode. And her heart.

The second best was probably the day he'd turned up, without warning, at the school gates. It had been a whole

month since he'd returned to face his mum at home in Berkshire. She'd had texts and emails from him, to say that he'd got a load of grief and been grounded 'for the rest of his life'. But Vee had convinced herself that during their time apart he'd probably forget about their All-time Greatest Snog and the reasons he'd even liked her in the first place. She'd probably never see him again, she thought.

Then she'd walked out of the Technology Block and seen a hunched figure, with a long fringe over his eyes, cute peach-fuzz on his top lip, one knee bent, his foot against the wall. She'd been so excited, she'd almost hugged one of the passing junior-school trolls. She'd sprinted across the teacher's car park, narrowly missing getting squashed under the wheels of Mr Kemp's reversing Honda. *That* snog had been awesome! And in front of the whole school! Almost #1 on the Snog Chart but not quite.

Now they met up every weekend. They laughed sometimes about being tied together in the boot of a car and how each one of their early romantic moments had been ruined by Eden and his minions. Verity's stomach still did a sickening backflip when she remembered what had happened to them. Just like it had flipped when she'd seen the news story.

EDEN VANISHES

The internet had buzzed with chatter about Eden Greenfield since the YouTube video and then all the other incriminating documents that had been leaked to the media. The handsome tycoon, once adored and admired, had turned out to be a liar, a crook and a thoroughly unpleasant bloke. There followed endless speculation about what he'd do next – hire lawyers, fight the authenticity of the damning evidence, end up in prison or make a run for it and go into exile. The police charged Kevin Burridge (Mud) and Chardonnay Pollock (Rain) with a long list of nasty offences and issued an arrest warrant for Derek Greenfield (Eden). Then Eden disappeared.

Six months later, Verity was playing *Demon Streets* version 5.0 in her room. She was supposed to be doing her maths homework, but *Demon Streets* was way more fun than maths. Maisie Malone and Ben Blades had joined forces with Steve Speed, Zac the Knife and a resurrected Veronica Vamp to create an invincible gang – The Pearl Gang. They worked together, collaborating, gaining more points than any other online players. There was now a Pearl Gang Facebook page, several fan sites and a club in South Korea where members dressed up like them every weekend (they were all under ten and all girls). On Level 48 the Pearl Gang met a new foe. He was a good-looking demon with a hair-trigger temper and he was called Guy Gorgeous. Guy Gorgeous had a unique ability for a demon. He was completely immune to mother-of-pearl.

Introducing Scarlett...

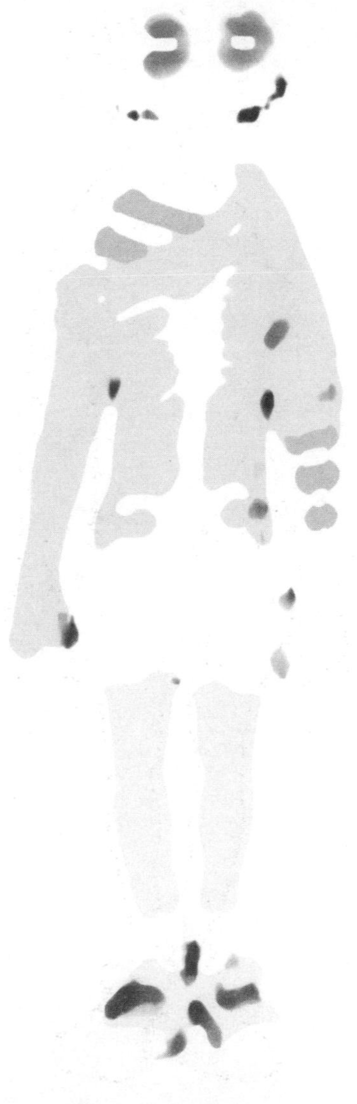

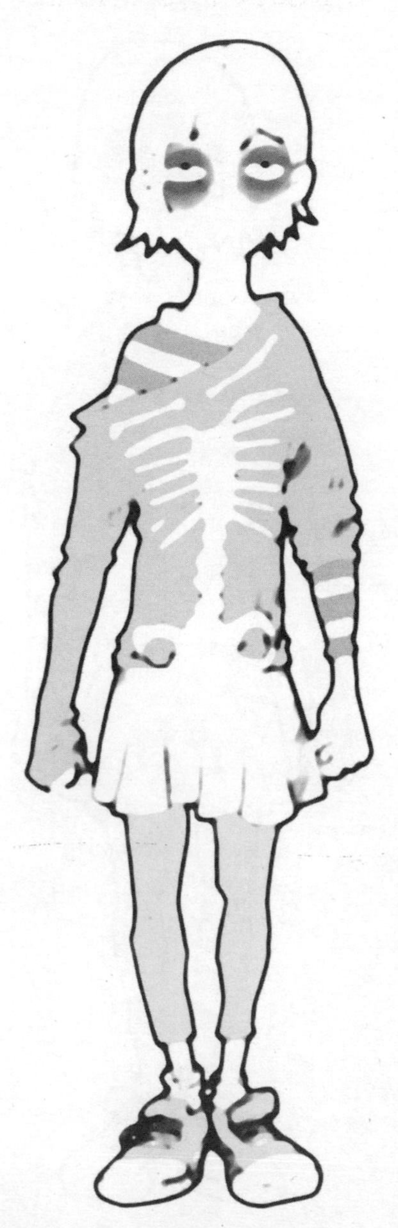

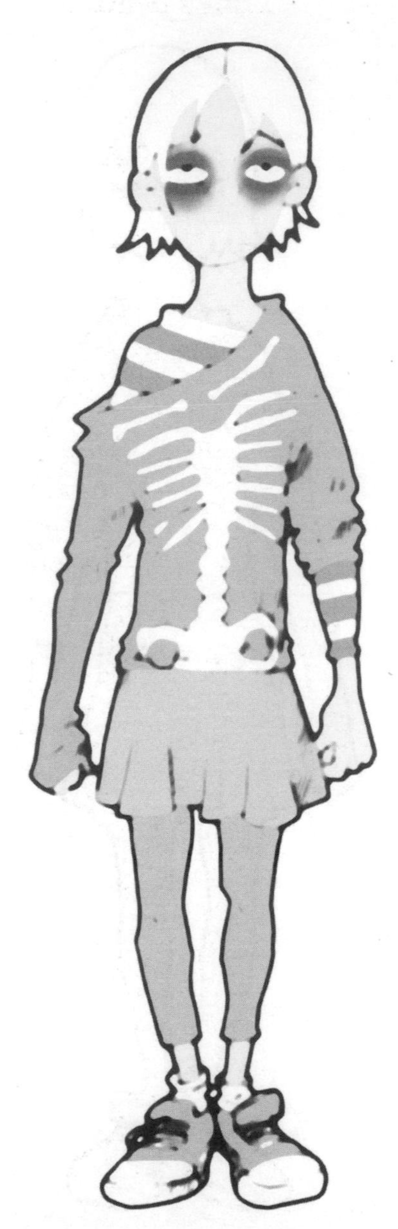

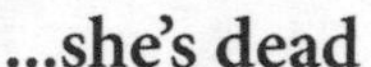
...she's dead

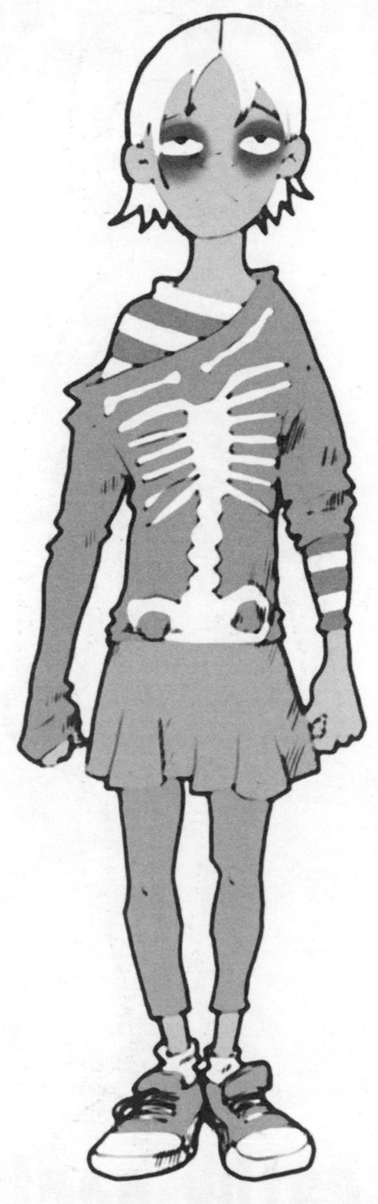

Scarlett Dedd

by cathy brett

EMBER FURY

cathy brett

HAVING CELEBRITY PARENTS ISN'T AS HOT AS IT SOUNDS.

YES, THERE'S MONEY TO BURN, FAME AND SOME TOTALLY SMOKING GUYS...BUT WHEN YOUR DAD'S MORE INTERESTED IN BLAZING A TRAIL TO THE TOP OF THE CHARTS THAN WHY YOU GOT KICKED OUT OF SCHOOL, *AGAIN*, IT CAN MAKE YOU SERIOUSLY ANGRY.

AND IF THERE'S ONE THING EMBER KNOWS, IT'S THAT THE SMALLEST SPARK OF ANGER CAN IGNITE A WHOLE HEAP OF TROUBLE...

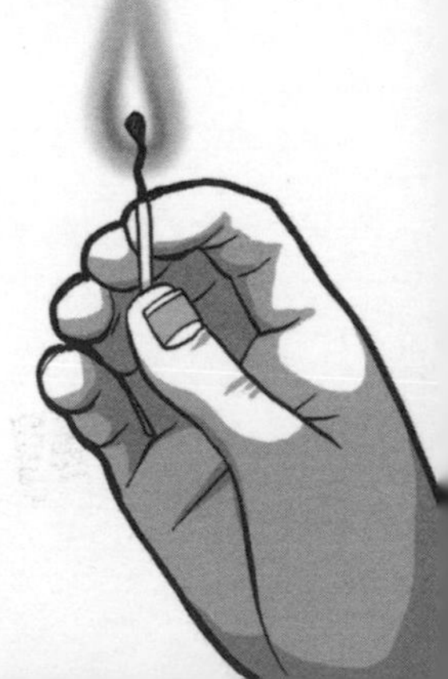

Praise for EMBER FURY by Cathy Brett

'Amazing graphic novel' *Bliss*

'It's as much a work of art as it is and awesome story'
teenlibrarian

'A brilliant accomplishment' *WondrousReads*

'This is a quirky and cool book and I thoroughly enjoyed it'
Chicklish

Read an extract and watch the trailer at http://bit.ly/iaFOC

Read Cathy's blog at http://cathybrett.blogspot.com and follow her on twitter.com/gingerdoodles

Find out more at
www.facebook.com/booksfromthebword